The Moonling Prince

Book One

(a starshiptopian romance with gothic moons and ghosts, empaths and tortured princes, and hummingbird ships)

by

Wendy Rathbone

For Della

companion of my heart, and beyond

1.

Tahir

The Realm of the September Stars sent an entire fleet of hummingbird ships for me. I couldn't begin to calculate the expense.

Their silver wings spun in constant gyrations, giving them a fluid, liquid appearance. The bodies of the ships had the grace of line only the designers and metalworkers of Lyric Prime could accomplish, each starboat a work of art, all slightly different from the other and individually autographed by the construction and design teams.

On the galactic market, the hundred different styles of beautiful starships the culture had produced over uncounted generations were no longer available, except for used, older models.

Of course, Lyric Prime no longer existed. Twenty Earth-years ago it was attacked and pillaged for its fine metals by an unknown alien force, and then destroyed. Many people died. The ruling family lost five of their children to the sudden and relentless war before moving to the nearby civilized moons and constructing a safety net. The survivors now lived beneath a veil of security and privacy they have rarely breached since the invasion.

For twenty years that area of the galaxy known as the Realm of the September Stars had remained mostly dark.

Until today.

One of the ships landed in the tallow field beyond the Temple. The rest of the fleet stayed in orbit.

"Tahir."

I turned, lowering the black hood of my robe. My master and mentor, Zash, moved gracefully across the tiled courtyard. His hood was thrown back. His dark gray curls reflected blue and gold in the strong sunlight. He was past middle age now, but his face was still beautiful, perhaps even more so due to the wrinkles of age. He looked helplessly from me to the huge gleaming ship fifty yards away.

I reached out and touched the roughness of his cheek. "I will miss you most," I said.

"Please. You can still change your mind."

"I agreed to go weeks ago. My decision is final."

"But the wave says they will want to keep you for life. And you are still so young."

"They need my help. The youngsters with the necessary talent aren't ready for a mission like this. The old ones are too set in their ways and would not be as flexible to change. I am the only one who can help. I am going."

He nodded, mouth frowning. "May your journey be strong but restful. May you find happiness along with growth. Be cheerful but authentic. My love will follow you through the stars."

My eyes blurred. My throat constricted. "Zash, this isn't easy for me."

As acolytes of the Onyx Temple, we were instructed in many disciplines, unofficially including not whining. But right now my voice came out thin. My chest began to shake. "It is the ending of one life, the beginning of the next, right?" I said.

Zash put his hand on my shoulder. "When you came to us as a tiny one, alone and crying in the rain, I had little hope you could be trained and no clue as to your natural talents. I confess, you surprised me. You are the most talented empath I've encountered in my lifetime. You grew wise, big and handsome. Your heart is generous. We masters are not to have favorites, but if I had a favorite it would be you."

I blinked, trying to keep myself in check. I ached with

grief, but I could not turn back. I knew in my heart I was making the correct decision.

As if reading my mind, Zash leaned in and gave me the empath's kiss for the Pain of Leaving, taking all of it into himself, his cheeks overflowing with tears before he pulled away.

A wind blew through me, fresh and clean, rain-scented with the memory of the storm I'd been lost in as a child. Flickering green like new leaves. A taste of spring warmed from his tongue to mine. The memory of the grief of departure remained but the pain itself was gone. I could move forward with impeccable vision. I could see without the blur of tears the blue sky, the drifting bits of yellow grass on the air like confetti, and the silver hummingbird, giant and silent in the field.

My future.

I moved toward it, heart lighter. Zash had taken my tears as a gift. With his empathic talent he'd taken my aches and made them his. After a few hours they would fade from him but we'd both retain the memory forever.

We empaths were a rare breed who could turn suffering into relief. Our strength was in bringing strength to others. It was our calling. Our talent. And this was what I was called away to accomplish now. My life's work finally coming to fruition.

I walked up the gangway and entered the ship, never once looking back.

The hummingbird waited to take me to my destiny.

2.

Arulu

The pain came in small bursts, budding up through Arulu's body, zinging along his skin like electric needles, then ebbed slowly to a somewhat manageable level.

After eight hours, the drugs were wearing off and it would soon be time for him to close himself off in his rooms and have the servants bind his wrists and ankles. He moved in and out of the pain as if through patches of fog. But he would have some reprieve between bouts of agony for another hour or two. Then it would be a painful twelve hours before he could take another dose of his medicine, a combination of powerful drugs that left trails of poison in his liver and on his heart. One dose a cycle was all his body could handle.

The Realm of the September Stars was one of the oldest cultures of all the galactic reaches. Ancient and formal, forbidding and renowned. Though its central world, Lyric Prime, and its dozen outlying, colony worlds were gone, the populated moons thrived.

What was left of the royal family lived on the smallest moon, Firgone.

It fell to Arulu, the eldest royal son, to rule and to see the next generation flower.

But under Firgone's dome, under wild stars flickering beyond scintillating purple glass and the warm lights of fake dusks and dawns, Arulu battled mind-numbing pain and its accompanying insanity. In his present condition, it was impossible for him to rule beside his father.

When Arulu was ten years old, his father had saved his life. How he hated him for it.

Arulu's mother had wanted him put down the day the

splinter-bombs came, the day his twin brother, Arku, and four little sisters all died within sight of him. For her thwarted but honorable gesture of mercy, he loved his mother the most of any human in all the moons. The rest were nothing to him. People whose lives could never touch him. The pain kept all emotion, except anger, resentment and hate, introverted within him. He'd grown up disconnected, disassociated.

He was still a baby, just a little kid, when it all happened. He resented his survival. He should not have had to live with what he saw, what he felt, and what he now went through every day.

Perhaps if he had not been the oldest twin, filled with all the hopes of his family, his father would not have been so cruel.

He liked to think these thoughts during the long nights when the extra sedatives he was allowed to take almost relaxed him as he convulsed and moaned through nightmare visions and the physical tortures that were the side-effects of the splinter-bomb's radiations.

Cool darkness beckoned Arulu every day. Every night he dreamed of graves. He dreamed of his twin's peeling face, skeletal and screaming. That ghost yet haunted him. He longed for his own essence to be obliterated. Finally freed. But the act of suicide was forbidden to him. His father needed him alive.

The walls of Arulu's rooms were insulated with meteorite. Thick against echoes, impervious to sound, they muffled his suffering. They enclosed him. Sealed off from others who might hear him, left alone on a soft bed (and most times tied if the convulsions got too bad,) with only the walls to reflect his pain, there was nothing there he could use to hurt himself save his own mind.

Every day for twenty years he spent close to twelve hours in those rooms, his prison in the moonling's keep. Sometimes, when he wasn't passed out from the pain, his agony sent him into throes of madness and nightmares he couldn't always remember. Not remembering was good, for when he did remember, what he brought back with him from his daily nightmares were horrific images, bloodbaths, tortures, and atrocities being done to others, or to him, or by him.

But in his saner moments, when the drugs were working, when he could function a few hours a day in normalcy, Arulu realized he wanted a life. He didn't want to die, and he had every reason to live. He simply had no time away from his condition in which to live. So he held himself back from life, from emotion, from any connection with others save his beloved mother.

And his ghost of a brother.

His father called him aloof. His mother called him bitter. Both were right, but his mother was the more honest of the two.

Arulu's father, Kean, had been an engineer, a fixer. It was his nature. He had worked in the starship-yards for ten years—a king doing ordinary labor out of love for the art of it—before Arulu and his twin brother were born. As a result, he could not accept that any puzzle was unsolvable. Anything could be engineered if a person focused long enough, worked hard enough. Kean spent years searching for solutions to Arulu's problem.

Now, Arulu walked the open, curving stairs to the throne room, the day's first pain-wave tingling out through his fingertips. His brother, Arku, followed unseen at his side, a wrecked phantom with ripped skin and a coarse voice that often raged bitterly in his ear. Arku's ghost had grown up alongside him and walked six feet tall in identical height to Arulu. He was invisible to all but Arulu. Arku whispered now, "Dear old dad, what the fuck does he want today?"

Arulu saw his father standing by the front column, eyes down, and approached.

Without looking up, Kean said, "I may have found a new solution to your problem. I will spare no expense to test

10

it. I expect you to be present at the moon base landing field when the hummingbird ships return."

"Another cure?" Arulu had not known the fleet had been sent out into the galaxy. What was his father bringing back this time? They did not look each other in the eye, though he noted that his father wore his formal gold robe of authority and order, and his hip-length silver hair had been coiled into the Braid of Ruling.

Arulu himself wore his dark hair down, the bangs too long, and no braid, signifying no power.

"Yes. Another potential cure, my son. I will not stop looking until the day I am gone from this universe."

"Poppycock," Arku the ghost hissed.

Protocol dictated Arulu could not deny Kean's demands. But he hated the public moon-base and Kean knew it. "If you insist I try this new cure, have it brought to me."

Arku snarled at Arulu's passivity.

"No. I command you to be there. I know you don't like to go about in public, but you being there will be a gesture to the people that the tragedy of our world need not be an end to our continuation."

"The continuation of the royal family, you mean," he said. "That I will inherit the throne? I cannot rule. By your side. Or ever. You know this. You'll only be building a fantasy. It's a false gesture, Father. Nothing will come of this. Nothing ever helps me. You've brought me so-called solutions dozens, no, hundreds of times. Why do you keep trying?"

"Because you are my son and I love you." He moved closer to Arulu, the gold brocade on his hems flashing in the artificial candlelight of the dragon-head sconces.

Arulu moved a step backward. He had not let his father touch him in ten years. No one but his mother touched him. And the doctors who administered the drugs. He was 30 now. He'd given up on his father's trial-and-error solutions long ago.

"If you loved me, you would have shown me

compassion and put me to sleep years ago as my mother wished."

"When you were a small child," Kean said softly, patiently, "you were full of love. You embraced life fully. Laughter echoed through the halls of the palace. Your true self is that person, that boy. You are enshrouded, blinded and deafened by pain. It is not who you are."

"It is all I am."

"No. I fight for that boy. And I will not stop."

Kean spoke of hope which Arulu could not see as anything but a false promise, something to set him up for disappointment as had happened again and again in the past two decades.

For the moment, Arku was silent. Odd.

Arulu said, "Then you keep me in agony for as long as you live for I am commanded to obey you. Your will curses me."

"My will is a gift to you, my son, Arulu. And someday you will see this."

He sighed, letting his long bangs hide his eyes. "I see nothing but broken light through a haze of torture."

And yet it was true that the drugs he took to give him a precious few hours a day of pain-free existence were his father's doing. The medicines had been concocted, by the king's command, just for Arulu's use. A hundred physicians had worked on the recipe for a year until they had gotten it right. By age eleven he knew blissful moments of pain-free existence. It was both a gift and a curse. The drugs gave him just enough time to remember that existence was not merely horror. And just enough reprieve to enhance the dread of oncoming, nightly torture. It made his life all the worse.

His father had given him back what life he could, but it only served to emphasize Arulu's loss. It was a tease at best.

Arulu was convinced this new solution Kean was bringing to the moons would most probably fail. Kean had not said what the solution was and Arulu had no desire to ask. He had simply made up his mind not to put himself through its tortures as well.

He would not cooperate with this new scheme of Kean's, but he told his father otherwise. "All right, then. I will be at the landing field when the ships return."

"Good," Kean said. He handed Arulu a digital scroll, thin as paper, containing a calendar to adhere to. "See that your medication cycle is fresh just before they land. Adjust the timing of your pills if you need to."

Arku entoned softly, "You're not really going, are you?"

"No," he murmured.

Arulu crumpled the digital schedule as he walked away.

3.

Tahir

I had never been on a starship, though I'd seen holos of them both inside and out. My education at the Onyx Temple included general details of star-travel even though few of us ever left the grounds of the complex, let alone the planet, Alluria.

For healings, people were brought to us from all over the galaxy. Rarely did we travel further than the next town.

I did not expect such a lush experience.

The air on board the ship smelled of rain. The bulkheads gave off an inner greenish glow as if the energy of light was trapped just beyond the surface.

When I first entered the ship, I saw plants growing in built-in pots along the decks and walls, healthy and verdant. I recognized none of them. One had leaves that sparkled red as if they were on fire.

As my guide led me to my private stateroom, I asked her what the plant was called.

"The Phoenix Vine," she replied. "It is very rare."

During this short journey through the alien corridors, I also learned the starship's name. *Harbinger.*

Obsessed with meaning, I wondered if putting me aboard a hummingbird ship of that name to bring me to a broken realm had been intentional. A harbinger can be a foreshadowing omen. Did they already expect failure from me before I ever arrived? Why, then, would they send for me at all? Or perhaps the omens they looked for were those of hope.

My stateroom was decorated with elaborate tapestries, fine silks and pillows sprawled across three rooms: a bedroom, a living area and a huge bathing area complete with an inset tub the size of a small pool. I did not understand the mechanics of how starships recycled water and oxygen, or how they also generated these things from the particles of space itself, so it all seemed utterly mysterious and magical to me.

My guide set my small case on a table. It contained my few possessions which I realized now were redundant since everything I could possibly need was provided for me in these rooms.

She turned and said, "Would you like to see the rest of the ship?"

"Can I see the bridge?" I asked.

"Of course."

Down the hall and two lefts later, two doors that resembled framed, paper curtains opened to reveal a large room with a central view screen overlooking a star field which appeared close enough to touch. I could almost feel the warmth from that scintillating, endless night.

The bridge's bulkheads curved away from that view, their surfaces painted in filigree patterns of brown bare branches dripping with orange and gold seedpods. It was alien and beautiful, a delicate but enduring scene as if these people who had been displaced from their destroyed homeworld still brought it with them wherever they went.

Control panels for elaborate computer systems encircled us. The consoles were carved with sculpted dragons and griffins. The air processors gently blew with a faint scent of tangerine.

In keeping with the reputation of the Realm of the September Stars, *Harbinger* was a work of art.

In the mess hall behind the food conveyers a mosaic of intricate detail depicted Sinarha, The God of the Wine Black Sea. Sinarha's long black hair tangled in surrounding stars. His cape was made of black warships shaped like missiles with huge fins They curved around him to form the shroud. He held a trident tipped with stardrive crystals. A dragon nebula hovered above his head.

Everywhere I looked there was some new depiction of beauty. A sculpture, a plant, a painting.

At meals I was served the sweetest fruits, the most tender steaks, and delicate wines of lavender and gold. The food was all synthetic, but I could not tell it was synthesized from the exquisite tastes. Before my first sleep cycle, thin, fine chocolates were presented to me on ceramic plates hand-painted with pink lotus blossoms.

That first night I asked my guide, "Is there any instruction for me?"

"What do you mean?" she asked.

"I assumed I would have a message to tell me in detail what is expected of me. And how to prepare."

"You were not told?"

"I was only informed of the desperate need for an empath in your realm. The message was marked with the emergency code. I answered the call because of my training. And because it was the right thing to do. But I have no idea what is required of me."

Her pale hair had been elaborately braided into an X on the top of her head. She bowed to me, showing me more intricacies of braids under the X, tight against her scalp.

"The queen did not send for you, so you are for the king. He will meet you when we land on Firgone. That is all I know. Nothing but your presence here is required for now." Her long, fake lashes fluttered twice, two blinks. Dismissal. She turned and moved away from me, leaving me alone at the threshold of my stateroom.

The ship's night cycle did not coincide with my own schedule, but after the elaborate tour and meal, I was tired.

I prepared myself for sleep. As the soft, alien bed enfolded me in its cushions of silks, I slipped into a dream of swimming between the stars.

4.

Arulu

Draped against the bone gray backdrop of a throne room carved from a demi-god's skull, the creature flicked its arrow-tipped tail. It stood ten feet tall and had a triangular head with a mouth that, unhinged, showed multiple rows of knife-edged fangs and teeth. Pieces of human flesh still dangled from that mouth. Torn bodies of children littered the floor.

It said in a voice of hisses and threats, "Crown Prince blood is the sweetest. After dining on your brother and sisters, the prince and princesses of the realm, I have saved you for last, Arulu."

The boy hid behind a crumbled pillar. His bare hands pressed against sharp dust-shards of destroyed columns and walls leaving behind bloody handprints as he tried to crawl deeper under more fallen debris.

The creature laughed, fangs glinting, and said, "You think you can hide from me? As long as you have a mind, I will find you. Look at all I have destroyed. I have just begun."

Deep within the palace walls, alone in his private pain-room, the moonling prince watched his story again and again. In his own mind the tale always repeated with horrific variations.

Playing hide and seek in the throne room with his giggling twin brother and his little sisters. Playing to the death.

Hiding from the splinter bomb of no escape.

A red caress. A spray of red. One, two sisters gone in an explosion of red.

Arulu's twin says, "Ari, I'm scared."

Arulu holds tight to his brother's hand only to realize it isn't attached to a body anymore.

Two more sisters scream.

In this, one of a hundred various nightmares, it is a demon who murders them all this time, a naked dwerger with blue-scaled skin and burning-ember eyes. Tomorrow it will be a dove-winged angel straddling Arulu, smiling beatifically as it slices away his skin inch by inch while the open eyes of his siblings watch in frozen dead relief.

When the dwerger finally leaves, Arulu is impossibly still alive.

His mother looks down on him with red-eyed grief.

His father finds all the pieces of him and orders the finest physicians to put him back together. After awhile he starts to look whole again. But the splinter-bomb is clever. It winds its way through more than flesh. It slices the mind in searing jolts in open places of the brain where the mind cannot forget or hide. It continues its work until the victim ceases to be.

It is said the rare survivors of the splinter-bomb are technically not survivors. They are simply victims who have not yet died.

5.

Tahir

I liked to read. I liked myths.

A myth that spanned the galactic sweeps, common in thousands of realms, told of the Void-God Sinarha who was born of three suns that fell into each other in inescapable velocities of gravitational love. Their ecstasies created a rent in spacetime that formed The Ghost Abyss. Out of that great abyss Sinarha rose, covered in jewels. As he flung them from his body they formed all the known galaxies. The most beautiful jewel called Mind broke apart and formed a spiral that became the Milky Way, home to a vast array of self-aware and intelligent life-forms.

The myth of Sinarha is, like any other myth, a story about destruction and creation.

Known as the God of Awareness, he is also called The Aeon of Death.

The myth speculates that before Sinarha's coming, all life was immortal, self-healing and self-renewing. The immortals lived countless lives in the weaves of time, forever searching for further completion of their universe. But this completion could never be met until they endured the last, most dreaded experience, one that could eradicate them all if they forgot their origins. That experience was mortality. But the trick of it was that to become truly mortal, a being must believe it is going to die. The only way to truly believe is to forget its own immortal self.

The immortals realized they could not evolve without fully understanding this final concept. They had no choice but to take the gamble and erase their memories, risking total annihilation of all life in the universe.

Thus, the final word in every re-telling of this myth: *Remember.*

To me, it was fitting to see this myth in various artistic forms on *Harbinger*. The mosaic in the mess hall was but one. Sinarha's visage, a figure holding a trident, was also stamped on the insignias of the uniforms the starship's crewmembers wore. And he appeared on labels, stamps, silverware, jewelry.

For a beautiful and artistic culture that was almost wiped out, the myth offered the idea that even in dark times, no effort is a waste. Nothing is really gone forever.

The fifth day of my travel aboard *Harbinger*, I woke early so I could witness our approach to the September Star system.

My guide allowed me to be on the bridge for the occasion.

I stood before the view-screen. My body trembled with the thrill of the approach to an alien destination. My throat tensed at the glory of the star fields. I did not expect that the swarms of stars I saw would turn out to be, as we came closer, the million pieces of their destroyed home world.

Chunks of ice-encased rock floated past the cameras and sensors. Silent. Grave. These cold, rotating pieces of earth had once been places where people walked, ran, laughed, loved, ate and slept. They had once been fields, seas, houses, trees.

Some of them hit the shield of the ship and went spinning. The rest of the fleet behind us sparkled as debris fields with remains as large as boulders and as small as grains of sand hit their shields.

My excitement faded. The grief of these people became all too real to me as I was getting a first-hand glance at the holocaust they had survived.

My guide said, "You were hoping to see only the still-intact moons."

I looked at her but did not answer.

She gave me a soft smile. "Be patient. In a few moments, you will."

I was embarrassed at my naiveté that I might be spared

in seeing residual horrors from twenty years in the past.

Of course I would be exposed to it. As an empath, what other reason than grief, illness, or pain would there be for me to be called to travel here?

I remembered the single sentence my guide had told me. *You are for the king.*

Did more horror await me?

For a moment I wanted to turn back. I saw Zash's kind face in my memory and my chest ached. Tears filled my eyes.

I blinked against the vision of the dead chunks of planet that drifted before me.

My guide said. "Do not weep for us. We are a strong people."

Shame swept me. I would never admit to her that I was mostly feeling scared, missing Zash, sorry for myself. Everything in my life was changing. I had chosen this path, yes, but that did not mean I wouldn't face overwhelming moments like this one.

I stood my ground. Lifted my chin. "I only hope my presence brings you honor," I softly replied.

I pulled my black hood up in the formal bearing of an Onyx Temple acolyte.

"Look," she said. "We're passing through the security net."

The path through the curtain, though it appeared open, darkened. A black fog surrounded the ship for about three seconds. And then we were through.

"I've never seen anything like that," I said.

"This defense technology is of our own invention. We have not yet shared it to outsiders. So you would not have seen its like even if you were a seasoned star-traveler."

"I understand."

True to my guide's words, a darkness beyond the shapes and shadows of their former, now broken world seemed to open, as if a black curtain parted to reveal a hidden room. Beacons of green, blue and lavender lights flashed in the dark void's distance.

A curving string of brightness.

A necklace of moons orbiting a giant yellow sun.

I counted ten moons. Half of them had rings like rainbows of stars. "Beautiful," I breathed.

"Four of the moons are for mining resources only, sparsely populated."

I could hear it in her tone. *The aliens didn't get it all.*

"The rest are habitats. The rings are artificial," she said. "They are satellites, space stations, star-ports, construction sites."

"You still build your starships, then."

"Of course we do. But at a much slower rate. Soon we will be ready for galactic commerce again. But such things take time."

"Yes, they do." I bowed my head.

She spoke again. "At the end of the line of moons, do you see the tiny one with the purple-pink glow?"

I nodded.

"That is Firgone. The royal palace is carved into its very bedrock. That is where we are headed."

Though small, the moon was a lovely orb of lavender/fuchsia light. It grew in size as we approached, unshadowed, whole, a living jewel. It was to be my new home. Apprehension and excitement warred. This was both an adventure and a blind dive.

"Do I need to do anything special to ready myself to meet the king?"

She looked me over. Gave me her first smile in five days. "Be yourself."

I smiled in return. I needed all my strength. There was no going back now.

6.

Arulu

Through the archway of the palace entrance, Arulu could see the splash of raw ruby and amethyst that was the moon's transparent dome reflecting the sun. Beyond that, a festive group of lights glimmered in the dark sky.

The fleet of hummingbird ships had returned.

Days ago he'd torn his father's digital schedule into twenty even pieces and tossed them over the edge of the palace keep to the rocky surface below. Yet his subconscious mind still adhered to Kean's schedule out of habit and respect.

Freshly dosed on his meds for the current day's cycle, there was no reason he could not descend the five flights to the surface below and walk the two blocks to the moon base landing field. The pain, for now, had dissolved. His mind was clear.

That would last about five to six hours. If he was lucky.

He had dressed for the day as well, like a child seeking his father's approval. Red silk jacket of veils. Brocade trousers. Gold bands at his wrists and on his fingers. A fancy gold filigree communicator fashioned into a necklace hung close to his heart.

He wore his long brown hair down. It swept against his back.

He started down the first flight before hesitating at the landing. His father wanted him at the base as the ships came in but he hated going out of the palace. He hated being seen, and seeing other people.

At the base there would be guards and workers. And sometimes there were onlookers from the Firgone's only city, Xia. Watching starships orbit and land on the moon was a beautiful sight.

But that meant there would be people. Arulu did not like people. He did not want to be around them. As the crown prince, he'd be noticed. He would have to acknowledge the people who saw him, smile, nod, pretend all was well with him when it wasn't.

And what in all the moons was his father scheming this time? What were the hummingbird ships bringing back from the far reaches of space?

Whatever it was, he had no hope for it. None whatsoever.

He stood on the edge of the next flight of stairs and stared in the direction of the moon base, a sick feeling forming in the center of his stomach.

His fists clenched. A cold sweat broke out along his spine. A fake wind blew the diaphanous triangles of his sleeves back. With it came the landing field's chemical scent of storm and ash.

His necklace chimed.

He switched it on, only to hear Kean's annoyed voice. "Arulu. Where are you? You should have been here by now."

"Father, I told you I'm not coming."

"You said no such thing. And you need to be here."

He leaned over the railing, holding the necklace toward his chin. What he really wanted to do was throw it down the remaining four flights of stairs. "Whatever you are doing, Father, just stop. I don't have the energy for more experiments, or more of your newfangled, magical snake oils."

"This is different."

"You say that every time." His voice almost cracked. He took a deep breath and steadied himself.

"But this time it's true."

"No, Father. Just. No."

"I went to great expense. It's very special—"

Arulu switched his necklace off and headed back up. He'd wait in the throne room and that was that.

Then, after his father came and Arulu rejected his next "solution," he would go to the business chambers to check on his mother. She was far too busy to acknowledge Kean's pet projects concerning Arulu's health. The only way he could see her before the medications wore off would be to seek her out himself. He looked forward to sharing his annoyance with her. She would acknowledge it. She would tell him no one understood him better than she did. She would hug him. And he would try not to remember the long ago days when that hug meant love, not pity.

At that last thought, Arku appeared at his side, his ruined face showing mostly raw skull, and gazed over the balustrade at the moon-base and the incoming ships. "Another expensive gift from the king. When will it stop," he said flippantly.

7.

Tahir

On the bridge view screen, I could see the dome over the moon form a sort of vortex. We sailed right through it and before I could take my next breath the ship lowered straight down and landed on a vast, sandy tarmac surrounded by low buildings with blinking red lights. In the distance, I saw a dark city with a shimmer of white lights. Its skyline silhouetted against the fiery twilight backdrop of the dome and the dark that was the net peeking in from beyond.

Closer in the foreground loomed black pillars and spires adorning a large keep. It was a castle, no doubt about it, like some gothic palace from a child's fairy tale. A work of art.

My guide saw where my vision focused.

She murmured into my ear, "The Royal Palace of the Realm of the September Stars."

I fell in love with it at once and wondered if I would live there. I hoped.

"Come," my guide said to me when the ship stopped humming.

She led me to the same gangplank I had used to board *Harbinger*. Now we descended into a dry, dust-scented atmosphere, completely different from the ship's air. But for processed air, it still felt quite fresh. My boots touched, for the first time, the crumbling surface of an alien moon.

A procession of colorfully dressed people approached, twenty or so, clad in silk robes and jackets of brilliant hues, peacock blue and green, goldenrod and magenta.

In my black robe I felt dour and foreboding.

It was custom for me to keep my hood. But somehow I felt wrong to be hidden by so much shadow. I wanted to ask my guide what to do about my dilemma. I didn't want to come off as a fool or a snob. But before I could speak, the head of the procession came right up to me and hugged me to his chest.

"Welcome," he said to the air over my shoulder. He let go and stood back. "I am Kean. And you must be Tahir."

I nodded.

"I am king here, for all that entails. But enough about that. I've been waiting for your arrival! Welcome, Tahir. Welcome!"

"Thank you. It is my first time off-world from Alluria where I grew up."

"Then we shall make it as comfortable for you as possible."

I tensed. I still had no clue what I was doing here, but obviously my talents as an empath and healer would be employed. So his words had somewhat of a veiled meaning to me. Healing was not a comfortable art. Not for the healer or the patient. But I did not dwell on that for now. Instead, I took in my surroundings, and tried to believe this wasn't all a dream.

Kean was dressed beautifully, his trousers layered in purple silk, his shirt and jacket dripping with trains of the stuff, some of the plumes long enough to furl against the rocky ground. His silvery hair grew long, its ends plaited in four straight braids.

My own pale hair, which I kept combed straight back, barely reached the bottoms of my ears. A few strands of errant bangs wisped against my forehead. I decided I would grow my hair long to fit the fashion of the culture. My first effort to fit in.

Though he wore no crown or fancy jewels, Kean had a regal bearing. For all the atrocities his family and people had faced, his smooth face had a serene stance, an angular beauty.

"Come, come," he instructed. "You must be ready to see where you will be living and learn what made me bring you to my court."

"Yes," I said, though I was still overwhelmed. His entire party was so colorful, so attentive.

He draped his hand against my shoulder and led me down a lighted path across the tarmac. Dutifully, his entourage followed.

Everything was new, a mystery. But I liked this friendly man. He seemed honest and open. I sensed no ploy from him.

Kean said, "I want to hear from you, in your words, all about your Onyx Temple where you are from. I am so curious about your intriguing life."

I turned to look into his dark eyes. "And I, too, am curious about a king's life."

He laughed. "A king's life is drudgery and duty. My designs for starships are much more fun to talk about. I actually preferred that job. But now I'm older with many things to oversee, and I have no time for it."

"That is unfortunate."

"Yes, sad, I would say. But it is the way of my life now. They say life is something you do not plan. Life is what happens. Although I must confess I do like some form of planning if I can. I find it comforting."

After the destruction of his world and the deaths of his children, I could certainly see that finding comfort in planning ahead might be the understatement of all understatements.

Because of the tragedies of his culture, I expected a far more grim man to greet me as ruler of the Realm of the September Stars. But this man was cordial and friendly, not paranoid or gloomy as I had imagined. He did not act or speak as a victim. I was already impressed.

"Yes, there is comfort in preparation for whatever is to come." I hoped I had not overstepped any boundaries in my statement. I added, "And this emergency you sent me for? I only hope I can help."

"All in good time," he replied.

I pressed my lips tight and said nothing. I didn't particularly like surprises any more than he did. But he must have had a reason for waiting for the proper moment to outline my job.

As we approached the low buildings that surrounded the tarmac, a square hover transport appeared. It was unlike any I'd seen before. It had rails and a gate but no top. Several benches lined the middle of the deck. It was painted red and the rails were draped in red velvet cloth. I could see no exposed controls.

The king stepped through the gate, and led me to one of the benches. His entourage boarded. All remained standing except the two of us as the craft took us gently up and moved toward the dark palace.

Under our feet came a soft vibration and low hum. We seemed to drift up toward the dome. The dome sparkled in sunset colors all along the horizons, but straight up toward the center it revealed the clear black of the net. No stars glimmered there.

As we drew near the castle I saw a great open-air stairway curving to a giant upper floor balcony and patio. Two fountains shaped like swans splashed the air.

An archway at the top of the wide stairway led to an open room beyond the patio and the hover-craft fit right through it.

The throne room.

Two giant black chairs sat in the middle of the room. The room itself looked carved out of gray rock, rough-hewn, natural. Lights that scintillated like trapped flame (bigger than candles) were scattered about the room in hanging lanterns and sconces. Pillars of silver-veined black marble added to the distinctly medieval design. Not to mention the sculptures of griffins and dragons that dotted the huge space. Ornate rugs surrounded the thrones. I caught a faint whiff of incense.

By one of the pillars, standing to the side of it and half-hidden from my view, a man in a red silk jacket and brocade trousers stood as still as a shadow. He had long, warm brown hair, unbraided and shining along his back. That was all the detail I could see. His face remained averted.

We disembarked. Kean moved toward the left throne and I thought he was going to sit in it, but instead he merely leaned against the thick arm. He glanced toward the man in red, then back at me.

The entourage formed a loose grouping behind the throne, with two who remained, as if sentinels, by the entryway we'd come through.

Finally, Kean spoke. "I would see you without your hood."

I reached up and pushed it back. I already knew from the flinch of my guide on board *Harbinger* that my appearance would provoke a reaction. Of course there are blonds among the people of the September Stars, but not as blond as I.

"Your hair is quite white," Kean said frankly. "It is considered rare and exotic by my people in one so young. And the blue of your eyes is so pale they glisten."

In truth, I did feel exotic by the very fact that they sent a fleet of starships to bring me to Firgone, and because I was amidst a culture alien to me, a place I had only begun to study in the days before I left the Onyx Temple. I had the download programs of their dialect of Galactic Standard, but not much else. I was alien, to be sure. And then, well, there was my rare talent. Empaths are born, not made. Which was why, I later figured out, my family had abandoned me at the entry to the Onyx Temple one rainy day. At first I thought I'd been lost, but Zash told me they had to have known of my talent, and that they chose the Temple for me as my rightful destiny. But in my mind it was still abandonment.

I'd been only six years old.

"Tell me," Kean said, "are you a true healer?"

"In what sense do you mean true?"

"What they say—and why I brought you here. That you can take pain away. And heal the sick or injured."

"Yes."

The king turned to the man at the pillar. "Arulu, did you hear him? His name is Tahir. Please come forward and greet him."

The man did not move and still stood half-facing away. "I can see him from here."

His voice came out strong, a resonating timber conveying strength and annoyance. After the king's friendly greeting, this newer man's reception was a shock.

"How can you see him or greet him if you are turned away? Come, son. I command it."

At the word "son" I realized this was the prince of the kingdom.

Without a word, the man turned so I could finally see him. As he moved toward the king, I noted his stiff bearing, his tight lips. He had dark slanted brows, a beautiful face. He looked no more than 30.

When he reached his father's side, he looked only at him.

It was at that moment Kean chose to dismiss his entire entourage, except for the two flanking the door as if guarding it. They all quickly left.

Kean said to me, "This is Arulu." He turned toward his son. "You must welcome Tahir. He's come a long way. He's a great healer."

Arulu finally turned and stared at me for a moment with hollow dark eyes. "Really, Father? Another doctor?" His eyelids closed half-way, and he turned away from me in disgust.

"I don't think you understand, son. Tahir is an empath of the Onyx Temple."

Shoulders rigid. Arms pressed tight to his sides. "So?"

Already the son hated me. I could read that much from him. And I could feel his held-back pain if not psychically, then through his inflexible body language. Had I been brought here by the king for him?

If so, I could already see that he might prove to be a difficult project. But he did not know me yet. He had no reason to believe in me. Or my talent.

Kean tried to explain as Arulu turned to face the back wall, hands clasped behind his back. "He has a rare talent, son. I believe he can help you."

"I'm tired, Father. Of all the promises. All the attempts that fail. This time I refuse. I will not cooperate only to face more pain and failure."

So. It *was* the son, Arulu, that I had been brought here for.

"People who have been sick a long time and have tried cure after cure became understandably cynical," I said calmly. I took a small step forward. "If I may explain? In private?" I addressed the prince, who still refused to look at me. "Surely you have time for that after I've come such a long way."

Arulu turned with a snarl, looking me up and down. "It takes more than a gentle voice and exotic—" he hesitated, as if looking for the proper word. He hissed. "—robes to impress me. Father, can you not see this is just more hollow, make-believe nonsense? The last one of these 'believers' in healing you brought had me reclining on hot rocks and telling me to go to my safe place!"

"Tahir is different," Kean insisted. "Hear him out."

"No! I will not allow him in my rooms. And you cannot

force me."

"I can make it the king's will."

Arulu took a sharp breath. "Then I will appeal to the queen to circumvent it!"

"Arulu, what harm can come from just listening to this man?" Kean asked.

"What harm? Are you serious? Father, you continue to harm me by keeping me alive every day for the last twenty years. At least respect me enough to stop throwing yet more supposed cures at me. Cures, I might add, that never work."

I had not been able to get in another word during this sudden argument. I watched the conflict with interest, understanding dawning. Though I still had no clue what ailed Arulu, the tension suggested nothing minor. And yet, if Arulu had some terrible disease for twenty years, why did he look healthy? Why had the affliction not killed him over such a long period of time?

At the moment, he seemed to suffer from anger toward his father, and a not so surprising shyness, or perhaps abhorrence, when it came to facing strangers. His anger suggested a resentment of his position, and possible depression. Was that it? Was I here to mediate a father/son quarrel that had lasted decades? A family dispute?

Since I had been twenty years old I had healed people who came to the Onyx Temple to seek out the rare empaths there, but those healings usually took less than a few minutes. The aches and pains were ordinary, if severe. I soaked the pain into myself and they were relieved. My body digested the pain I took until it faded from me. The recovery process for me usually ended after only a matter of hours. If the pain was severe and affected me at all, which was rare, for the time I needed to filter it I would be cared for gently and lovingly by the other acolytes.

Now I had been brought to the Realm of the September Stars to live. An emergency situation. A dire circumstance. The king wanted me to be his healer, no doubt living in the palace, my duty solely focused on him. And, it seemed, his son. Arulu. Who clearly wanted nothing to do with me.

Kean finally said to his son, "This one is different. Why don't you hear him out?"

"I am uninterested in anything this off-worlder has to say."

My instinct was to immediately back off so this prince had less reason to hate me. "It's all right. I would never force my ways upon anyone."

"It is not all right," the king said sharply. "I brought you here for him!"

"For this one person only who does not want it? Surely you have others in your kingdom that might need healing."

"Well," he said, "It will be good to have you around in case other situations arise which our physicians cannot take care of. But most illness has been cured on our moons. And we age spectacularly slowly. Pain from accidental injury is temporary, and we have the best medication here."

"I don't understand. You brought me to live here," I stated, stepping closer to the king.

"My son's affliction is on-going. It never ends. I'm not sure even you can heal him, but if you can ease his pain—"

"Father!" Arulu interrupted. "Must I stay and listen to you discuss me as if I'm not even here?"

The king continued, ignoring his son's outburst. His voice grew soft as he said, "This is about a splinter-bomb from twenty years ago. It is about Arulu, the only survivor at ground zero. I brought you here for him and him alone."

My veins instantly chilled. I looked at Arulu. How was he still standing?

Kean continued. "I say the term 'survivor' loosely because the bomb affects him to this day. It has never left our presence."

I had heard about splinter-bombs but never seen their damage first-hand. I knew surviving a ground zero splinter-bomb attack was next to impossible. The rays of the bomb affected the nervous system of the body and brain, set it afire. The body eventually exploded, killing the victim if they had not already died from shock. The bomb also affected non-corporeal material within its vicinity by slowly disintegrating matter. Organic or inorganic material. It didn't matter which, the bomb destroyed all of it flawlessly.

If what the king said was true, Arulu should not have been standing there.

My entire body recoiled as if it could feel the fires of that horrible attack on a now-dead world from two decades in the past.

Voice a near whisper, I said to the king, "How is he alive?"

Before the king could answer, Arulu said loudly, "Because my father is an unmerciful ass."

Kean said, "His physical body was flawlessly put back together by the physicians. But nothing could be done about the fire inside him. He can only take so many drugs before they, too, commence to destroy his body. The safe doses he now takes give him only a few hours a day to function. Such as you see him now."

Arulu glared.

My eyes filled with empathy. It was my way.

Arulu grimaced in hatred as he mistook my tears for pity. His body was tensed to flee. I could tell only the command of the king kept him rooted to his spot.

What a horror for this man to have suffered such an atrocity and still be standing. His kingdom itself was fractured. But unto himself, Arulu was a world of drowned and missing pieces.

Arulu faced his father. "May I go now?"

Kean sidestepped the question. "You will make plans to see this healer as I command it."

Arulu bowed his head, the first time I saw any obeisance from him. "Please do not make me do this."

"I feel it will be different this time," the king said

kindly.

"You say that every time!"

"Tahir is special."

"Father, it is a fact proven again and again that nothing can help me. You fail to see this. And this man is no more special than any other cure you have brought me over the years."

"Unlike your mother, I will not give up," Kean said.

It was not so odd to hear them discussing me like this. I'd heard similar discussions from patients at the Onyx Temple. People did not believe because they did not want to be disappointed. My results as an empath needed to be felt and seen first. I understood that. Many things in the universe sounded far too good to be true.

But I could also see that, despite this king's charisma and power over his son, despite his infinite love, Arulu had lost all hope long ago. A hopeless man is a stubborn man. Worse, he can be a danger, both to himself and others. Without hope, life is a meaningless pursuit. And yet, the king, with all his hopes and unbending need to fix what was broken, prolonged the torment of both his son and himself.

Hope had at its core an agony that left many people thinking they were better off without it.

There was no easy answer.

"May I speak?" I asked.

The king turned his soft gaze upon me. Arulu stiffened and would not meet my eyes.

"I will not touch your son if he does not consent," I said firmly. "But perhaps there is another way I could show you my talent. Prove to you that I have a gift that might aid the suffering of others. My ability is very rare. I'm not a boastful man and I am not perfect, but you will not encounter many like me even in one single, long-standing lifetime."

"Would you allow him a demonstration, Arulu?" the king asked.

"It would not be a demonstration on you, sire," I said

to the prince, who still would not glance my way. "But someone else. A volunteer."

Arulu said nothing. He was suffering, and seething because of it. I had met and helped a lot of desperately ill people. But I could not imagine the hell in which he'd lived for two decades.

The light sconces bred tentacled shadows upon the rock walls that held them. Nothing else moved in the room. Even the king's entourage seemed to be holding their breaths.

When Arulu still did not answer, the king prompted him. "Well, son?"

"A demonstration would prove nothing. He might take away the pain from a broken arm. That is nothing compared to a splinter-bomb's effects." He addressed only his father, as if the rest of the room did not exist.

"Please, Ari. One time. Will you try?" the king asked.

The prince appeared to deflate at the use of the nickname. "Father, please don't ask—"

"One try," Kean said quickly. "Just one."

Slowly, Arulu turned toward me. His dark eyes were fixed and cold, as if he did not see me at all. His hands clasped to fists at his sides. The red silks of his blouse wavered like wilted feathers. "Will you have to touch me?" he asked.

"Yes." I knew then that he would not go for it. As soon as he discovered the touch from an empath required a kiss to establish the healing connection, he would balk. He would laugh as he tossed me off-moon, the echoes following me all the way through the milky stars.

Did the king even know? Had any of these people researched the process at all before they'd sent for me?

The prince's dark eyebrows pinched together. The angle of the flickering light of the throne room drew his visage into a determined frown. He was breathtakingly beautiful, even with that frown.

"One try," he said in a monotone voice. "I will give you one half of a 20th cycle."

35

My mind translated that to approximately half an hour.

The king breathed out a long sigh and put his hands together in a soundless clap. "How long will you need to prepare?"

"Not today!" Arulu stated.

"It wouldn't work now anyway," I said. "It must happen when you are, ah, not drugged."

The prince turned away again.

Now Kean looked worried. "You can't do the healing while he is lucid and not incapacitated?"

"I can if you time it right. The moment the drugs he is taking wear off there will be an interim where I can reach the pain, pull it out. He will still be lucid but succumbing to the bomb's effects."

Arulu started to say something but Kean held up his hand to stop him. I heard him say softly, "If it doesn't work, you will pass out anyway. You won't even remember since you forget anything that happens during the minutes when the pain takes over."

"Small comfort," Arulu retorted with a hiss. "I don't need to remember every detail of what he does to know that your foolishness in trying to fix me is fraught with constant failure."

But it was a comfort for me. Arulu would not have to be told the touch was a kiss, then, until the very last minute. He would not have to try to withhold his disgust, or embarrassment until then, and by then I would have fail safes in place.

Some empaths had been accused of fraud, perversity, or worse from people who witnessed the procedure on holovids but did not benefit from it first-hand. There were people who thought it was all some horrible trick. The kiss was an unexpected intimacy to many non-believers, but the reality was that the energy was exchanged and entered the mind, breath to breath, healer to patient.

"Tomorrow, then," the king commanded. "Is that long

enough for you to prepare?"

I nodded. There wasn't much in the way of preparation that I needed to do for myself except make sure I had a comfortable place to recover, water, and protein of some sort. And I did need to make sure during the moment of the kiss that Arulu did not bolt. For people like him, we often employed strap-downs. With his condition, he had no doubt been strapped down before for treatments.

But I did want some time to look up information on splinter-bombs and any other known survivors of them. It would have helped if I'd been able to do some reading about it on the voyage, but no one had given me any details of why the king had called for my presence.

I still felt Kean knew more than he was telling. There was a reason he'd invited me to come to stay. A reason I was asked to immigrate and not just come as a guest.

He said to Arulu, "I will give orders for the surgeon on call to withhold your noon hour dose. You will have the morning dose only."

Arulu shook his head. Mumbled something I couldn't hear.

"It must be this way," I heard the king say to him.

"Now may I leave?" Arulu asked.

The king waved him away with his hand.

I watched Arulu depart, back straight, gait stiff. He may not have been in physical pain at the moment, but his body suffered still, his muscles quite obviously strained.

"Do you have a library? Or computer room?" I asked.

The king said to me, "All you need has been provided for you in your rooms. All access to my kingdom, nothing denied. You will have escorts. They will be discreet. If you do not want them present during your time with Arulu, they will wait at the door."

His wave dismissed me as casually as he dismissed Arulu. I had thought he might talk to me more about his son in private, but he seemed quite finished.

8.

Arulu

She wore satin inlaid with velvet that always looked too warm for any room, even the vast airy rooms of the upper palace that sported cold drafts.

Her name was Winter. She preferred the old-Earth Chinese version, Dongji, the language of her ancient ancestors, though Arulu liked the sound of Winter better, and he had heard his father call her by that Galactic Standard translation thousands of times.

She wore her dark hair always up, pinned with crystal insects that glittered around her like a halo. Butterflies, ladybugs, and dragonflies adorned her neck. She had rings shaped like birds. A snake bracelet on her upper arm.

Today she sat before an array of monitors, her fingers flickering over the screens too fast for Arulu to follow. Ten assistants worked around her on their own arrays.

His feet felt the hard tile beneath the soles of his boots. The room was all cool light and antiseptic. The humans in it didn't even seem real.

He didn't want to interrupt her, but she always insisted on seeing him at least once a day during his medicated phase. She never visited him when he was down from the meds and insane. Or if she did, he never knew.

"Mother."

She turned, graceful as always, her cool scrutiny and her attempt at a hug perfunctory.

Arulu understood her distance from him. For what mother could bear to have a son like him?

He admired her for her honesty. Her beauty. And he

loved her still, despite her coldness, because she was his mother. Warmth settled in the pit of his stomach just from being around her. She had lost five children. He was the sixth. Her brave front was in inspiration.

"You met with your father?" she asked.

"He ordered it."

"Did you see the healer?"

Arulu nodded. "From a distance. No real meeting. Just another man with another bag of tricks."

"The king is a hopeful fool."

Arulu bowed his head, said nothing. If he began to speak against his father, he feared he'd never stop. His misery would compound.

"You will follow his orders then?" she asked when he remained silent.

"I don't intend to see this through."

A hint of a smile crossed her perfect, doll features, though her red lips only quirked. Her dark eyes half-closed, shadowed by her heavy lashes. "Then you intend not to cooperate?"

"What would be the point?"

"Exactly. I could speak to this healer. Dissuade him. Send him away. Or?"

Arulu blinked. He knew if he said the word, she would even have the man killed. For him. People had disappeared before under too much royal scrutiny. The family ruled beneficently, but they were not all pure of heart.

He was well aware of the frozen landscapes that lived inside his mother, well aware she'd become her name. He harbored those steppes and plains and plateaus himself, the icy tundras that comprised his soul. Oh, yes, they were a pair, mother and son, leaden and weighted with the emptiness of suffering, and that final emotion-killer, grief. The splinter-bomb had succeeded in that quite well. After twenty years, his mother had not changed. On the surface she appeared healed, but the scars she carried in the shapes of her dead children ran to the core of her heart. She was damaged forever. It was a damage Arulu understood like nothing else in the galaxy, and he had no hope to be healed from it.

Winter had no maternal instincts left, nor sentiment like the king. The only reason she saw Arulu was because they were alike in this one way, desolate and vague, functioning only out of duty. They both knew the urgency of need when mind demanded occupation, distraction. Work was Winter's comfort.

Arulu studied when he could concentrate, spoken languages, art, fable-telling, but no longer the art of the starship-making of his father, a childhood dream gone forever save a few sketches here and there. Nor did he learn computer language like his mother. He studied anything that took him away from the hell he inhabited. Ancient Earth history. Philosophy. The nine billion names of the gods.

He would not have his mother kill for him. If he wanted that done he'd do it himself. He'd dreamed of killing enough times to undo an army. Doing it for real might feel good. But to take that one final step? The innocent boy in him rebelled.

"Maybe send him away," he finally answered her.

"I'll speak again to your father." She always called him that. Or "the king." Never "my husband." Never "Kean."

Arulu glanced up, his hair brushing his cheek where it hung forward nearly hiding his face. "No. I'll do it myself." His voice came out angrier than he'd intended.

"It is your right to refuse this alien."

Refuse your father. That part went unspoken but he heard it anyway.

Arulu nodded, but suddenly all energy drained from him. Kean had ordered this. Arulu had stood up to him in the past, only to be thwarted in every way. He'd never won against his father. In this case, what might Kean do?

Strap him down. Immobilize him. Drug him. Imprison him.

Winter understood the consequences and still encouraged him. It was utterly sadistic of her. She was his ally in word only. In deed, he could never actually refuse the king who would force his way no matter what it took.

"I will not make any of this easy for the healer or the king. I guarantee that," Arulu stated.

Winter touched him on the shoulder, her palm barely resting there, so light he could not feel any heat. "My son," she said.

He felt something prickle briefly inside him. A weird mixing of anxiety and hope, the two things associated with his mother's love. Well, her type of love anyway.

He loved her. How could he not? That was where the feeling came from. Not her. Because she didn't love him in the same way. And she never would.

"I see him tomorrow."

"Does he have a name?"

"Tahir."

"By the following day, you will have forgotten it," she assured him.

The room's walls sparked with blue light from window screens and consoles. Her viewer was filled with strange scribbles and curls. Not anything like one of his fluent languages.

He wanted to believe her. Needed to. "Yes."

It was all strangely beautiful. Her place, her space. The mild electric aromas on the air. The thin blue light of artificialness, constructs of logic and elements where not even dream's own cider-light could invade. No fancy. No warmth.

She moved closer to her desk. "I have work."

"Of course."

He turned and left her there. And wished for the same peace. Wanting cold existence to anesthetize his pain. Wanting this Tahir problem to just go away.

9.

Tahir

After the interview with the king, I turned away. From the flowing silks. The amber scents. The dark-aired throne room. From the king who mourned a son undead.

Two escorts led me down winding stone stairs—so Earth-medieval for the technological marvel this palace was—and through corridors lined with high sconces that ghosted the walls with flickering gold.

I had thought my journey had started with the hummingbird ships, their glory and beauty, their ability to astonish with their gyros of movement. The way they mastered the stars.

But I saw I had been in error. Despite the fancy greeting from Kean, my journey was only now just beginning, here on a tiny moon amid a grave of worlds, a morbid fairytale sealed in the stone of a spell.

The way Arulu's eyes, dark and beautiful to be sure, lacked luster when he looked at me did not fool me to believe for one minute I was welcome here. Maybe Kean was an ally, but if I failed him, what could I expect even from him? He had his own agendas, his kingly duties to repair and rebuild an entire realm and culture. He had accomplished a lot in twenty years, but he had so much more to do. If I did not make myself indispensable to him, I would be forgotten.

I glanced at my escorts, wondering how much, or how little, they'd been instructed to help me. One was female, one male. Both wore coats of dark blue satin, the tails of the cloth reaching to their calves. Their boots curved out at the knee, heavy and black. They both had long hair braided back in fine tails and gathered in one band.

I deliberately slowed my pace, forcing them to notice. When I had their attention, I said, "I'll make a list of the things

I need."

The female's eyebrow rose.

"Do I give this list to you?"

"Yes," she replied, and her voice was as dry as the moonrock beneath our feet.

"What are your names?"

They answered almost in unison. "Taridia." "Sovat."

"Do your names have meaning?" I don't know why I wanted to know.

"My name translates from an archaic alien language to Sunrealm in Standard. But please don't call me that," Taridia said, still dry. But it was the first human-ness I'd seen from either of them.

I looked to the man. "And yours?"

"Sullen." His lips curved up. "Or close to that. So I've been told. The language of my name is unknown to me." His smile brought out dimples. So they weren't robots after all. And he, despite his name, was the lighter of the two. "You can call me that, if you want."

"Sullen it is."

Taridia smirked at him.

They had to have been children when the attack on their homeworld happened. So many had died. I wondered how they'd escaped, or if they'd been born on one of the ten moons. Twenty years was not long enough to heal such scars. It was the decimation of their universe. Shadows of that would encroach on their culture for decades to come.

We had passed many closed doors. We turned a corner, leaving behind the echoes of our footfalls, and both escorts stopped. "Here is your room," Sullen said.

He pushed a lever. The door slid into a slot in the wall, leaving the threshold open.

The room smelled of fresh linen and talc. It had a window framed in velvet that I immediately saw overlooked the distant city. Even though we'd gone down some levels, we were still several stories above-ground.

The room was filled with rugs, plush chairs, tables with colored-glass lampshades. A large bed piled with pillows. A separate alcoved bathroom. A computer and other gadgets on a dining table. On one wall was a mural of a black sun slashed through the middle by red spikes. Black crescents fell from the slash marks like tears.

Opulent did not begin to describe my accommodations.

"We will be outside if you have any needs or questions," Taridia said.

Sullen added, "Give us your list when it's complete. We are here for six more hours before the next shift."

So I would not be left alone. It was both a comfort and a gesture of distrust. Could I blame these people, or their king, after what they'd been through?

"Thank you."

Sullen pushed a lever and the door closed.

I looked around. This was ideal. More than I'd expected. It would be a great place to rest, recover, and re-energize after my session (or sessions if it came to that) with the prince.

Healing for an empath was an art. Never quite the same for any two people. Sometimes I would briefly feel the pain of the other, sometimes not. It took a lot out of us.

I noticed my belongings from the ship had already been delivered. My case sat, unopened, on a white bench at the foot of the bed. My few belongings consisted of a grooming kit, underclothes, an extra temple robe, some money (useless here,) a tablet with a library I'd constructed of my favorite writings, lectures, vid-plays. And holos of Zash and my other Temple friends.

I vowed never to forget brothers and sisters at the Temple.

Also, stashed among my things, was a gift Zash had sneaked in at the last minute. I'd discovered it my first night in transit. It was a small, hand-made box of oak wood, intricately carved with Temple phrases:

Be uncertain and certain at the same time.

Assume both the worst and the best at the same time.

Stand by your word, or do not speak.

Thought forms reality.

The King of Healers is Love.

Zash knew me too well. They were all my favorite phrases.

Inside the box sat a fat, faceted jewel that rippled in color from green, to lavender, to gold. When I touched it, the cool surface of the stone instantly warmed and sent a surge of energy into my skin.

The worry stone was priceless. Not every acolyte at the temple had one. Not even all the elders had one. They were considered amulets for service that had been inspired beyond the conduct and confines of the Temple.

Zash had to have stolen it. Or maybe an elder had given it to him.

I had not even started my service, or earned it, but the worry stone was a gift I cherished. Now I took it out of the box and held it in my palm, fingers closing over it. It shifted in the room's light, yellow-peridot-amethyst. It felt alive in my hand. I brought it too my lips, touching lightly. When I did, my whole face tingled.

Its properties were easily explained by chemists, the fusing of elements, their lightning reaction to heat, to touch. But lore said the stone housed a god.

Reluctantly, I put it away. An item I should not have.

I went to the computer and found it not too different from others I'd worked. I pulled up a report Kean's aides had helped him write, detailing the effects of Arulu's condition. I needed to know what he went through every day. I found out that he could become violent, fully able to hurt himself, or others. And that his doors were locked for the long cycle.

Most of the time during his pain regimen was spent passed out. The shock to his body should have killed him over time. His doctors were the best, though. They gave him just enough medication to get through his shock during his down-time, and to function mostly pain-free for half a moon-day.

I began to make my list to give to my escorts.

I spent a long time on it, reminding myself to go slow, remember all I had observed, and consider every variable.

Arulu was already unwilling. All the circumstances and consequences of splinter-bombs were irreversibly destructive, and hideous. People simply did not survive them.

I carefully carved out the list. No drugs. That was not the point of my healing. And Arulu's body was already poisoned enough.

When I finished the list I lifted the lever to open the door. Sullen and Taridia greeted me. I handed it to them.

Sullen took it and quickly looked it over.

He said, "The trauma equipment is always available and easily accessible near the prince's quarters. As for the rest of this stuff, no problem. But the portable bed with ankle and wrist restraints is not necessary. Arulu's bed is well equipped."

"Oh," I said quietly. "That one's not for him. That item will be for me."

His mouth hung open.

Taridia said, "How can you heal him if you're the one strapped down?"

"It's for after the healing is complete. Make sure you, or anyone else on duty during that time understands that I will need a period of several hours to rest and recuperate. If his pain touches me I cannot predict how I will react to it. But I will be too overcome to walk, that is for sure."

"You mean it takes that much out of you?" Sullen

asked.

"No. I mean I take the patient's illness into me. It passes through me, but not all at once."

Both began to look worried. "The effects of the splinter-bomb are not a normal illness," Taridia said.

"Yes. I understand that. I'm planning on it taking some extra time for me to recover. In the meantime, I'll be quite incapacitated. The bed with the restraints is a precaution."

Sullen folded the list and put it in the pocket of his blue jacket. "If what you're saying is true, we might need the trauma equipment for you."

"I hope not." But as he spoke, I felt my pulse quicken. I was quite experienced. I hadn't had a bout of "stage fright" since my eighteenth year. I'd healed everything from long-lasting colds to knife wounds to bodies broken beyond belief. I'd healed cancers, bad hearts and brain tumors, taking all the illnesses into myself and disseminating their toxins into the nothing beyond all thought. I was trained to do this, born with the gift of drawing energy, imparting healing and life energy, and opening mental doors to send the poison/pain/death energy away. At age 30, it was like breathing to me.

But the more I learned about the splinter-bombs, how their energy wormed its way not only into the nervous system to deliver the greatest amount of torture, but into the mind as well, creating nightmare hallucinations and all dismembering of reality, the more I understood that I would need all my instincts, strength and training.

A weak, untrained empath might not survive it.

Sullen left to deliver the list to people who could gather the things I needed for tomorrow.

I said good-night to Taridia, not knowing what actual time of day it was, and closed the door.

One of the tables contained a bowl of fruit, and there was a tiny kitchen with a cold-box and sink. Water, wine, and juice had been provided, as well as crackers, cheese and protein sticks.

But I wasn't the least bit hungry.

The trip here had been uneventful, smooth and easy. But I was still exhausted.

I lay down on the soft blankets of the bed by the window. For a time, I gazed at the dark glow of the distant city until I fell to sleep.

10.

Arulu

A night of horror awaited him. Every day, even before the drugs began to wear off, Arulu's body began to shake. He could not hold his hands steady for much beyond sweeping gestures. He dropped things. He could barely feed himself. But he never ate this far into the day anyway.

His body remained on a schedule he was helpless to change. It felt the wearing off of the chemical pain inhibitors, remembered pain was to come and braced for it. The skin seemed to draw up into cold coils, as if covered in snakes ready to strike. But when Arulu looked at his hands and arms they appeared normal, untouched.

It was the mind, though, that played the most devious tricks.

Sometimes he thought maybe the dread of pain was worse than the actual pain. At least the pain sent him away even if toward realms of slithering, gray horror. Past that, if he could pass out entirely, sometimes the terror would blank and he would know nothing for a time. But it didn't really matter. The nothing was never long enough, nor permanent enough. If only he could stay there forever.

Arulu moved shakily down the hall to his private room. Normally his mind would be anxious and paranoid. He would find himself turning quickly to see if anything followed him, all the while knowing nothing was there. His eyelids would flutter. His breathing would turn to short, sharp gasps as if he were trying to get air past an obstruction in his throat. The panic made his body tense up. It wanted to flee, run, even if it meant breaking down walls to get outside. It knew only that it needed to escape. His thoughts were only of fear, internal voices muttering: "Unsafe. Unsafe."

But tonight anger fueled him. Resentment. Fury. The acid taste of rage. The ultimate sensation of having been put through an unfair trial, found guilty for something he didn't do, and sentenced to be executed. All he could see was Tahir's face and that stupid, heavy robe he wore, black and lifeless. Ugly. Foreboding.

Stupid healers were all alike, believing in some faithless guru or god, expounding on virtues of clear hearts, meditation, diet, or an upbeat attitude. There was not a one of them he hadn't envisioned slaughtering.

But this one. Tahir. Even the name curled through his blood, boiling it. He wanted to roar. To beat on something, feel the tearing of flesh on his hands as he dug through something hard be it rock or wood or skeleton. The urge was primal and irresistible. He was a cat in the woods, his hot eyes piercing the dark with hunger. He needed to stretch, to hunt, to burn.

Off to the side, in his peripheral vision, a skull with flaps of flesh still attached spoke to him. "Brother. Come with me."

A skeletal arm came around him. He burrowed into the bitter, bent embrace. A splinter of bone dragged across his back. Razor-shudder. Frigid void.

His twin was cunning. Played games and tricks. He was often impatient and he always taunted, but Arulu loved him hard enough to weep over it. "Ari, you cry-baby," Arku would say, but pull him to his bony chest and trickle his petrified fingers through his long hair.

Tonight, Arku's dead tongue waggled black from his

moon-bone face. A strip of black hair, still attached to a scabbed piece of scalp, dusted his face like a wisp of storm-cloud. Arm around him, holding him close, he whispered into Arulu's ear. "Let's go up tonight, while you can still walk. To the guest rooms. It'll just be spying, no more. See what he's up to. This Tahir."

He felt himself turn, focus away from dread and onto his brother. Yes. Something to do. Something to wear off this biting tension he could no longer bear.

Arku, lazy and casual, wanted to use the anti-grav platform to rise, but Arulu needed to run. He wanted those stairs. He took them two at a time, flying up the levels, his boots tapping an endless rhythm of power, purpose, rush. Arku floated beside him, grinning all the way.

He skidded around a corner on the fourth floor and stopped abruptly when he saw two of Kean's guards standing at the end of the hall. He didn't remember their names. Didn't care.

Arku began to curse in at least seven ancient Earth dialects.

Arulu smirked at him. "What problem? I am allowed to talk to any of my healers at any time!"

"Oh yeah, I forgot. They let a madman wander the halls unguarded here." It was sarcasm, of course.

Guards spied on Arulu all the time. These two would be no exception. It wasn't paranoia if they really were watching you.

Arulu looked at the gleaming skeleton beside him. That was what he would look like dead. He should be dead. He and Arku, buried together on a moon of long shadows and infinite silence.

Instead he was here. Locked in a nightmare of pretending to be alive, and sane.

He approached the two, blue-coated "escorts" (Kean hated the word "guard") with conscious effort to appear relaxed, keeping his hands behind his back to hide their shaking.

They moved to the side, acknowledging his presence.

"I came to speak to my healer." He congratulated himself on how normal his voice sounded. Not even the slightest waver. At the moment, Arku was nowhere to be seen.

"We know of no appointment," one said.

Arulu shrugged. "I didn't know I needed one."

"The king said—"

"The king knows," Arulu interrupted.

He didn't really look at their faces, but noticed one shifted uneasily, and the man's coattails fluttered, threatening to turn into some kind of winged thing clinging to the guard's backside.

"You are here to guard the healer, not me, correct? He's the stranger here, the alien," Arulu said.

One guard replied, "We were instructed if he needed anything we are to be here for him. Also, he does not yet know his way around."

Arulu nodded. "Of course."

They stood, awkward and silent.

"Well," Arulu prodded. "Chime him, please." How normal he sounded. Twenty years of practice. He'd be an actor's dream.

"Uh, yes, sire."

One of the guards palmed a panel.

Arulu clutched his hands together, palm to palm, against the small of his back.

The three stood waiting. No sounds came from within for almost an entire minute.

"Chime him again," Arulu demanded.

But as the guard's hand rose, the door slid open.

Tahir stood on the threshold, black robe, hood back and at rest against his shoulders, light-blond hair like light on glass and pale eyes blinking. Looking at those eyes was like looking through a prism of ice at approaching dawn. There was no monster there.

But Arulu was not fooled by the glint and glare surrounding a softness that turned his stomach. This healer was no one. And he would make sure the man knew it before he made sure he went away. One way or another.

11.

Tahir

I had no idea how long I'd been asleep. Or how long the moon city through the open window had been staring at me in my dream-state. Something had awakened me. The echo of it still shattered the quiet of the room.

I knew immediately where I was. I had no disorientation, which surprised me because everything was still so new. I was on a moon called Firgone. In a room in a gothic palace where what was left of the royal family of the Realm of the September Stars lived.

The black sun on the wall seemed to shift and bleed within its red slash-marks.

I turned on the bed's coverlet, saw a red light blinking by the door.

I got up, still sleep-dazed, and put on my robe.

The door opened to the touch of my palm and I inhaled the cool hall air.

I saw the two escorts. Sullen. Taridia.

But the third man was unexpected. His hostility and resentment had been clear when I saw him in the throne room. He wanted nothing to do with me and he'd protested our meeting tomorrow.

Was this why he was here now? To argue me out of a job?

I had no idea what time it was, but a part of my brain

told me his meds should be wearing off soon. I was not prepared to deal with that right now.

Instinctive politeness forced me to bow my head in greeting. "Prince Arulu."

"You are the healer," he stated. His voice seemed carved of a distant wind, airy but with concealed depths of power.

"Of course. You saw me earlier today."

His mouth opened as if he were about to say something else. But no words came. He glanced away.

"You wished to speak to me?"

His eyebrows narrowed as he gave a curt nod. But his body language was poised for flight.

Something whispered in the air alongside him, movement, or maybe a sound. It was too quick for me to discern, gone before I could blink. A trick of the eye, maybe. A breath of a shadow.

He wore red, which became him. His dark coloring deepened within the scarlet frame of long, shimmering sleeves and trails of scarves floating off his shoulders. The hair hung loose, as it had been when I'd seen him earlier in the day, straight and glossy. But the eyes. They bore heavily. He wasn't exactly frowning, but his stress made the irises look like triangles.

The face was youthful, but the rigidity of his posture made him seem older.

My escorts shifted nervously but did not yet intrude.

Arulu finally found his voice. "I wish for a consultation."

"Now?" I asked.

"You shouldn't be here. You don't need to be here. I need to make that clear."

I had overheard him speaking to his father. He thought I was a sham. "You don't need my help, then."

He glanced over his shoulder, but not at the escorts. At the wall? At the air? Was he seeing things? "I don't," he said.

I took a deep breath. "What harm could it be to find out?"

"Harm?" His voice rose a bit.

Something tapped, echoing down the corridor. Other people. Those who looked out for the prince, perhaps, but staying unseen.

He lowered his voice to an almost-whisper. "The harm is that you think you can affect one fiber of what I am."

I nodded, familiar with the self-preservation in many patients which kept them from any hope that might be dashed. "Would you like to talk privately?" As I said the words, my skin prickled a warning. The stage fright I'd felt earlier, perhaps. Was I so intimidated but this angry, fractured being?

He started forward.

Sullen stepped toward me. "That would be unwise." He did nothing but move closer to me, never raised a hand. But Arulu glared at him as if he were vermin.

I wanted to ask him why letting Arulu into my rooms was unwise, but not in front of Arulu. I already understood he could be unpredictable when the drugs started to wear off. But I knew from reading reports that the dangers he imposed were mostly to himself.

"What is it you think I will do to you?" I asked.

Still glaring at Sullen, Arulu said, not answering my question, "He doesn't get a say in what I do. A private consult is what I want. May I come in?"

All my instincts flared again. I could read people well. But trying to get a "read" on Arulu beyond the obvious— broken, suffering, angry, out of control—was difficult. The heavier emotions associated with his intense agony, and the memory of agony when medicated, blocked his intent, and his true self.

"We do need to talk. I am as un-informed about you personally as you seem to be about me."

"Talk? Yes." His smile held no humor. "I came here to

assure you you cannot help me. No one can." Those three words came with a sound like a laugh. But it was no laugh. "I came to convince you to leave."

"I'm here at the king's behest. I gave my word."

He glanced sharply at Sullen and Taridia. "I have more to say. About that. About the king. I would like to speak only to you."

When I met Sullen's gaze, he gave a slight shake of his head.

My unease with the prince annoyed me. It presented a hurdle. I'd have to get over it, or he'd be correct. I'd be of no use to him. Tomorrow. Or ever.

I looked at Sullen and Taridia. "It's all right."

"The door should remain open," Taridia said.

Arulu rolled his eyes.

I moved aside to let Arulu pass. The satins of his clothing rustled. He smelled of deep wood, freshly cut as he moved through the door. I'd not been this close to him before and something about his presence, only inches away now, produced a reaction in me that combined mystery, wariness, tenderness. And no small amount of alarm. For without even one touch between us, I could pick up on the horror of his life from here.

He had had no release from this state of being for two decades. All normal functions of his mind and body had been reduced to a misery of mere survival. The heart beat. The lungs took in oxygen. He could speak. He could understand his environment and his predicament. But he could not live within it. Not in any normal way.

He did not know me. He did not know I could help him. How could I blame him for being hostile?

I noted how tightly he held his hands behind his back. I didn't know how much time he had before he lost all control.

I motioned for him to sit in one of the plush chairs that came with the luxurious quarters. I sat in the chair that was next to him. I had thought to offer to make tea, or something

55

friendly like that, but intuition told me this was not a time for such pleasantries.

The door stayed open and Arulu glanced at it as if it offended him. Then he looked behind him again, as if something invisible had followed him here, then at me. He kept his voice low. "I have things to tell you about my father. He's not completely right in the head, but it's not spoken of. That would be treason."

I said nothing.

"And when it comes to me, his son, he's understandably extreme. My past. The things I—" He suddenly stopped as if gripped by unseen hands that distracted him. He brushed at his arms, his legs, making the gestures seem casual and routine. But he was nervous as any patient I'd ever had. He had ticks and tells. I wasn't fooled.

"My father thinks he's doing his best for me. He's not. And I am not willing to play his games. So I have an offer."

"An offer?" I waited. He was coiled so tight into his tall body, despite pretending nonchalance, stretching his legs, tilting his head.

"I am wealthy. What price would it take for you to go away, pretend you never arrived, never heard of this place, or me?"

"You want to pay me to leave you alone?"

He nodded. "And leave here. Immediately."

"All this before you even try to understand me?"

He let out a chuckle. "What is there to know? You have some miracle cure up your sleeve for me? For this? Are you completely deluded?" He ran his hands up his thighs, clasped them tightly together. They were shaking. I pretended not to see.

"But have you even asked anyone, your father, me, what it is I do?"

"I don't need to know. It's all a farce. And I won't play in it."

"It's always been a farce for you in the past, perhaps.

56

But I'm an empath."

"I don't care what you are, or what you call yourself. I only want to know what it would take to get you to just leave." His voice grew rough, unsteady. The anger made his eyes flash. The air seemed to glitter around him, like an aura of electricity manifesting before my eyes.

"Have you ever had an empath in this palace?"

His lips flattened.

"Have you ever met one?"

He stared me up and down now. The left side of his face twitched. "Black robe. Acting all superior. I'm not impressed."

"I'm not trying to impress you. I'm here to do a job."

"Well, let's say your job isn't working and move on, not waste our time any further. How much?"

Money. I'd never thought about money. Never had much of it at the Temple. Never needed it. If I had not come here, the only place I ever wanted to live was the Temple. It was my home. My old home, now. But money meant nothing to me.

I shook my head.

He looked momentarily confused, as if this ploy had always worked for him in the past. "You don't want to be rich? Do whatever you want? Not have to play these games with people's lives, their minds?"

"I don't play games. I am what I say I am. I am doing what I want to do. What I am gifted to do. Beyond that, there isn't more." I startled myself with my words. I had meant them to be factual, self-explanatory. But they came out sounding as if I were limited. My identity sounded so small to my own ears.

His eyes lost focus for a moment. His voice echoed my words. "There isn't more?"

Back-tracking, I said, "This is what I do. What I love to do. Help people." My skin prickled a warning. What the splinter-bomb did: made people crazy if it didn't outright kill them. And those around them could be influenced, perhaps?

The glimmer surrounding him shuddered. He rubbed his hands together slowly, with force. The red hues of his clothing creased with darker shadows, the satin melting with the light, lending him a sort of fierce, fiery armor.

"You have given up your life." He looked down, seemingly grinning. "Like me."

"I have given up nothing. This is who I am." The reds blurred. Suddenly, I couldn't get a focus on him.

"So you won't leave." He did not look up. "There's no price?"

"One healing between us. It's what I agreed to. That's all I ask. All the king asks."

It was a lie. The king had asked me to remain here indefinitely.

"That is not all he asks!" Vehement. Teeth gritted. He still looked down, but at the brown tile floor now, his hands closed to fists pressed together.

Play along, I thought. Keeping my voice calm, I said, "What else does he ask?"

"Only everything from me." His voice came strained. "My torment. My entire life. He asks this of everyone he encounters. He's a tyrant." His chest heaved on that last word.

I had signed away my own life to be here. To do what I could for another realm and culture in a distant point of the galaxy I couldn't even see with the naked eye from my skies of home.

For a moment, Arulu's eyes glistened with tears. "He takes and takes. Without stopping."

"I've only been here one day, but it's very apparent to me he loves you."

His entire demeanor went dark, as if a light had dimmed, his skin shadowed, dark pools of it under his eyes.

"My mother wanted me put down right after—after the attack. I was ten. She is the only person in the galaxy who truly loves me." That bitter and brittle gaze now came up to meet mine.

It was more information, a new detail I hadn't heard before. I didn't falter. "I am a healer. The purpose is to avoid death."

"So you say. But if you can't?"

"If I cannot get to them in time? I can't bring anybody back from the dead, if that's what you're asking."

A snarl. "Yet you're going to try to bring me back."

"You're not dead."

Without warning, his shoulders jerked. His face contorted. The shadows loomed long in him. I could see them, elongating his face, stretching his limbs. He gave a groan and then everything settled.

The drugs were wearing off.

I could reach out to him. I could take that into me, the torment and horror, the strange interphase that came over him, and the pain. But I was exhausted from the trip. I had had no time to prepare my energy.

"You need to leave this place." Arulu's tone was harsh and unwelcome. "I have no more patience for healers or anyone else in my life. Unless you would do the honor of killing me. That would cure me permanently."

"What? No!"

"I won't tolerate anything less. Or would you force yourself upon me? You? A healer?"

I had to work to keep my voice controlled, calm. "There are many patients who fight treatment of all kinds."

He let out his humorless laugh once again. I could hear it echo down the hall. Saw the glimmering around him again as if something invisible incased him, imprisoned him, rode him.

He seemed on the verge of losing all control. His fists came forward on his knees. The fresh tree scent of him turned acrid. His body jerked forward. His soft lips stiffened, opened. "A warning, then, Healer. If you force it, I will kill you."

From beyond my throat, a bitterness came onto my

tongue. People who came to me were suffering. It made many of them irrational, crazed. They said horrible things, cursed their loved ones, their gods, their own souls.

"That won't happen," I replied, remaining very still.

"You don't know what I'm capable of. They haven't told you everything. They haven't—" He seemed to choke. His eyes widened. His words stopped with a gasp, a cry, and in all his red silks and dark, flowing hair, he tumbled to the floor with hard thump. His body writhed there as he screamed. Before I could stand and go to him, the escorts came running.

Echoes of his screaming. They were like nothing I'd ever heard. The sound went through me like arrows, hot as melted lead, and it was as if the room filled with small white dots. It was my vision blurring.

I moved to him but the escorts blocked my way.

Between Arulu's screams, I yelled, "Give him something! Do something!" Before my words were out I realized how quickly I'd forgotten in this seeming emergency that this happened to him every day. That he could take no more drugs into his system. And that his pain was to last at least twelve hours before he could take his medicine again.

All my instincts cried out to help. But my reserves were tapped.

In my personal experience with the power of healing that came with my gift in being an empath, my assessment of my ability to heal came with a sensation from a part of my brain that seemed to reside near the top of my head. A tingle. A tremor. A trickle of pleasure. The gift slid into my brain like laughter, and a feeling of fullness. I could tap that when the reservoir was full, and the feeling of fullness was accompanied by warmth all over my body, and an urge to expand it. My fingertips and my hands, and most especially my lips, felt the greatest pressure, and when I had all of that, I knew I was ready.

None of that came over me now, and yet seeing Arulu

struggle and suffer, I still had the instinct to touch, to kiss. The pressure was building inside, but wavered, simpering. After traveling so far and being in a new place, my energy was very low. I needed sleep. Then food. Then a period of silence and stillness.

I had only just arrived. I had not gotten any of that yet.

"Help him," I whispered, unable to stop myself.

"We can't."

I knelt beside Sullen, watching the young prince thrash, eyes all whites now, foam at the edges of his twisted mouth.

Sullen had hold of one of his arms; Taridia had the other. My hands reached out. Automatic.

I had to consciously draw them back. If I tried anything now I would certainly fail. The king would know and question my intent, and the prince's already hostile trust issues would grow even more out of proportion.

Sullen continued, "We can only take him to his rooms, make him comfortable, strap him to his bed. This is the way it is. And has been for twenty years."

More people came, all dressed in the blue coats, all with braids tied back in flowing bundles on their heads. They got him up and into a floating chair. Strapped him down even as he struggled, as his muscles bulged against his sleeves, his pant legs, as if trying to tear out of his clothing, and his very skin.

Arulu's head bowed forward. His limbs twitched. His vocal chords heaved in a rhythmic rant, the screaming hoarse, rough, but the edges of its blade dulled out of pure exhaustion. His hair tumbled across his sweat-drenched face, sticking to it like a tangled net. He was caught in the jaws of this thing and could not find a way free.

I noted my heart rate had doubled. I'd dealt with all measure of diseases in humans of every age and every degree of suffering. But nothing so cutting, so blinding and outright evil as this.

12.

Arulu

The sky darkened as if a cape had been thrown over the entire planet of Lyric Prime. Something wet pressed against Arulu's cheek. Tears? Blood? Slime?

He tried to open his eyes but found they were already open. He could not see a thing.

He cried out. "Arku!"

Emptiness filled him. It had claws.

No more people, family, love. Only memory made of dust, searing wind, and howling, howling everywhere. Who he was. What life made. This. Feral boy of nowhere, nothing, netherness. Out alone in a whipping, nosferatu night that never ended.

Shards unseen pierced his way-flung body. A thousand needles. A million spikes. Tearing.

Make it end. Make it stop.

A mother's voice. "Put him down for his own good!"

A father's cries. "I cannot."

None of it real. Just echoes on the cyclone of his pain.

Arulu opened his eyes that were already open and entered another dream. Four walls of a room, lavender, gray, white. A window. Blurry edges of a bed, a ceiling of shadows, the dim gold light of a future fading.

His mouth felt full of sand. Tasted of grit and the dust of coffins.

Fire zipped up and down his body, following the nerves, igniting all the way.

He heard his voice, raw, crying. *Stop*, he thought. But he could not speak aloud.

The pain had not receded but his body had actually become numb from it. That happened sometimes. The pain still ravaged with fangs and flame. It boiled. He floated in that container of acid so constant it became almost a background noise to him, though his body railed and jerked.

He blinked and could remember, through that haze of agony, where he was. Who he was. In his own bed. In his room in the second palace—the first being the destroyed one on Lyric Prime—carved of black rock on the tiny moon of Firgone.

He tried to turn in his bed, but straps held him firm. Still, he could move a little, turn his head.

Arku lay beside him, half skeleton, half zombie, looking at him with deep, brown eyes. "Hi, brother. Are we having fun yet?"

Bone fingers moved over Arulu's face as if to wipe away his tears. The skeleton of his twin embraced him, trying to comfort him.

When Arku first started appearing to Arulu, he had still been a child. They had both been ten when the splinter-bomb took out the royal palace on Lyric Prime. Arku died instantly. But six months after, his ghost returned. As Arulu grew, so did Arku, his skeleton elongating, his raspy voice deepening. In the nightmare realm, they grew up together, brothers bound in blood and death. And non-death.

Arulu's cries softened. He wept against his brother's open rib-cage.

"It hurts. I know," Arku said. "Embrace the roar. Become the blackness. And you'll come fully to me. As we've always wanted."

Arulu wanted to. How he desired it! But something he could not define always held him back. Perhaps a simple survival instinct. Perhaps something more insidious. But he could never make that final step to join his twin.

A sudden thought. Healers! That was the problem. And his father the king always bringing them around, more and more of them to fuck him up.

"Yes." Arku always read his mind. Now he whispered against the damp hair above Arulu's ear. "That is why we want to kill them."

"Them?"

"That annoyingly arrogant new one. Tahir. And Kean."
The whisper moved over Arulu's face with breath scented in
loam and mold. Lips that were mostly teeth and bone moved
across his cheek. "Killing might be the final step. To send you
over to me."

Arulu groaned and felt tears trickle down his temples.
Every day. Every night. Unbearable. The evil twin cliché. The
desire to be with his brother unquenched. Old wishes would
never go away. He could not have the past. He could not have
the future. Why did he continue on?

He had anger and rage, such rage, but the killer instinct
they said every human had remained a chained wolf in his
heart. He'd killed in all his nightmares, in his delusions and
pain-terrors, but somehow his brain and his body always
knew the difference between acts of thought, even in dream,
and reality.

He had never harmed another human being or animal.
But Arku's soft cajoling, night after night, year after year,
begging for them to finally be together, wore at him. Killing,
Arku had discussed, might send them both over the edge. But
at least they'd be together.

He'd hit a plateau in the last years. Hearing his
brother's sing-song voice as white noise, much like the pain
receding to a cloud of orange surrounding him, always
burning, but his mind going numb, bored. For that time, Arku
remained with him, but mostly silent. Just a ghost.

But the arrival of Tahir disrupted his plateau. The last
healer Kean had brought to the palace on Firgone had left in
disgrace, a sham, a charlatan. The pall of that experience led to
many years of non-interference. Kean did not force Arulu to
partake of magic waters, or swim with dolphins. He didn't
make him drink strange elixirs or chant alien alphabets
backward.

It had been blissful to be left alone.

But now. Tahir.

Overnight everything had changed. And now Arku became vocal again, aggressive, mad.

Arulu kicked at his restraints. Yelled something that sounded like a word but wasn't.

His lips were dry. His throat ached, a minor pain in comparison to his usual torture that twitched his limbs. His eyes sought the clock on the wall, trying to remember when his next dose of medicine would come. "At twelve. Always at twelve," a voice chanted. Arku nuzzled him. "But remember, Ari, not today. You don't get any today. The damned king's command."

Yes. He remembered now. Tahir would be coming to do—something. What? He had never asked. Not had time. How did it work? Would there be hot rocks, needles, or candles this time? Would there be leeches?

Arku laughed so loud it caused a deepening of the rawness in Arulu's throat.

Arulu pulled at his restraints and screamed through that laughter. "How can I kill him if I can't get free?" he asked. His voice came out a whisper. His vocal chords were that depleted.

Arku said, "I have a plan."

"Too late, brother," Arulu hissed. "Always too late. Go away!"

What was left of Arku's mouth scowled. "You don't trust me? Pity the poor baby."

"You're free. I'm not. Am I not tortured enough?"

"I? Torture you? My loving sibling, I'm helping you. Listen. Just listen." His dusty, dead whispers filled Arulu's ears, whether he wanted to hear him or not. Plans for treason. Vengeance. Murder.

When he grew quiet, Arulu turned to him, wrists and ankles aching as the restraints went taut. "I can't."

"It all comes down to you, brother. Control in the face of a splinter-bomb legacy. I know it's hard but you have it in you. You can do it. We'll only need a moment, seconds, not even a minute. You fake that you are healed. Fake that you are well. Keep the seizures at bay for that long, then put your hands around his neck and press. Hard. Hard as you can. He'll fight but you're stronger. After everything you've been through, you'll be the victor. I'll be right here with you all the way."

Death had made Arku insane, but no more so than Arulu in his dim farce of an existence. He understood why Arku had turned, these past years, to such extreme plans. He was trapped and suffering. Just like Arulu. He'd do anything to break out of it.

He thought about his hands around that black-robed healer's neck. Watching his calm, know-it-all face bulge, go red. Watching as the blood vessels in the eyes burst, feeling the heat of the skin go clammy, the limbs fold in, the body slump. The fantasy was almost too much to bear. The pleasure of having control over something for once in his life. The power.

He wanted to do it.

"But I'm not strong enough."

"Don't simper!" Arku smacked him on the forehead. The hard bone of that slap would leave a bruise for sure.

Arulu screamed.

Arku screamed as if to mimic him.

After awhile, Arku said, "Don't you want to be with me anymore?"

"Yes!" He yelled the word past his burnt-out voice.

"Good. Because you'll love it here. I promise. Our sisters are here, too."

"Sisters?"

"Remember them?" His sharp hand gestured to the center of the room.

Four little dark-haired girls abruptly appeared, standing in the middle of the floor lined up by size, ages four to eight. They were holding hands, rocking their arms.

66

Their images quickly blurred as more tears slid from Arulu's eyes. He craned his neck, trying to see more details, trying to recall their pretty little faces, their sweet voices, their smart games.

But his head fell back. He bellowed to the ceiling. He fought. His body contorted. Slicked with sweat. The salt of tears.

Arku's voice kept whispering, "Kill and it'll all be right again. Kill and you'll be finally able to rest, my love."

13.

Tahir

My hand trembled. Hot tea spilled over the edges of the cup and dotted my fingers, making my breath catch. I stilled my hand just in time to keep the cup from completely tipping.

I leaned back against the downy pillows on the bed, sipping the steaming liquid, watching three bright lights that hovered over the gloaming city in the distance. They were three of the other nine moons. I'd seen a list of their names but couldn't remember them all, words like Seedglow and Snoglobe and Wolfeye. I did not know which three these were. For now, they were merely bright, close stars, the only stars against the black backdrop of the net, a triumvirate of diamonds in an unmoving arc against the black sky. They followed the orbit of Firgone precisely, and they never rose or set because Firgone did not spin.

I could still hear his screams.

I shook the echoes from my head.

The city pulsed blackly.

My mind clung to that horrible sound Arulu had made.

67

It had to have found its way, over twenty years, into the very walls of this haunted place, embedded into the tiles, the very infrastructure. I could bury myself in the luxurious and plentiful pillows of this bed and still hear his yells.

The city. Concentrate on the city. Xia. Translation: Sunglow. It couldn't have been a more inappropriate name for such a city as loomed in my window. I kept staring, trying to clear my mind. There was no sun there. Lots of white lights, though, and hulking shapes of fat and thin towers, long square walls of ashen stone, crooked buildings with strangely curved buttresses, and fences on rooftops that looked like spikes. At the furthest point were groupings of eerie spires and steeples. The land around the city was dotted with the lights of more modest buildings, personal dwellings, houses, cottages. But all of it, because it sat on the black bedrock of the moon, appeared to be floating.

Such a dark place from my vantage point.

Again the screams.

The sounds and the images of Arulu would not leave me, the prince splayed on my floor, draped in his feathery red clothes, his body awash in agony, tossing itself again and again upon hard tile. A once beautiful face contorted itself into a distorted deformity. It seemed to crack, though the skin stayed together. And, again, the noise emanating from that throat. A divisive song of clinging torment that schemed through his body and evilly plotted to do the most harm.

Now, I kept seeing that face, the tightly drawn eyes, the thick lashes smudged against his cheeks glittering with tears.

This. I would be taking this into me. Sick frenzy. Wild anguish. A mad universe of monsters.

Not to mention the pain.

Stage fright and second thoughts had been drilled out of me when I'd been an apprentice empath. Now that training seemed a distant memory. I tried to remember the comfort of temple litanies.

Let your energy sustain you. You will float upon the disease, not within it, until it dissipates. Let your natural empath energy keep you safe. You take the pain but it is not yours. It surrounds you, but does not touch you. You see it, but it cannot see you. You are the carrier but not the host.

On and on the litanies played in my brain. I'd learned 800 of them.

But never before had I seen the effects of a splinter-bomb. Never before had I been faced with taking the damage of one into my very being and forcing it to melt away.

Just like any other disease, I told myself.

But Arulu's suffering had already entered me as I had watched him thrash upon my floor. My heart was still tight with that horror. It seemed I would never relax. But after awhile the tea began to work. My muscles calmed. My heart slowed.

I was able to focus again, close out the bleak city and the images of the damaged prince, and go into my own tranquility, a concord I had woven with my own mind, a connection and access to my deeper self I'd begun when I was a child.

Normally it would take me a good four or five hours to prepare for a healing such as this. Rest, teas, good food and focus. But I could not stand the thought of Arulu suffering any more if I could help it. Without rushing the process, I stepped things up.

I went deep into myself and consciously opened all the conduits to my energy, letting it build, doing everything I could to focus harder, rev myself up. I chanted every mantra I could think of. I thought about Zash, and the other disciples at the Onyx Temple who'd become my lifelong friends. I allowed my outpouring of love, and my homesickness for them, to gather and spin, filling me up.

All the things I loved came into my energy. Zash who taught me compassion and a father's love. Thunderstorms and good books. Stars on smoke-filled winter nights. The way dust spins in a shard of sunlight. My healing, and all the gracious looks on my patients and their loved ones' faces when I could bring them solace, and an end to their pains.

The tears of healing are pure and sweet. Like rare diamonds, gifts from time itself. They taste of childhood and wonder. The first bloom of love.

I remembered that as well, adding it into the mix. Turning twenty. The boy from a farm down the road who had teased us acolyte boys from afar. Then we'd grown up and the teasing stopped. Now instead of insults from across the road, he'd meet my eyes, nod his head. He had bluish black hair and green eyes that made my whole world seem spun of emeralds and spring. In secret, we met often for one hot summer, down by the Silver River, and learned the ways of love until adult distractions and duty took us in different directions, me to my life devoted to healing, him to a farm that housed his soul.

But the memory of that still churned my blood.

Zash had known of me and Nik, but never spoke to me of it. It was understood that by committing ourselves to the Temple we would probably never leave, never marry or have regular families of our own. But chastity was not taught, nor required. That was our own business, and Zash did not interfere.

I felt the power of the empathic gift slowly pour into me. Its warm rain dotted my body. My skin heated. My chest felt that familiar tickle I'd come to know that meant my gift was close to looking for a recipient. The energy would soon flow, wanting to burst free along with my instinct to pull back, take in, ebb and flow. The empath nature, the aspect we were born with, was the part of us that latched onto disease. It was as natural as breathing, once we understood the function of the gift. Scary at first for us kids, yes. Meeting torment face to face. Taking something so horrible into us and seeing it inside and out was terrifying. We learned the grace of calm, and of detachment. We rode the waves of other people's suffering and horror with strict discipline. We still got stung sometimes, a backlash of the sickness, but it was only temporary. We had beds ready in which to recover. The skills Zash taught us saved us from the greater shock of all we observed, felt, and took away into ourselves.

But now I was alone. Experienced, yes. But Zash was not here. Nor my brothers and sisters who gave me the only sense of family I'd ever known. I knew I would need all that training, and all my reserves, to meet Arulu's demon head on.

I had only myself to rely on. I needed to take very good care.

Slowly I fell into a dreamless sleep where I replenished my physical strength, and where my mental senses were surrounded only by the chemicals released by the love I'd brought into my mind.

14.

Arulu

"Arku!" he yelled.

Coming up from delirium was like staving off drowning. He grasped for help but there was none. He knew he was alone. Always alone at night in his rooms where only lightning-rod specters of the splinter-bomb paced and his body jerked and heaved with the perpetual feeling burning knives.

Answering the plaintive call, Arulu's twin plopped onto his bed wearing nothing but rags of skin. What was left of his face was bloated. His teeth showed through his mashed lips where his mouth would not close all the way.

Arulu was used to Arku's appearance, but he always expected an accompanying stench of sewage and ruin. Instead, only dusty essences of dry air surrounded him, and sometimes a loamy fragrance as if the ghost had breath from the grave.

Arulu tasted salt on his tongue and decided he must've bitten it.

Arku said, "Remember our plan."

"What plan?" Arulu stretched his numb mind. Pain made thinking a slogging, slow mess.

"The healer, you idiot. He's coming!"

Arulu frowned, tried to concentrate through all the chaos that left his psyche lost, blocked to normal understanding, sometimes even simple words. He tried to make sense of what Arku was saying.

"Fake that you're healed. He'll take your restraints off and then you can kill him."

"Kill?"

"Yes! It's what you wanted, isn't it? The glorious experience of wrapping your hands around his neck."

He tried to remember, to think. Did he really want to kill? He said, "But if he fails, and he will, Kean will send him away."

Arku laughed. "But that's not as fun."

"I can't," Arulu said. "I don't have the strength." He could feel the screams again, welling up in his sore throat. Soon they'd be pounding to get out. His hands felt as if they were on fire. His entire body flamed, and the nerves sizzled. He could not imagine pushing himself through all that to grab a grown man about the throat and throttle him. It was ridiculous. Tahir would be able to defend himself at the very least. Arku's plan was, as many of his plans in the past, insane.

Arku whispered, "You may be my older brother by eleven minutes, but you were always the weaker."

"I was not," he gasped out. Slowly, he was falling back into the blackness again. His body shook, felt cold and hot at the same time.

"Were, too."

Silence.

Arulu thought Arku had left him and turned his blurred gaze toward the edge of the bed. His brother sat looking at him, the bone sockets around his lidless eyes caked in blood.

"Not weak," Arulu managed to force out the words. "Cursed!"

"Yeah, okay, brother. You got me there. But all I'm saying is you already promised the healer you'd kill him if he touched you. I'm simply agreeing with that tactic. One hundred percent."

Arulu started to cough. The reflex turned to choking. He focused on breathing, knew he wouldn't choke. The mild sedatives he was allowed to take at night made sure of that. Despite pain, despite endless torment along his nervous system as if he were being burned alive, his airways remained clear. His lungs and heart functioned. His brain lost no oxygen.

But every night he faced, the pain seemed worse than the last. How could anyone live like this and not die?

Still, he kept breathing. His damn body wanted to live.

Three A.M poured like black liquid around the edges of his vision.

Before he passed out, he heard Arku say softly, "I'm on your side, brother. I'll never abandon you. I'm here for you."

He thought he heard Arku laugh as he began again to scream.

*

He held a strange, curving sword. He had never learned the arts of fighting in any system, sword, knife, rifle, laser, hand to hand, so he did not know what this was called.

Didn't matter. He seemed to instinctively know how to use it. Because it gleamed in the firelight of the distant bombs, and dripped with pearls of ruby blood.

It was beautiful, the red freshness of spilt life against silver, like berries in snow.

Hacked and headless torsos surrounded him. A mountain of them. His foot was on a caved-in chest still spraying red. He could smell salt in the air, charcoal on the wind. Burning cities and burning souls that made the sky white.

He could breathe. He was free. No pain.

He remembered now. As he had killed, the gray cloud of pain began to lift. One slash after another, a head falling here, a body there, and he could feel his limbs lighten, his cold heart warm, as if all the weights of the splinter-bomb were cut away.

Orange sparks of light in the distance. Scattered novas ablaze to show off the silhouetted ruins of the city.

All around him were the slick and the bones, torsos shipwrecked on a scarlet sea. All of it, his doing.

This was his domain now. Ecstasy and relief. He wanted to crawl into the salt and stench of it, roll, get it all over his skin, then bury himself in death and never leave.

A white flash. Then he saw him. Arku. Moving like a dog on hands and feet over the dead. He looked revived, whole. He shone. He wore a white gown that left his arms bare. It was spotless. No blood stuck to it. His hair blew behind him like a shining flag. His teeth shown white with his smile the closer he got.

When he reached Arulu's feet, he said, "We are whole now, brother, and you have joined me." He stood without effort, like a dancer coming up from a crouch, and embraced Arulu who moved his arms up, the curved blade still dripping, and pressed himself, blood, blade and all, into his brother's arms.

It had all been worth it. He felt no more pain.

He closed his eyes. The carnage vanished. Then turned his head and met his brother's lips, grin to grin.

*

Arulu came to, coughing, still screaming, but grinning as he looked up into the healer's unnerving, foam-blue eyes. Irises that were so pale they looked almost white.

74

He gagged as the pain abruptly returned upon waking from his dream. And yes, it had been a dream.

It took him a moment to reorient. Room. Bed. Restraints. Another stranger who peddled hope because Kean would not give up. He shuddered. His body recoiled, jerked, seized. But he forced the words out of his hoarse throat anyway.

"Give my my drugs."

"Not today," said Tahir.

"If you touch me I will kill you."

"So you've already told me," the healer said, bending over him, blocking all the light as well as the walls and ceiling of the room itself. "But what if I am the real thing? What if this is the last day you will ever suffer?"

Arulu let out a half-yell, half-laugh. "No one can ever make a promise like that."

"Hmm. One thing at a time."

Arulu winced when the healer had the gall to smile. All white teeth but different from Arku's smile. This smile was one he wanted to cave in with his fist. This smile offered him nothing.

Arku's voice whispered in his ear. He felt the bony hand on his shoulder, though he could not see him. "Remember the plan. Pretend you are healed. He'll take off the restraints. You can do the rest."

How he wanted to. After the dream and how good that had felt. But he didn't see how he would find the strength.

"I'll be right here with you. Right at your side," Arku said.

Something flamed to the side, brightening the air, and the face of Tahir moved away from his vision. He smelled an aroma like burnt honey, something sweet and sticky.

"Make that stop," he cried out.

"Relax." The healer's voice came soft, the tone going into him in a rippling way he didn't like. "It's not for you."

He felt tears slide out of his eyes as his muscles pulled

and released, pulled and released. "It stinks." Voice rough and shaking. "What is it?"

"Incense for my own relaxation."

He groaned. "Put it out and go away!"

His eyes opened and closed. Dark. Light. Sweat pooled at his throat. He still wore his clothing from last night and it was soaked through.

He turned his head back and forth.

"Get me my drugs?" This time he heard a bit of a beggar in his voice. He wondered if he looked like one. Hair plastered to his neck and face. Tangled on the damp sheet. His satins ruined by the liquids from his skin. At his belly, the top of his garment rode up. He couldn't move to correct it.

He heard himself whimper in frustration and tried not to be ashamed. It didn't matter anyway. This man would be dead soon.

Tahir mumbled something.

"What was that?" Arulu asked harshly.

"In my language, I simply said, 'Serenity through longing, warmth and love'."

A fucking prayer! He muttered, "Utter garbage."

"I said it for myself, " Tahir said softly. Again his voice went through Arulu like a warm tide. "You don't have to listen. You don't have to participate at all. This is my work."

"You look and sound ridiculous." The pain hit him hard that round, and he cried out.

"I'm sorry you have had to go through this, but it will be all over very soon," Tahir said.

Through gritted teeth, he answered, "Not real!"

Arku had been strangely silent throughout this conversation. Now Arulu heard him chuckle. A tickling sensation in his ear.

He heard Tahir speak again, but again not to him. Another person, or persons, was in the room. "And when I'm done," his measured, easy voice intoned, "guide me to the chair and take me back to my room. I'll need time to recover."

"Excellent," Arku gabbed into his ear. "The stupid, fake process wears him out. He'll be weak. You can do this!"

"But there are other people in the room. We won't be alone," Arulu said.

Tahir came into view again. "What?"

"I'm not talking to you." He convulsed in mid-sentence. The last words came out a strained sigh.

"Who are you talking to?"

Why was that voice so soothing? As if someone had scooped scented oils and lotions upon his skin. He could only turn away, ignore him.

But not for long. Tahir stood over him again and all he could see, smell, hear was the healer. His weird eyes, his black robe, the almost-white of his too-short hair. But he smelled clean like a winter wind. And something about him, an energy, or maybe just the heat of him, quelled a tightness deep within him. Of course it had to be his imagination.

And when he looked up at him, it seemed almost right the way Tahir's eyes swirled, the fringe of silver-blond lashes so perfect he could see each individual hair matching the silvery brows that were like two frosted lines below the golden skin of his forehead. It was as if the face, cheekbones, lips, nose, eyes were slowly pressing into him, a delicate and gentle web he'd walked into accidentally. No harm. No spider. Just the strands of silk that made a home.

Arulu's mouth opened to moan. Instead he made a single resigned sound.

He heard Arku snarl, "Coward. You gave up hope years ago. If you grasp at it again, you will hurt like you never have. Hope has always destroyed us. Hope kills us, and keeps killing though we can't die."

Tahir's face came close. Closer.

Arku raged over and over, but the whispers were retreating. "Don't let him touch you!"

Silvery hair against his forehead. Breath upon his tear-stained cheeks.

"Stop him. Fight."

Nose to nose. Eyelashes brushing his own.

"Don't let him touch you like that! Push! Turn! Bite!"

Eyes. Lips. Moving air. Lips. Lips.

"Stop!"

Touching his.

"Stop."

Moistness. Taste of rain.

"St—"

Pressure of mouth to mouth. Like air coming into him slowly, filling him up, sweet air he'd never breathed before. New. Different. As if for twenty years he'd only been breathing dust and dirt, dark and void.

His eyes had closed. He saw Arku on the rim of the blackness, distant, but it looked like he was dancing, gesturing. Heard curses, whispering. Saw the rictus of his mouth widen.

But he could not move. Could not go to him. Something else was happening. Something had him in his grip. Rocking strong. Holding hard. But slow and gentle, too, pulling at the thing inside him, all the splinters and knives, the needles and swords. All the blue lines of fire that mapped his arms and legs. His heart.

Oh his heart. It turned, uncurled, opened, bloomed. Soft breezes and stroking sunlight. Ice melting. Where dark still stirred, the coin-light of the moons of the people of the September Stars rose over the hills of his restored being. He did not remember a time like this. Not even before the bomb.

He saw blazes of light, not fire but spirit. Life. A sensation like adrenalin but less burning, more of a tickling, pleasure, comfort.

In this transformative, unbelievable moment, he had lost every vestige of the pain.

This was no fake sham.

A part of him wanted to rise up, an essence spilling, coming up from his body as if to float, to fly. That was it, a need to soar. Wanting to burst from the seams and flood every room, every hall and alcove of the dark moon-palace.

He felt more conscious than he had in so long, he'd forgotten what it was like. To be awake. To be alive.

There was a man hovering over him. He was dark like a shadow except for a halo of light at his head, and a scent of soft breezes. And this man was kissing him! He had never been kissed before. Only by nightmare versions of what could be. Only by ghosts. And he'd never been kissed like this.

There was breath, too, sweet and warm.

The lips molded themselves to his, strong but pliant, hot, soft, giving, taking, reverent.

Reverent? This was just a healer. Didn't he hate healers?

His wrists pulled at his restraints, but not because of seizure, or pain. It was because he wanted to reach out for once in his life, touch, and embrace. He wanted to pull the man toward him, feel him against him, all over. He wanted to touch him.

Out of a depth of some remembered darkness, now far away, an echo of a nasty voice wavered. "If you touch me, I'll kill you!"

Could that have been him saying those words?

That darkness like ink spreading on a white page, spiking, bleeding into all the crevices to form endless spider legs making their way through time and space—what was it?

The longer he looked at it, the bigger it got.

The man who was kissing him shifted his weight and Arulu felt him tense. A whirl of wind shook the air and seemingly the very stone of the room. He smelled ion and thunder. A sharp metallic taste spread throughout his mouth and down his throat.

Arulu felt the healer's hands barely brushing his shoulders, more a balancing touch than anything. So what was it that raked across his chest now? And pressed his hip and thigh? Something sharp, taloned. A grip of bony fingers.

He tried to see, open his eyes, lift his head, but lips held him in place, and a heaviness sunk into his head as the dark swept up his mind, through his thoughts.

His eyelids closed tight, squinting shut so that colors edged the dark. Plum, citrine, lava. The ever-present shock of green lightning. Dancing shapes of white-gold. Patterns formed a grotesque face. Arku's skeletal features emerged.

Slowly, the skull with missing chunks of hair and skin morphed into a child. The brother of his flesh, his cells, his identical DNA.

In a boy's tremulous voice that echoed throughout his brain, Arku said, "Please keep me. Don't let me go. Don't let go!"

The buried memory of so long ago came rushing back.

Playing in the throne room on Lyric Prime. Running. Laughing. Hair streaming. The giggles of four little sisters, the patter of feet.

The explosion came from nowhere, unpredicted and shocking in its concussion.

The throne room tore to pieces. The sound like planets crashing, end of the world. Arulu found himself clutching a torn piece of ceiling or wall—he couldn't tell which—and coughing violently, breathing clouds of white dust as he knelt on the gritty floor.

Something touched his hand. He looked down. Arku. Eyes almost all whites with fear, eyebrows lost beneath his bangs. His lips moved. "Ari, I'm scared."

Arulu grabbed his hand, pulled him up and clung to his shoulder as he tried to get his bearings. His brother felt damp where his hand touched his back. Sticky.

The air was almost solid white, but he could make out, through the debris, a red patch on the floor, unmoving at the front of the big room. One of his sisters. He looked around for the others. No sign of them, only the whirl of the wind left behind, only sounds of continuous, structural cracking as if, in seconds, everyone and everything would cave in completely.

"Ari…"

"Shh."

He heard another sound, then, a strange caterwaul of agony so intense it seemed to stab the very air. He felt the core of himself shift, uncurl, as if he were going to turn inside out.

Arku wailed. "No. Make it stop! Ari, don't leave me. Don't leave me!"

Arulu clutched him tightly, the pain heaving, drowning each part of his body in slow increments. Whatever it was made sure he felt every moment of it as it spread like some internal fungus throughout his system.

Arku was screaming now, but the fog of his own pain made that sound more distant to Arulu. He didn't scream himself, yet. He was too far in shock. Too afraid.

He felt his brother against him suddenly go still. He looked down. Whatever had entered him left his eyes for last so he could see.

He watched in horror as Arku's body simply came apart, as if sliced by a thousand invisible knives.

He held only liquid flesh, pieces of skin, pieces of his blue tunic dark with blood.

Now Arulu flailed. Panicked. His body spinning in a frenzy as he slid away, trying to get up, to run.

A strange voice said, as if pressed right up against his head, "No. You can't get away. You are mine, now. I will never let you go."

He began to scream and scream.

For twenty years he had not stopped.

Now, in his mind, the little boy stood before him, whole and unhurt. Beautiful. "Ari. Don't leave me."

He started to move toward his brother. But the healer was suddenly there, dour in his black robe, pale hair flashing dares to the dark.

He continued to move forward, angry now. But the healer caught him easily, holding him back.

Arulu tried to jam through him, pummel, jab, kick. The healer never budged. He was strong.

Arulu screamed. "Let me go. Let me go to him!"

But Tahir held firm, impassable as a rock, a mountain high as the stars.

Arku begged, cajoled. "Don't leave me, Ari. Don't leave me!" His voice shrill. His cries unbearable.

Arulu fought to get to his brother. Arku begged, wept.

The dark wavered. Arku went silent. Arulu stopped fighting, held tight within the clutches of Tahir's black robe. But he could still see around the man, through the robe which was like diaphanous silk now, transparent as glass. Arku, still in the distance, was moving forward.

Arku's shape distorted as he walked. Swelled and lengthened. The skin and blue clothing of the child flaked away as Arku, growing into the ruined adult Arulu knew well, began to run toward them.

Tahir held firm, arms around Arulu. His back was to Arku but Arulu could see everything. Arku's speed increased. Strands of flesh and cloth trailed behind him like ribbons made in Hell. Arku was a whirlwind of scattered bone, skin, gristle and blood.

When he hit the back of Tahir, Arulu felt the impact as they were both pushed back.

A sensation of falling.

Then he heard a voice. Tahir. "What was that?"

Lips no longer pressed to Arulu's mouth. Surprisingly pain-free, he opened his eyes in time to see the healer, eyes wide, stagger back.

Something caught him. One of the palace guards. Arulu did not know which one, could not make out his face.

But he could see Tahir fall back, the body go limp, the jaw shaking as he heard him say, aloud to the room, "The splinter bomb is not just a weapon, it's channeling an entity."

15.

Tahir

I knelt in a grove of springy grass. The Silver River sang loud. Lyrics spilling over rock, reflecting clouds. *I am cool and deep. Come and live in me forever.*

The sky soared so blue the eyes ached to look at it. Air like taffy cooling in a kitchen.

Loam. Bark. Fresh leaves.

I was wearing drawstring pants, loose and thin. A white shirt with the cotton sleeves rolled up to my elbows. I'd left my Temple robe by the fence, folded tight behind a rock.

My bare arms dappled in the light through the leaves, the skin turning gold to brown.

This was where I could come to relax, be free, sit inside myself and just breathe, gaze at nothing. At life. At peace.

I lay back into the shadow of the tree trunk, knowing the illusion for what it was, knowing I was really deep in the dark keeps of a moon-palace in a far distant realm of the galaxy, but soaking the forest in and drawing up the essence of strength and home.

This place by Silver River was where I often came after healing, to this place in my mind. It was a very real place, but whether I was there in mind or body didn't seem to matter. Its affect was always the same. I absorbed the energy here. It was a high yielding point of earth where ley lines and vortices of winds met just right. The place stirred me from deep inside until I could stand it no more, and I jumped up running, turning, a spiral of human made light.

Here I am again, I thought. The beauty of the river mirroring greenness, the trees like long-lost friends, swaying. But something was different and I tried to force myself remember.

I returned to the base of the tree and sat again.

I'd been in full empath mode. Of that I was sure,

because my body trembled as I sat there, pinches of strained muscle, darts of nerve pain fluttering up and down my spine and the backs of my legs. I made my hands into fists, stretching them to get rid of the pins and needles feeling.

A cloud moved over the sun, making me look up. It was shaped like a bird, the beak, the wings all in detail, painted in flowing ivory. The wings wisped and moved as if real.

For a moment the glade darkened. Normal, of course. Just cumulous on high. But something wasn't right.

I glanced around, saw only the velvet curves of grass ending at the stones of the river, the river itself dancing, the trees beyond the far shore tall, emerald, proud.

Beyond them, I saw a flash and squinted. Nothing. Underneath their thick branches, that part of the wood was caught in quiet shadow, frozen from the hidden light, still nothing out of the ordinary. They were liquid and cool as the river, those shadows. Part of the world of branches and thick life and teeming growth.

The flash came again, just beyond that shade. It blinded my eyes for a split-second, making me blink.

I shook my head, trying not to be distracted. Remembered I was here to gather my strength. I'd been in healing mode. Had helped someone again. This one had been serious. I needed to rest.

The disease, as usual, would ride all around me, beneath me, possibly even affect me with fleeting pain, but never enter. I could feel it lap, press, pull. The heaviness around me stayed out as I concentrated on making my body light, weightless.

What had it been this time?

Sometimes it took me long minutes to remember.

Scraps of images. Hummingbird ships. Xia, improbable name for the city-in-gloaming. A necklace of moons.

I frowned. Yes. I'd taken a trip. A long trip which I'd committed to for life.

A man in red flowing sleeves, satin feathery trains, his long hair hiding his face, came to mind. Arulu. Prince of the Realm of the September Stars.

Now I remembered. I'd come to heal the prince. The only survivor of a splinter-bomb attack that had destroyed the system, all but ten of the moons.

I remembered: Arulu wracked with terrible pain. Arulu an invalid for twenty years with drugs that gave him only hours of reprieve each day.

It all came back to me. How the man, insane with his suffering, had fought me. Cursed me. Threatened me. But I'd borne it all and gone to him anyway, giving him my gift, proving my talent.

I'd performed the empath kiss and now I was here.

But something odd had also happened. Within the tortured side effects of the splinter-bomb, within Arulu, I'd found something strange. Other. Alien.

An entity.

A being that seemed to live within the splinter-bomb effect.

Under the friendly tree, the sky of noon, the light of an ancient, friendly sun, I gasped.

My body chilled at the realization. I shuddered all over, moved up to stand again, my eyes peering beyond the glade, over the river's sheen.

That flash was not normal. Nor had my healing been simple routine. I did not have the usual sensation of the disease I'd plucked, nothing like it had been with other patients. Usually I could feel it like a heaviness surrounding me, sense the talons looking for footholds, smell the ice of destruction just beyond my own body.

But there was nothing like that. Only the two-time flash in the wood. As if all that it was and had been had drawn back, but was watching me. Observing. Waiting.

Hunting.

I had not done a battle like this before. Nor had I ever

heard of such a thing. None of my teachings spoke of an experience like this.

Every healing was the same with minor variations and difficulties. Some took longer to recover from, but the routine was the same.

I glanced nervously over my shoulder. I felt nothing.

If the disease and aftereffects of the healing really were gone, I should be waking. If the king's escorts had done what I asked of them, I'd be in my bed now. Asleep.

I tried to think of myself waking. Nothing happened.

I recited a litany I'd learned to calm my mind, protect the body.

For a moment I thought I felt the plushness of the bed, the pillow at my cheek. I focused on that, tried to move. Nothing.

Zash had taught me that when faced with the unknown, fear could be the great destroyer. He taught me to learn to think creatively. When I had once complained about the necessity of taking an art class, annoyed that it was a waste of my time, Zash had said, "We have a system in place that trains your gift, of course. But not everything is predictable. We aren't machines. Your imagination, apart from your gift, is what will save you through your life. Use it. Grow it."

I learned to love those classes that took me away from the sometimes all-too-serious, all-consuming purpose of the Onyx Temple. Poetry. Drawing. Music. They were what made the world thrive apart from disease, disorder, chaos. Zash had been so patient. I had been so naïve.

I looked around the glade once more. Then spoke. "Hello?"

My voice reverberated through the air, catching itself in the river's soft chatter before it bounded up and shattered on the glass-blue sky. Beyond the furthest bank, something white flashed again.

I spoke again. "Hello?" Softer. Radiating outward,

chiming among the tiny waterfalls created by recent storm-wrecks.

The skin along my neck prickled. Out of nowhere, a hand touched my shoulder.

I spun, knocking the hand aside. Cat-green eyes. Tousled black hair. It was the boy down the road from the temple.

"Nik," I greeted, but stepped back when Nik smiled. Something wasn't quite right. We'd been summertime lovers the year we'd turned twenty. I knew Nik pretty well, the planes of him, the muscled lines, the graceful stature. It seemed I had memorized his every expression. This man looked like Nik but leaned to the left, as if injured. His smile beamed, but the lips crooked to the left, weird. He looked as though he might be suffering.

"Tahir," Nik said. It was almost the familiar voice I'd known, but not quite.

Nik reached out. Instinctively, I backed up.

"What?" Nik asked. "Not even a hug after everything, after all this time?"

I said, trying to sound casual, "Not when I'm healing."

"You're finished, though. Resting. I can help you relax."

"Thank you. I'm fine." *And how do you know this?* my mind wondered.

Nik tossed his head. His bangs shifted against his brow, curling up. "I see that."

I watched him, amazed. Had what I'd taken from Arulu formed into this almost perfect replica of Nik? Or was this something more? Hair wind-blown, mouth slightly damp, t-shirt and jeans fitting his farmer body just a little tight in all the right places. I did not feel pain from the presence of this entity. Nor did I expect to. But Arulu certainly had Or was this a separate phenomenon altogether? I had seen Arulu's twin just before I broke contact with the prince. Arulu had tried to go to him. Had not feared him. I thought if I had not blocked his compulsion, I might have lost him, lost the healing. The damage the splinter-bomb had done had been nearly irrevocable. And it had apparently used love and companionship to keep up its malevolent work. Loneliness and a craving for love could be used as the victim's own poison.

I saw the bigger picture now.

Assessing Nik, I wondered what my former lover would do. Or rather, the former lover from my memory. The true Nik was thousands of lightyears away. As much as it seemed like him, it couldn't be him.

If the man came at me, I could defend myself, but not forever. I could run, but was sure Nik could run faster. This was my realm but Nik's game right now.

And yet, none of it was real.

But the effects of the splinter-bomb itself were very real.

I was so confused.

I tried to wake myself again, concentrating on the part of my mind that wove consciousness. I could feel the cushion of a bed beneath me and, against my left side, maybe a long pillow.

"You're not going to leave so fast, are you?" Nik asked. His arms crossed in front of his chest. He leaned one hip against the trunk of the tree in a rather "fashion model" stance that I found entirely cliché. *That's from my mind?* I wondered. While I'd spent time on the webs growing up—the Temple did not censor its acolytes—I didn't think modeling poses would be forefront on my conscious mind. I'd had a wide range of education, and this is what this entity chose?

Of course, I was not technically conscious.

As if it were reading my mind—and perhaps it could—Nik said, "I know you well. Insulting me insults only yourself."

It was actually something he'd said to me once when I thought I was complimenting him when I told him he was the romantic standard for tall, dark and handsome. He'd actually been offended.

I could almost grasp the edge of the coverlet at my left side, felt my fingers curl against smooth cloth.

"Remember how much you liked it when you would lie naked in my lap and I would stroke the back of your neck with just the tips of my fingers?"

Warmth heated my skin at those words. My teeth clenched, more in anger at myself than at the image before me. I was usually in much better control of all my faculties. *Just words*, I told myself. The entity might use them like any weapon. They were the constant after-spray of the bomb's innards. But the memory the words evoked was strong, and it knew that. Nik had been so sweet. Since him, I had not had a lover in years. Not wanted it. Not really thought about it. My fellow acolytes, my brothers and sisters, called me Iceman behind my back. I told myself it was because of my extreme light eyes and hair. I knew better, though.

"Remember how you'd trace the lines of my chest, press your hand to my heart, lean in and kiss me?"

It all threatened to tumble in like it was just yesterday. The imagery so green and warm, the salted scents, the lingering slickness between us, aftertastes of clean skin and bright love.

"You made such endearing, aching sounds," Nik said.

I tried to focus on my fingers, the cloth of the bed, and move awareness up my arm, through my chest and to the rest of my body.

"How am I not him?" he asked, again reading my mind. "Because you are very endearing. You deserve the compliment. I always told you so."

My farmer would tease me like this. Yes. But this could not be Nik. It just couldn't be! His laughter when I couldn't help but moan was not meant to be mean like when he was a kid who didn't know any better and bullied us from across the street. It was just the way he was. Perhaps a bit uncomfortable inside himself, but beautiful to me.

"And the way you kissed. Your non-healing kisses were sublime."

He was so real!

Had Arulu faced an entity like this his whole pain-filled life? It was strangely wonderful but maddening, but just couldn't be real.

I felt pulled in two different directions. I needed to wake, but I had a fascination with what this entity truly was. Also, I had to be sure that when it was gone, it stayed gone.

And yet engagement felt intuitively dangerous.

I turned away. His voice followed.

"Tahir, why are you turning from me. Don't leave me. I'm all alone."

My fingernails clawed at plush coverlets.

"I need your help."

I pushed with all the force of my mind to open my eyes in reality.

"The pain Arulu felt with his own ghost will not happen to you. Your gift protects you."

Somewhere on another plane my legs stretched, kicked.

But here wind rustled, shimmering the sun-gilded leaves. More white flashes. Little soft rains of light.

Nik said, "I am real. Tahir, you're special. I need your help. I think you are up for it."

I saw Nik's hands reach toward me.

I clutched hard at the bed I still couldn't see, feeling my body arc up. For some reason I didn't want him to touch me again.

My body in the glade took a step back.

In the guest room of the palace, I could hear my own screams now. And other voices, other hands on my limbs. Holding. Soothing.

Beneath the canopy of my memory, stabbing into and distorting the sacredness of two youths in the pure innocence of discovering themselves through lovemaking, Nik came at

90

me faster than humanly possible. Before I could even think to run, his palm touched my shoulder. "I'm so sorry," he said.

He pulled me to him, arms strong, hot, hard.

I screamed.

And came up on the bed in my room gasping, sitting up, my hands pushing against my thighs, slapping at them, then at my stomach, my chest, my head. I looked up at the faces of my two familiar escorts, as well as three others I did not know.

At the foot of my bed stood Arulu, in fresh garb, a long, gold jacket and white lace shirt. He was so beautiful. Relaxed. I couldn't take my eyes off him. Had I done that? Made him relaxed? Made those eyes that looked at me now pain-free? He stared at me. Face impassive but eyes bright, burning with knowledge, tears of familiarity. For he knew exactly what I was feeling now as I slapped at my raging body.

"My skin," I heard myself say. "It burns."

16.

Arulu

The room ran in shades of pink and gray. Arulu looked around as if seeing it for the first time. It was sparse for having been the accommodation of a boy and young man for thirty years. A painting adorned one wall, blended golds and purples of some abstract twilight. Arulu had not chosen it for his décor. His father had, stating, "The room needs color." That had been years ago.

His bed was stuffed in a cold, gray, corner, coverlets black on black. Disdained restraints for ankles and wrists dangled to the sides of the cushion like discarded ribbons of a gothic torture wedding. The pillows were arranged in a row on one side, black, gray, more black. He had more colorful ones in his cabinet, but he never used them.

While he'd been in the anteroom dressing, someone had come in and made up the bed.

He had various touch screens and communication gizmos on a table (a ridiculous number of toys for any and every technological function which Arku had laughingly called gizmology) but had actually collected, in his life, nothing much more than fine, royal clothing and accessories which were housed in a separate closet.

This was the room of a boy who'd been dead for twenty years.

Now that he had come back to life, everything looked different. New, or drab, or waiting for a fresh touch.

He still could not believe what had happened and his mind had trouble correlating it all.

Tahir's touch. The lips. No one had ever kissed him like that. That kiss had brought the essence of the man who was Tahir around him like an embrace, gentle, encompassing, but solid and strong.

This was healing? He would not soon forget the way the pain waved off him like falling water and drifted away. He never thought anything like that could be real. In twenty years he'd given up all hope. He saw no beauty, no happiness, no world that might ever exist to contain him without the constant raging of death unpromised, the howling of his soul.

But in the middle of that upswept hope that caressed with soft hands and breaths, Arku had appeared. Crying out. Reaching into the swell that contained the pain, scrabbling forward, crawling through the death and loss. He had not wanted to leave him behind to this hell. Couldn't imagine it.

But Tahir held him tight, took it on. And he wouldn't let him go to Arku. He knew it was because somehow all this, the splinter-bomb, the pain and Arku's ghost were all tied together. But leaving Arku behind like that was wrong.

Even after the healing, after showering, trying to

straighten his mind, trying to recall if Arku had actually managed to touch him before the healing ended, his skin still tingled. The relief of no pain was like stretching too long unused muscles. He'd finally been freed from his cage of spiked flesh.

He had Tahir to thank for that. All the pent up hostility from yesterday for the man had simply vanished. But they were not done. He needed to talk to Tahir about Arku. So far the ghost had been absent ever since the healing. That was not right at all.

He heard a rustle of fabric and the tap of soft footsteps.

Kean and Winter stood in the open doorway.

Arulu's father had already visited his son right after Tahir had been taken away, needing to see for himself his tired but pain-free son healed for the first time in twenty years. Kean had been beside himself with joy, teeth gleaming, hugging his son so hard, a son who had not allowed himself to be hugged in so very long.

Now he came forward and hugged him again.

Arulu allowed it, knowing he should be more thankful, but still not able to hug him in return.

His mother, wearing white today, hair adorned with dozens of white crystals, and looking as if she were carved from the very ice of her name, came forward and put her arms loosely around him. How cold the embrace was from the person who loved him the most. He understood her perfectly. She'd lost five children and would never forget that. She still did not trust the situation and he couldn't blame her.

Kean asked, as he, too, could not quite believe. "Do you really feel fine?"

Arulu nodded. His body thrummed with life. It was as if he could feel every cell quivering. No more pain burned him. No more pain numbed him at any physical level. On the mental level, however, the place inside himself where Arku had resided was a very big hole. He had never told a soul that he lived with his dead twin inside him all these years.

"It's a miracle," Kean said.

Arulu allowed himself be assessed by his parents. He held still. He kept calm. But now he looked up. "A miracle?" he asked.

"Yes. The healer didn't lie. I told you he was special. And now you see. He was what he said he was. It's wonderful. Aren't you happy?"

"To be pain-free, yes," Arulu replied. "But, Father, do you know what you've done? You've allowed my torment to be transferred onto another."

Kean shook off the criticism with a nod. "He volunteered. It's what he does. And for him it passes. Will pass. That's how empaths are."

"It doesn't matter. It isn't right."

"It's temporary. Didn't you have a talk with him? This is what he does. He takes the disease onto himself. He's trained to handle it."

Arulu frowned, remembering when Tahir had said something like that, when Arulu had gone to his room the night before the healing to bribe him to go away. And to threaten him. "Maybe, but I was there. This surprised him. Father, I didn't have some minor disease!"

"He knew that, darling," Winter said. "What does it matter now? The job is done. The healer will be compensated. And he will stay on to attend to palace concerns of this sort, as they come up. In the end, he doesn't matter. You do."

It was a cold statement. Ungracious. And as true to Winter's soul as could be. She had her son back. Arulu thought, *Why should she care about anyone else?*

Arulu said, "I was there. This was different. He was shocked. He said the thing in me was an entity. It pushed into him. It hurt him. I have to see him."

"You don't have to," Kean said. "He's being taken care of as he commanded. We are seeing to his needs. You aren't responsible for him."

"But I am. If what was inside me went into him—" He

swallowed hard. It was unthinkable that what he'd endured could be passed to another and dismissed. He needed to understand this more. And selfishly, he needed to talk to Tahir about Arku.

"I have to fix this," he said.

"Don't be ridiculous. Arulu," Winter said. "There's nothing to be fixed. It really is a miracle. We honor the healer. But don't be foolish. You needn't have anything more to do with him."

But there were other reasons Arulu was not finished with the healer, other than guilt that the horror of his pain might become another's agony.

Like night and day, one moment to the next, things had changed for Arulu. Coming to and finding himself free of the splinter-bomb phantom had been a welcome surprise. He was free of agony. But apparently, now free of Arku as well. That part was not easy, nor welcome. He loved Arku. He'd had Arku, the ruined ghost with skin flapping and bloodied bones, when he'd had no one else. Arku was his twin who had suffered as much as he had. He loved him unconditionally.

Yesterday, he'd wanted the healer dead. It had been Arku's idea and now he knew why. Arku did not want face the possibility he might be parted from Arulu. Arulu could hardly bear the thought. To have his brother taken from him. Twice. It was unbearable.

He automatically had to wonder: What if Arku had moved into the healer? Was there a way he could get him back? Could he have his brother and be whole and sane at the same time?

Things had so quickly and drastically changed, which was why he needed to see Tahir. Much as he'd wanted to wrap his hands around that healer's throat, now all he could think was he never wanted this, pain for Tahir, and maybe Arku trapped within that mind.

"I need to see him."

His parents stood together, the first time he'd seen

them look united, not arguing, not trying to escape each other's presence. "As your mother stated, the healer will be well compensated," Kean said. "And we don't know the outcome yet. He takes illness into himself. He did tell you this, yes?"

"Yes."

"But I will say this again, it dissipates. Doesn't last."

"He was taken screaming from my rooms," Arulu protested.

Kean nodded. "Give it time."

Arulu merely shook his head. "What if it doesn't take time? What if it's permanent?"

Kean bowed his head, his silver braids brushing along his upper back. "You are jumping to conclusions, Arulu."

Arulu looked into his eyes now, something he never did for years on end. Kean had always been the bright one, the most fortunate of men, before the day of the attack. Now the view of the black net above them, and all the moons, were all they had left. A still-dying realm. He'd never stopped making these ultimate sacrifices to save a single son to rule over – what?—desolation, despair, the scarred human remains of a people who once were great but could barely maintain their own concord? A people whose ships and stardrives had reputations of grandeur exceeded only by their quality, but now could not even hold their heads up, and had constructed nothing new in years?

"Father," he said softly. "Was all this worth your time and cost? And if he doesn't recover, would you still say you succeeded, all to have a healthy son to pass on what is left of the ruins of our culture and civilization?"

"I didn't do this for the Realm," Kean replied.

"What for, then?"

Kean looked up now, the lines of his tears dividing his face. "I'm your father. I did it for you, my son."

*

Arulu looked down at his own hands. His richly dressed body. He could not believe it. No drugs. And the pain was gone.

He watched Tahir thrash upon the bed. His black robe had opened in the middle, parting all the way down his chest. Beneath he wore a simple, stretch cotton shirt with short sleeves, and loose black shorts. His chest heaved. His hands clenched and unclenched in the bedding, as if he were fighting a battle those outside his mind could not see.

Arulu knew that battle all too well.

He didn't think this was right. The healer never mentioned suffering as a part of his recovery from the healing process. But everyone else seemed to think it would pass.

The healer. Thinking of him in such terms felt distant, mechanical. This was a being. And his name was Tahir.

Where had that sudden empathy come from? He'd not felt anything for another person in so long. And why did he have such an urge to reach out to him? Arku would have laughed as his sentiment.

Arku, are you here?

Was that a rustle in his mind?

He remembered too hard. What it was like. All of it. Every day. Every bloody night. The screams like sharp, cold, piercing stones thrown up into the night. It was all meteors, still, in the universe of his mind, each one a cold burnt shape of the pain of his voice. Quicksilver. Needles. Flicking away at tapestries of children's skin. Every night he'd dreamed images of slaughter, his own or another's. Sometimes his siblings lay shredded by his own knives of rage. Other times the monster came, that thing with spines like fangs that craved and slurped for blood. That scoured for whimpering children hiding behind pillars of dust with its ten red eyes. That smelled of obelisks of the dead.

Was Tahir seeing all this now?

Before passing out, the healer had said the splinter-bomb effect was an entity. But perhaps he'd misinterpreted Arku's ghost for the poison itself. And taken both into him. But Arku was not the poison. Was he?

He had to find out.

Tahir lay sprawled, body jerking. He was not restrained because he wasn't fighting. Yet. Arulu watched the hands make fists in the covers. Saw his eyelids flutter. His lips moved as if trying to form words.

The man looked strong but helpless at the same time. Arulu wanted to do something. Call his name. Shake him awake. He could still feel those lips on his, how strange that was, and had the weird thought to do it back to the unconscious man before him. To kiss him. *Why?*

On the edge of that thought, Tahir's body convulsed. His head came forward, then his shoulders and he abruptly sat up. His eyes opened, nearly white with shock, and even more beautiful in the radiating brightness of pain than Arulu had thought when he'd first met him. He looked at Arulu with such anguish, and said, "My skin. It burns."

He thought he saw a residue on the air over Tahir, like a shimmer or lace of mist.

Arulu didn't know what to say. He felt completely responsible.

One of the escorts said to Arulu, "Your doctor has been called."

"Good," Arulu replied. Then he said, trying to keep his voice steady, "Tell me, healer, that this is temporary."

Tahir blinked, rubbing at his thighs, then his upper arms. "This isn't normal. But it's always temporary. The disease always passes through me."

Arulu longed to speak to him alone. Said nothing.

Tahir said, "The pain is manageable right now. I just need time."

Relief. Guilt. Curiosity. "The doctor can give you what he gave me. It will give you relief for a half day, at least."

Tahir nodded, body still shaking. "It's not so bad. Just a

burning sensation." He lifted his chin. "Arulu, how are you doing?"

An emotion he could not name rippled through him. "I am—fine. I have no residual effects at all. After twenty years." *Except I've lost my brother.* He did not say that last part aloud. People were in the room. Strangers, though he'd known them all his life.

Tahir leaned forward, still rubbing absently at his arms. He looked so intently at Arulu it was as if he looked through him. He whispered, "It's a little like being possessed."

At that moment, the doctor came in, a small woman with a silver case over her shoulder. She set it on the table and took out some packages.

She approached the bed and said to Tahir, "Before I give you this, I just want to check your vitals."

She had done this half an hour ago to Arulu.

Arulu watched as she looked into his eyes and ran a buzzing box in the air over his head. She listened to Tahir's breathing, his heart. Asked him to describe the pain and the level of it.

She finally said, "I can give you one dose of this medication for the pain every 24 hours. But you know this."

Tahir said, "I understand. It should not last longer than a day anyway."

But to Arulu, he looked confused, and still dazed if not a bit lost. Well, he needed this man in top shape. He needed to talk to him, to know everything that was going on. Whatever this thing was, it still resided in this palace. For the moment. What that meant for Arulu was two things: guilt that the pain had been transferred to another human being. And hope that Arku might not be completely gone.

17.

Tahir

The brown eyes, so vivid and deep, pulled at me. Arulu stood at the foot of my bed watching as the doctor administered the drug for the new pain I had inherited in this bizarre aberration of my healing ability.

There was something there in Arulu's gaze. Still some horror there, mixed with need. But also concern, which surprised me. It meant I'd done my job. I'd healed him. It was obvious, and relief swept over me blocking out the pain for a few moments. But Arulu wanted something more from me. He didn't watch me out of pure empathy, though I did not completely discount that ability existed in him. The normal kind, of course, not the healing kind. Despite having just been released from unceasing madness, he was not a bad man. I'd seen that when we were connected. And I felt it when he ran at the image of his twin and I caught him in my arms, held him away and apart from that being.

I'd felt it. There was still love in him. A strange love, yes, but still love. An attachment had formed. I had seen the ghost of his brother. It appeared in our minds the same way Nik appeared later in my aftermath. I could still feel the touch of Nik's hand on my shoulder, though none of it could be real.

We needed to talk.

I assessed the damages to my body as the doctor packed up and left. My two escorts, whom I'd met the previous day, Sullen and Taridia, remained. Arulu remained.

I was exhausted. My body soaked in sweat. My limbs sore from muscle contractions. Even as the medication made the pain ebb, I was still shaking. My stomach heaved in a strange nausea. I wanted a shower. And I wanted sleep. Real sleep.

I moved my legs over the edge of the bed. My robe fell

open. There was a strange vulnerability in me.

Arulu said, gaze flicking over me, "Is there anything we can get you?"

"No. I need a shower and sleep."

"We'll be outside," Sullen said.

Arulu looked annoyed at being gestured out. He wanted to talk to me badly. I wanted to talk to him. It would have to wait.

I watched his body hunch, shoulders slightly forward as they had been when I first met him, as if he were in pain again. There was still a tenseness in him. Something unfinished. His desperate, sad eyes wandered over me once more before he turned and left with the others.

I could still feel him struggling in my arms trying to get through me and to the horror that had been his brother. So much left unspoken there. So much unexplained.

In my first night here, I had read sparse studies of splinter-bombs. Very little was known about them. For me, this was not a simple, physical healing I found myself involved in. It would be a psychological one, too, and ongoing. Not to mention managing the effects of it on me. The Nik charade in my mind seemed to be connected to the unfurling of the pain. I had no idea how much damage that had done to me. I'd never experienced anything like it.

Right now, I needed to concentrate on getting myself rested, regaining my energy.

18.

Arulu

Arulu's routine, if he could stomach it, was to work his muscles an hour a day to keep himself from cramping during the long nights. He often went for walks in the hydro-gardens, skirting the paths so he would not run into people.

After leaving Tahir's room, he'd taken a short nap, then decided he needed some exercise. His muscles ached from the long night before the healing. And afterward, he was still exhausted.

He walked through the slinky, golden shadows of the palace halls and took the beautiful winding staircase down to first-level. As he had come around each bend of a new floor, Xia hovered in the distance, brooding under the dome that let in the dark of void through its whispering colors. Broody, but domineering, that city had been formed in the shape of grief, built upon quickly and steadily as survivors of the war moved en masse to the moons. The lights of the city looked like sprinkled sugar on top of blackened, misshapen cakes. Climate technology created false, hazy days in the dome but never enough light to make more than perpetual dusk. Red reflections of light and shade bled along the edges of steeples and towers, like being on the wrong side of a monster's mouth.

When he reached the ground, Arulu followed a walkway carved of moon-stone that curved through rocky outcroppings and led past outbuildings and cottages. The desolate plains of the moonscape comprised of gravel and sand stretched toward a horizon of low mountains. On the other side of the moon lay the sun. Every half-year it rose on this side of the moon. Then the long half-year day would begin. That was still a couple months away, yet. Firgone celebrated the sunrise with a holiday called the Coming of the Light.

Arulu came to the long, low hydroponics building, one of ten in a row, and entered. The lush and misty smells immediately ignited his senses. Inside, the light was bright enough to hurt his eyes. The building held a captured jungle, humming and buzzing and alive. The effortless greens of the foliage surrounded him. He took a path that circled the gardens, one he knew passed by a bracken waterfall, and strolled beneath the canopies of branches and leaves.

A few people were there, distantly walking ahead of him, and he heard the voices of excited children, but no one was close by. No one bothered him.

He had time now to go over everything that had happened so quickly—too quickly—and to think about Arku. The idea of his brother kept coming back to him, and a feeling that he was lost now, scattered and alone and scared, and Arulu could do nothing about it. At least before, even with the pain and the horror, he had Arulu to cling to, and Arulu had him. Even if only in ghost form. They suffered and raged together. Arku was not alone in death and Arulu was not alone in an un-death that was not quite living.

He focused his mind. Searching for any sign, any touch or inner voice of Arku. Nothing. He could not help a pervading feeling of being sliced in half, unwhole. He needed to talk to Tahir. And soon!

Tahir had called the splinter-bomb an entity. But Arku was separate from that. He was sure of it.

He didn't realize his fingers had curled to fists as he walked. He consciously relaxed again, still unused to the idea that he was unmedicated and pain-free. He should be celebrating. With his parents and their friends. (He had none of his own.) How many years had he and his parents been told there was no cure? How many years had he lived with his only hope being hope-to-die? Even in moments of medicated clarity, he'd been haunted by dread every hour of every day as he faced the oncoming horror of the night.

He heard the waterfall before he saw it. The pounding rain of it. The metallic and mossy scent fizzing the air. The way the atmosphere grew more humid. He came around the bend and saw the sparkle and the flare of liquid, the way the colors played on the surface of the moving water: green, turquoise, ripples of pink. He became immediately mesmerized.

The children who'd been walking ahead had stopped for a few minutes but had moved on by the time he got there.

He was glad. He went to a bench by the side of the falls, where the mist lightly fell, enough to feel but not make everything wet. By the little dappled shores and grass and rocks, bees from the beehives to the north buzzed the green-tinged foam.

As he languidly watched them, he tried to clear his mind. Relax. Accept that things were completely changed now. That his world, once turned inside-out, was back in place now.

For awhile, sitting there, he experienced a kind of peace he'd never known. And a gratitude for being alive. It had been so long since he'd felt these things. For endless years he could remember only resentment, bitterness, panic and anger. He remembered hate, and how vicious his thoughts toward his father were, and toward anyone who tried to help him.

Those feelings still gathered in a dark space inside him.

He watched one tiny, yellow and black bee land on the edge of a rock, wade around the dampness, then take off. It looked so small, so mortal. His throat went tight and he was shocked when he felt tears trickle down his cheeks. His breathing went heavy. It all came as if out of nowhere. The choking. Overwhelming emotions he could not name rushed at him all at once.

Raising his right arm, he leaned his forehead into the inside of his elbow and wept. Long heaving sobs that kept coming until he thought they would never stop. The satin of his jacket became stained with salt.

Twenty years of his life lost. And a twin brother he missed more than his own soul.

Tahir had taken away one agony only to replace it with another, leaving Arulu grieving for all he'd lost. For who he had been and who he was now. A boy, still. Bereft and on the edge of becoming—at age 30.

He had no idea what to do.

During his pain-free hours, he had accomplished little in his adult life. He could not concentrate long enough. His focus was, at best, disassociative. He'd completed enough lessons as a child to function. He was literate. He did like studying arts and language when he felt well enough to do so. He could operate all of what Arku called gizmology. But he'd been little able to contribute to palace life. He'd had no identity apart from pain. No desire for it.

When the sobbing wrung all it could from him, it subsided.

He wiped his eyes and stared blurrily at the falls.

He tried hard to remember Arku's face. Not the destroyed ghost, but the child who looked just like him. Eyes a little brighter. Hair a little shinier. Arku, the beautiful one. The strong one. Eleven minutes younger and his best friend.

Even in ghost form, Arku had been his steadfast companion, the one thing in his whole screwed up existence worth living for. The only thing he'd ever loved aside from his mother. But while Winter's love was true, it was cold, honest but distant and cruel-edged from grief. He echoed that back to her and it was enough for him.

Arku had been his confidant. His fellow prisoner in hell. They'd shared everything.

His thoughts quieted but his grief remained. Finally, he was able to shakily stand and continue his walk.

It was good to have his body moving without pain. But in truth he was exhausted. After his emotional break, all he wanted now was his bed and a nap unfettered by nightmares and agony.

After that, he would see Tahir again. Demand answers. Probe his mind for the truth about the splinter-bomb. And Arku.

19.

Tahir

I woke to find a spread of fine foods and hot drinks at my table. The coffee was hot in its silver, swan-shaped pot and smelled of a perfect mix of bitter and sweet.

Covered dishes held meats, eggs, cheeses, bread and rolls. There were sweet cakes, too.

My empty stomach began to recoil, but as I sniffed and looked through each delicacy, it began to change its mind. The scents that wafted through the air caused a rumble of hunger. Finally.

I sat down and poured myself juice, and some of that amazing coffee.

I'd gotten rid of the robe and was wearing only shorts and a short-sleeved shirt. I had no pain. No seeming residual effects of the healing. But I also knew the medication that had been given to Arulu for many years had been given to me. It was still in my system. I had a few more hours before I would know for sure if my gift had gotten rid of the after-effect symptoms of burning pain, or if I had more work to do. More self-healing.

Already my mind was composing a long star-wave to Zash back home, asking him for advice and if he'd ever encountered anything like this in all his teachings and healings.

I needed to tell him about encountering the disease as an entity that appeared not only intelligent, but also malevolent. While diseases could take the forms of spirits for many, that was an illusion brought on by the mind. Illness was often comprised of viruses and bacteria, life forms in and of themselves, but they were mindless parasites. Not forming thoughts, not deliberately sadistic. Their behavior was about survival. They thrived on tissue manipulation and destruction and made people sick.

This splinter-bomb experience could be the very same thing, but at another whole level. I'd been prepared to treat tissue damage, but not something seemingly living that could actually communicate and *think*.

On top of all that, the psychological ramifications of twenty years of that thing affecting Arulu, messing with his body and his mind, could not be removed by a single touch from my healing kiss. My gift could mend brain chemistry, but not memory of trauma, past or on-going.

I had not expected, when an entire fleet of hummingbird ships came for me to bring to the Realm of the September Stars that this was going to be an easy job, or a quick one. But I had been self-assured enough to think it would not be beyond me.

Now, I was not so sure.

*

The city lurked out my window, icy-black tower-silhouettes against the stars. It crouched on the horizon, steeple-spined. It loured, a great city beast with beings clinging to it, inside and out. Did it notice the people passing through its heart every day, feel every stomp and fall of foot, hear every shout or whispered word?

My mind was taking strange paths, clamoring weird thoughts ever since I woke.

Showered, and with food in my system, I felt stronger. But I still could not get over the idea, and the fear, that a being might reside within me on a level a bit higher than bacterial.

It was an odd, creepy-crawly feeling, and my spine twitched.

I kept staring at the city out the window as if it taunted me.

I'd spent an hour writing a wave to Zash. It would travel at incomprehensible galactic speeds, but still take a day or more to reach him. His response would be at least another day.

So I had two or three days on my own to ponder my strategies. Use the imagination Zash had encouraged within me. Two days before I could count on any outside advice.

First, though, I needed to see Arulu. Have a real talk with him. Alone.

I had found some clothes in the closet that fit me. Grey shining trousers, a stark white shirt, a jacket of aquamarine velvet, the sleeves only a tiny bit long, which actually seemed to be in fashion here. I found shoes that fit me as well, soft black leather, ankle-high, with a thong that wrapped about them several times, tying them in place.

I combed my hair back. It fell just past my ears and wouldn't stay. A little gel and I appeared somewhat presentable, I thought, by palace standards.

I headed for the door. It slid open to reveal Arulu standing outside and just about to push the admittance button.

He said, "Oh," as the door opened.

"I was just coming to find you," I said. His clothing was brushed silk, all in plum and dusk-blue, the folds dark where shadows gathered on the shining cloth. His silken hair was held back with an oval comb of carved ivory. The comb was big, loose enough that the hair fell along his back not in a tail but a fall. His stature communicated a pain-free body, no longer tense. But the dark eyes shimmered. Anxious. Disturbed.

"You look well," I said, trying not to stare. In reality, he looked beautiful. I wasn't going to say that aloud, though.

"And you are rested?" he asked. "Not in pain?"

"Rested, yes. I can't know if the pain has disintegrated until the medication wears off. In the meantime, I found these clothes in the closet." I spread my hands and stood aside, beckoning him in.

"They are meant for you. My father had your room furnished for you. Everything in it is yours." His eyebrows rose as he looked at my attire, but he said nothing more about it.

"Did you come here to ask me questions? I expected it, of course."

He looked flatly uncomfortable, but quickly nodded.

I gestured for him to take a seat at my table. There were still carafes scattered about with juice and coffee, although I suspected the coffee was cold by now. Somebody had come in and taken away the leftover food when I must have been asleep.

I poured us two glasses of orange juice. I placed one in front of him. He ignored it.

For a moment I just watched him. He glanced around my room unhappily. I noted this because his eyes, slightly pink around the edges, were narrowed, his breathing quiet, shallow. His gaze came to rest on the sun mural with the black slash through it, surrounded by black crescents on the white wall. He stared at it as if reading something from the images, language, maybe? Something I could not detect?

I was alien here. While still at the Temple, I'd spent weeks with the implants at night to learn their dialect of Galactic Standard here in the September Stars. But even with all the learning, it would take a long time to understand nuances and symbols. So many things were unfamiliar.

Instead of barging right in to the difficult conversation of every horror he'd had to live with for twenty years, I decided to begin off topic. So I asked him about the sun.

"It's a symbol of rebirth. Like a reverse sun, starting over from the other side. Not dead. Just coming back into being in a different way. The bloody slashes through it are to show power."

"That's intriguing."

"I hate it," he replied. Now his deep gaze flicked to me. "If that's what it's going to be about, it should be more morbid. The moons should be half-skulls. The sun should have black thorns for rays."

"A bit of the artist in you," I said with a smile.

He actually glowered, turning back to the wall. "It's too simple. Nothing is that simple."

"How are you doing?" I asked.

"I have to admit," he said, not looking at me, "you have a real gift there. I felt it, all right."

"An empath's kiss is real. Some may pretend to be empaths, but the true gift is very rare. But I'm real."

The color of his cheeks darkened, much to my surprise.

"I don't have the pain anymore," he added. "So far."

"You shouldn't. It transferred to me."

"But it won't stay in you, right?" he asked.

"I've never had an illness remain in me. But this one is strange. Different." I hesitated.

He leaned forward looking suddenly interested. His perfectly arched eyebrows rose. "You said it was an entity."

"And I believe that to be the truth. Did you perceive this yourself?"

He slowly shook his head. Took a breath. "I...I did see someone."

"I saw him, too." I treaded carefully. I remembered how he'd tried to go through me to get to the specter. How desperate his action, how his voice cried out. "Your brother?"

He nodded and moisture spread through his eyes. "Do you believe in ghosts?"

How could I answer? I'd never seen one. They were stories told at night to giggling children. But I'd just seen something I'd never known to exist before this morning. An entity that seemed to be able to possess another through a psychic bomb. It sounded insane. But I felt it had spoken to me and touched me through the visage of Nik. "I can't say," I finally said. "I believe in the spirit."

Disappointment crossed his smooth features. "More than that. The self contained after death. Whole but trapped in non-physical existence. It's possible, isn't it?"

I knew what he was asking. Was his brother still,

somehow, alive? "After today, I would say anything is possible. But Arulu, the entity itself is like that. It appears non-corporeal but alive. We don't know anything about it. I've read all I can find that is known about splinter-bombs, which is not even enough to comprise a few articles in the wave system. It could be a program that goes into the brain that accesses memory and operates in a sort of dream-state, functioning as a being who communicates but really is infesting you the more you interact with it."

As I spoke, I saw his cheeks twitch. He glanced down at the table-top. His eyes brimmed but did not spill over.

I stopped talking, afraid that I'd hurt him if I said any more.

Arulu whispered, "My brother was more than that thing. Something other. You have to believe me."

I took a deep breath. Softly, "The spectre, or ghost, that I saw while in the healing mode could be an entity of the bomb's effects."

"No!" He swore. Turned his head away.

"But I only saw it that one time," I hastened.

"If that was the effect of the bomb, it was a trick. It didn't want to be dissipated. Maybe it pretended to be Arku." His voice came rough.

I was almost certain that was not the case. But I replied, "It is definitely a trickster at its core, whether the bomb is machine or being."

I heard him take a deep breath and clear his throat. "Is there some way we can find out?"

Find Arku. That was his unspoken question.

Honesty seemed my best course here. "I don't know."

"Could you..." He stopped, swallowing tightly, and looked up. "Could you do the healing again? Look for him in me? Or yourself?"

I felt a frown press my brow. I had not expected this. "You don't want to pay me to go away anymore, then?" I forced a smile, trying to lighten the mood.

"But what if it's real? Separate from that thing? What if it lingers? What if you have my ghost?"

My cheeks deflated, smile gone. "I've never—" I didn't know what to say. Any more words I might've had stopped in my throat.

He squinted. "You can try, can't you?"

I had taken part of his grief into me. I could feel it even now, an orange ash of poison drifting through my veins. Arku. The dead twin. There but for the grace of all the galactic gods go I. That was the sentiment every time he'd looked at him. I'd felt it when I was connected to him. Along with a kind of warped hope. *Please let me die. Let me go be with my brother!*

A haunted man who wanted to remain haunted. I knew he was in grief, but this was more.

I had grown up with other children in the Temple, but never had a real sibling and certainly not a twin. It ached inside me, this missing piece. It would dissipate along with the entity, I hoped. But everything was new here. Ghosts and moons. A black city that seemed to float in the stars. Corridors with light the came from dragon-head sconces. Dark, tortured princes in beautifully plumed satin coats. I didn't know what to expect next.

At least Arulu no longer seemed to hate me. But if I could not help him with this grief, there was no doubt he'd hate me again.

I wanted to try anything to avoid that. "You want a healing to try to bring back a ghost."

His face went stricken. "I know it sounds wrong."

Insane, I thought. Aloud, I said, "It is not a part of my teachings."

"I will pay you."

Again, with the payment. I had no need for money and he knew this. "I have everything I need here. This is where I live now. You don't need to pay me."

"What do you want, then? And I'll do it."

I leaned back in the chair, sighing. Thinking fast. Maybe there was a way to help him further. Zash had taught me that if you take away something a person holds dear, you must replace it with something else. A sense of purpose can be found in things you would not ordinarily think of. A creative gesture. The learning of new things. But also just beauty. A flower. A stone. A note. And love in any form. Any at all.

"I'm new and alone here," I said. "I have traveled far and everything is strange. Can you even imagine it?"

"Yes, but you agreed to this. You came willingly."

"I did. But that doesn't change the fact that I'm a stranger here. There is a discomfort in that."

"What does that have to do with this?" he asked impatiently.

Impatience and immaturity. It might be difficult. Even a mistake. But I said it anyway. "I just need a friend."

He blinked, and shadows moved across his cheeks. "Friendship?" He looked incredulous.

"Yes, friendship, and I will help you. Not as a job, but as a friend. You can tell me about him." Arku. I did not say his name. "Maybe together we can find him. But I am going to be upfront with you and say I can't know for sure."

"I understand." He paused.

"All right?" I asked.

He opened his mouth, started to speak. Stopped.

"Would it be so bad?" I asked lightly.

He tried to speak again. Finally managed, "I don't have friends. I haven't had any for twenty years."

It was a terrible thing to hear him say that. A child torn from his brother and sisters, left in agony for two decades, would of course not be prone to making friends. But it seemed such a terrible abuse, aside from all else he'd suffered. To have no one. No confidant. No real companionship. No love.

The gods help me. I said, "Well, can you accept that you have one now?"

The desperate look returned in his eyes. "I think I will

be a terrible friend in return."

"Why?"

"I don't know how."

"It's easy." Could I really teach this? "You show an interest in their feelings, their thoughts. You listen. You do things together."

"Like what?" he asked.

"Share a meal. See a vid. Play cards."

"Sounds—okay."

"And there's trust. It makes it easier to share. Secrets. Things you are dealing with that maybe no one else would understand." I hoped I wasn't sounding completely corny.

"I don't know anyone I can do all those things with." He hesitated. "Maybe not even you."

"I didn't say friendship was a magical thing that just happened over night. You become friends. The relationship grows after you get to know each other better. You learn pretty quickly if you're not compatible. I'm not going to force you to like me, or anything like that."

He nodded. "I'll offer friendship, then. We can try. And you'll try to help me find my—" He swallowed hard. "—brother."

"I can't make any guarantees. I want you to know that."

He shrugged. Almost smiled, but his lips stayed firm. "Well, the friendship isn't guaranteed. But you said you'd try. So I will try, too." His jaw set. His chin went up a fraction.

"Good. Then I want to ask you something."

He ignored my statement. "When do we start trying?"

I let out a puff of air. "Now. I think it's right now. We're talking, right?"

"But the healing thing?" He looked nervous again.

"That's what I was going to say. I can't do it while medicated. It won't work. I'm blocked. But when the medication wears off, I'd like to ask you to be here. I don't know what's going to happen. It would be better if I weren't

114

alone."

"I can do that." Soft. Not looking at me again.

"I don't want you to feel awkward. Listen. Just be here. If you can't handle it, if I go into convulsions or something, call someone to help. It's okay. Just be here."

His brows narrowed. "But I don't see how you can be so calm. I mean, do you think you'll go into convulsions?" Eyes wide. There were gold glints in the brown of the irises.

"I hope not. I have a very great gift. It has protected me well so far. Zash said it's very rare, my strength, my will, along with the gift."

"Who's Zash?"

"My teacher. One of the best. He was like a father to me. Still is. He's the one I told you I wrote a wave to asking for advice on all this. Anyway, my gift is strong. I'm hoping the pain will be gone by tonight."

"Me, too."

He pushed at his bangs, the ones not long enough to be caught in his hair-comb, away from his face. His forehead was tall. His coloring was all tans and browns. He looked so polished, refined, A true prince. But he was a boy trapped in there. He had grown in stature, a perfect physical specimen to look at, but inside he'd remained a prisoner of pain and fear of pain, and of an entity that told him his brother was alive.

This was going to be hard. Still, I would be his friend. Even if that meant being a friend who had to tell him a truth about his brother he did not want to hear.

I didn't know if either of us would survive it.

20.

Arulu

Friendship. Why did that word scare him?

Arulu had never known a normal life. Kept to himself. He visited his mother once a day. Tried to avoid his father. And took walks alone. Even in his times of medicated clarity, he never went out of his way to get to know any of his father's entourage, or the escorts who seemed to discreetly follow him around. Nor did he ever pay attention to servants.

It was really quite simple. He hated people. He believed this intrinsically. It didn't matter the cause, that he suffered so completely he was locked inside himself, introverted through anger, rage, pain. What mattered was he had learned to hate so fully, that coming back into the world, waking again after so long, made things, even familiar things, strangely frightening.

Before, he had not had to deal with taking any responsibility for his actions, no matter how hard his father tried to assimilate his ill son into his world. He learned hygiene and how to dress by rote. His clothes were provided for him, without a word, and he chose only what colors to wear. But anything to do with politeness or manners did not occur to him. If he did not speak when spoken to, or mouthed off to a stranger or servant, he barely remembered. Nor did he have any concern. He cared nothing for others and mostly did not acknowledge them.

Other healers had come and gone. He had been rude to them all, he was sure, though he could not remember every detail. He only knew he had despised each and every one of them. Tahir had been the worst because the king had made such a big deal out of it. All those hummingbird ships. Kean had never sent an entire fleet into the galaxy at large for any reason since the home system's destruction. And never as an honorary escort for a single person.

Arulu had hated Tahir instantly. Wanted him dead.

The empath's kiss. He felt his skin heat over that thought. He sat now in the chair, facing that man with such pale eyes framed by bronze skin, and that sun-lit hair that glistened even in the shadowy palace and the ever-dusk of the moonland.

He wondered how old Tahir was. They seemed almost of the same age. Which was something. At least the healer wasn't some old man trying to be a father to him. Or worse, a guru.

What did friendship look like? He could emulate vids, stories he'd read, when he could concentrate long enough to read. But it all seemed such silly fictions to the reality he lived every hour, every day, year to endless year.

Now he looked up. Tahir was watching him but pretending casualness. Or maybe he was casual for real, but how could he be when faced with such horror? The pain could be upon him at any time.

He did not know what to say. Remembered Tahir's words. "Be there for me when the medication wears off." Arulu calculated the hours. Hours he knew well, right down to the minutes, having faced this nightmare as his daily routine.

"You have three hours. If your body works like mine," he said.

Tahir nodded. "They gave me your dose. We are about the same size, I think."

Arulu had noticed but didn't want to say he had noticed. They were both tall, both narrow at the hips, although Tahir seemed broader in the chest. Of course that would be. Arulu thought his body appeared wasted, sometimes even emaciated, though his parents and the doctors made sure he got the nutrition he needed by ordering the servants to make fresh food available in his rooms at all times.

He knew his shoulders hunched forward often, a habit

he couldn't break. He had gone through gaunt phases and stopped looking in the mirrors, deciding he looked deader at times than Arku's ghost.

Awkard and hating it, Arulu said, starting to stand, "I will be back in three hours, then."

Tahir looked about to say something, silvery brows narrowed.

Arulu had more questions but wasn't sure how to articulate them. He wanted to leave, and yet he didn't.

As if reading his mind, Tahir said, "If you have more questions, I'm here." His smile was damnably charming. "You don't have to rush off."

Arulu decided to see the charm for what it was, a healer's ability to put other's at ease. To make them comfortable against their fears and nightmares. Was the prelude to friendship a similar ruse?

How could he tell? He had no experience. Could barely remember life before age ten.

Arulu finally said, "I do have questions, but I don't know where to begin." He stood all the way up now, his knees a little shaky which surprised him. He needed to move. Not face head-on the man he still did not trust but who had, in a single day, done incredible things.

He walked to the big square window that looked out over badlands of black dust and mountains towering over valleys curled in shadowed shame. The city, though teeming with life, could only be described as bleak by any standards. It was sorrow's road in every direction leading to that city and he'd often wondered why the royal palace had reconvened here, on the darkest of all the moons, Firgone. Even the mining moons had color in their mineral moonscapes. Some even had water, green with algae and plant life. One moon, Darkquill, was actually terraformed complete with hemispheres, a daily rotation, and seasons.

Arulu leaned with his palms down on the cool, dark-metal sill. The cold glass was leaded and thick with time.

Inhaling the dust-scent of lost memories that surely were embedded in the crystal, he said, "This palace is centuries old. 642 years to be exact."

He heard Tahir say behind him, "That old? Really?"

"Nothing changes here." He did not know what he was saying. Why he was even talking to his man! "Oh, the décor changes, the furnishings, the lighting. But it's all inside this old, cold mountain my ancestors carved into this place. Frozen and unbending. Always dark. I don't know why they built it. Maybe it was a vacation palace."

"I think there is beauty here." Tahir, still at the table. Soft and unchallenging.

"The artisans had an inspired design. The spiral stone staircases. The dragon-headed thrones carved from the bedrock itself. But it's dreary." He didn't know why, but he got comfort from talking about something apart from himself. Even if it reflected his inside emotions too accurately.

He heard Tahir give a short but kind laugh. "Dreary, maybe. But it's truly amazing. There are wonders throughout the galaxy I have never seen, but this is a wonder. An experience I've never known. It's all new to me. My first time away from all I have ever known in a tiny province on a planet in sector 24985."

Arulu said, "The backwater sector." Then realized maybe he'd insulted the man. He was unused to this. He hadn't had a conversation with another person that had gone on this long in 20 years. Not even with his mother. Teachers didn't count. And most of what he learned in any furthering of his schooling was by robots on the wave.

"So I've heard," Tahir said. "The term is arbitrary, meaningless to me."

And derogatory, Arulu thought, wondering why he'd said it. But he forced himself not to equivocate. He did not know this man. Why should he care?

In the black skies, beyond the purple sparks that rippled constantly over the dome, he saw three moons of dusky red and gray sheens, slowly slipping across the void, forever following Firgone. He had never been to any of them except Darkquill, where he'd visited as a child He'd loved it there. But he'd never wanted to travel after the bomb. And couldn't very well in his condition.

In that, he and Tahir were alike. Neither had ever traveled far from home. Until now. Tahir arriving in an alien realm, brave enough to embrace it and make it his home. What might make a man decide to do that? Just get up and leave all he had ever known?

Arulu very badly wanted to ask Tahir just that question. But it stopped in his throat along with old resentments, and a strange shyness that made him furious. Giving voice to that anger, he asked instead, "I wonder, does a man who travels far from his home for a long period of time do it because he is running from something, or looking for something?"

"Maybe he is looking to expand his horizons." Tahir's answer was smug, but his voice remained relaxed and passive.

Arulu felt himself hunch and forced his shoulders to relax. Bad habit.

"If you're trying to ask about me," Tahir said, "I have a calling."

Arulu turned half-way from the window, but not completely out of its shadow. "That sounds too altruistic to be true." These things like altruism, love and sacrifice—he didn't believe in them.

"I love my job," Tahir said. "My gift is an honor."

But flat, thought Arulu. *Impersonal*. He felt his lips smile at that. He could deal with Tahir on that level. He didn't have to get close or personal. This friendship could be forged on tiny links of commonality that had nothing to do with deeper reaches. Except for Arku. They would both have to deal with Arku.

The discomfort in his body returned at the notion. He

should just leave. That would solve everything. Leave, and come back in three hours.

A purple square of light shone from the window across the hard, tile floor, coming from outside. From the dome. He looked through the haze of the room and back to Tahir, who sat with one hand on the table, fiddling with a silver utensil, staring at it. He looked so still in that moment, boyish and vulnerable. Nothing more or less.

So why such apprehension?

It was all about Arku. That was it. His heart raced with the grief. He had had his pain taken away. But how could he live like this? Now? Without the voice of his brother anymore? Even if that voice said unpleasant things to him, sometimes, he'd loved it. Even if it inspired him to kill, though he never had obeyed it. Arku had only said those things because he wanted them to be together. He wanted it. Needed it.

Feeling bereft made him suddenly braver. He walked through the purple square and into the whiter light provided by a chandelier over the table. He stood before Tahir, fists at his sides. "You should know I'm not going to stop looking for my brother. Even if you tell me you can't find him. It's a mystical event and you have a mystical talent. Despite any proposed friendship between us that you hope might form, I'll hound you."

Tahir blinked up at him. "You don't have to hound me. I said I would help you."

Arulu shook his head. "And you don't have to tell me you don't believe me." Everyone humored Arulu all his life. "I can see it in you. You're all alike."

"All of who? Alike what? I am here to help. I don't know what else you want me to say." Tahir's voice did not rise. He kept himself so carefully in check, which Arulu found annoying.

"Just so you know. I won't give up."

Tahir nodded, "We are taking this journey together." So agreeable it was infuriating.

He almost snorted. "I don't even know you."

"I know." Tahir gestured with his hand. "Sit down again, if you want, and I'll tell you what you need to know. About me. About this situation. I know you don't believe me. But I am here to help you. It's a job, yes, but it's also what I want. I didn't travel this far into your realm and learn a new language and leave everything behind that I loved for pure altruism. The case intrigued me, I will admit it. I couldn't stop thinking about it the first time Zash told me of the proposition. I knew nothing about you, but when I found out I thought about you. What you might be going through. What you might be like. It was interesting. I've never had any adventures, really, in my life. Not aside from my gift. My gift was a means to get myself into one of those adventures. Maybe I was restless. I don't know. A lot of things came into play."

The speech was a long one but Arulu found himself wanting to hear more. Reluctant, but not having anything better to do, he sat.

"Every healing I do, I learn more about myself," Tahir said. "I wanted that in every healing, and didn't always get it. I craved more. Zash taught me selfishness of that sort is not a bad thing. We all feel need as living beings. We all want more than what we have, sometimes. It's how things are invented, how art is created. Culture and technology. All from wanting more."

"But you said you didn't want more. You turned down my offer of money," Arulu argued.

Tahir nodded. "It was the first day. I wasn't going to leave. Later, maybe, if I found myself so miserable here, I thought I could come to regret not taking your offer." He shrugged. "It crossed my mind."

Arulu liked hearing that. His bright and shiny healer wasn't perfect. Good.

Tahir continued. "I don't think altruism is a necessarily bad thing. You mentioned that word, so I'm bringing it up.

122

But a person cannot commit a life to that. It won't last. Myths of altruistic gods are just that, myths. Too good to be true. We also need to help ourselves sometimes. We cry out for it with our bodies, our hearts. Some altruism might fulfill that, but always it is temporary."

As the words came, the explanations and the seeming honesty—though he still wasn't sure he trusted—Arulu's body naturally relaxed. Pent up energy and animosity subsided to careful wariness, and no more fear. At least for now.

Arulu had spent life keeping his opinions to himself because he was convinced no one would share them. But it seemed Tahir did not believe in altruism any more than he did. A shock.

He thought of his father, always so desperate. Grief drove him. Wanting his son back. Selfish. His mother, less selfish, wanting to put an end to Arulu's misery because suffering was wrong. But again, selfish, because he knew it hurt her, and he agreed that no mother should have to see her child go through what he did. And even if love existed, from them to him, they were spurred more by their personal motivations than that one sorry word. He knew it was true. Could feel it when they looked at him.

In his bitterness, he'd dismissed many good things as fake or shallow. In his rage and anger, he saw them in a different light. He never imagined someone else might share those depths.

He wanted to explain this to Tahir. But no words came.

As if sensing this, Tahir said, "I don't mean to monopolize the conversation."

Arulu replied, "You're not. I mean, things have moved so quickly. I don't have all the words you have."

"But you have questions."

Strained, "Of course."

"You can ask me anything."

Arulu remained silent, staring at Tahir's hands, which

were both on the tabletop now, left covering the right.

Tahir took a breath. "I once healed a man of about forty years who suffered from total amnesia. I was only twenty-four. People can suffer temporary amnesia, or partial, but this was total, very rare. He had no clue who he was. He'd been that way for over a year and no other therapies or medicines helped him. When I took the fog from his mind his memory came flooding back. I saw parts of it. Terrible. He'd lost everything, everyone he ever loved in a shuttle accident. Only he walked away. But no one knew. It was assumed he'd died in the fiery wreck. He had never been reported missing. He'd wandered for months and no one could identify him because the accident happened on a world he was not native to. They had no records of him, and no way to know where to look in the vastness of the galaxy. When he remembered, it was horrible. I had made him worse by trying to help him."

Arulu leaned his head in his hand. "Why are you telling me this?"

"Because nothing is straight-forward. No healing is ever the same. You take away one horror to replace it with another."

Arulu scowled. He didn't know how to listen to anything Tahir told him without relating to it personally. He said tightly, "You don't believe in my ghost."

"I don't not believe."

Defeat ruled him in the moment. He asked. "What about that guy with amnesia? What about grief? Is that considered a disease? Do you heal that?"

Slowly, Tahir nodded. "Zash helped me with that when I left the Temple."

"But if you take away emotion as if it is a disease, what are people left with?"

"You don't take all emotion. You never can. The memory is still there. But the pain can be eased."

"What if a person doesn't want his pain eased?"

"It's a choice. Arulu, people come to me. I don't go to

them."

"You came here." But he knew it was a weak jab.

"Your father came to me first."

"And you answered."

"Yes."

Back to the topic at hand. "How are you going to help me find Arku? You'll go into my mind with, with that empath kiss?" Dammit. He felt himself heat at the words.

Tahir nodded. "Yes."

"Then you'll take that. Take him. You think I'm insane."

"No—"

Arulu interrupted. "Promise me you won't touch my emotions when you're in my mind. You won't take them. I don't want you touching them. My grief is my own."

Tahir leaned forward, looking straight into Arulu's eyes. Arulu saw his pupils so black in their surrounding ice-blue. "I promise. I won't. If that's a part of you that's sacred and you want to keep it, I won't touch it. We'll just look and see. See what Arku is, or where he is. If he's a part of you he needs to stay a part of you."

Arulu finally found words to express his greatest fear. His throat felt choked as he spoke. "I'm afraid you've already taken him away."

Tahir bowed his head and raised his own palms as if looking into them. Reading them. "It would not have been deliberate."

"But it was. You held me back from him."

Tahir frowned, looking up at Arulu. "I believe you may have Arku in you. But during the healing, when we both saw him, that wasn't him, I assure you."

Arulu pressed his lips tight. Inhaled slow and long. "Maybe. Maybe not. Can you be one hundred percent sure?"

"He was coming at you," Tahir answered.

"You interpreted it that way. But Arku would fight for me. Just as I would for him."

"Okay, I believe you. But we can't find out until the medication leaves my body. But I promise we will find out."

His hands were shaking now. Arulu had to get out. To breathe outside of these rooms. He rose. "I need to go for a walk," he said. He'd just come back from one. But he wanted out. Now.

Without looking back, he said, "I'll be back in a couple of hours."

He heard nothing from Tahir, not a sound, not a movement. The door hissed open. The corridor stretched in two directions under snow-gold, artificial light. His lungs heaved. The guards at the door pretended not to see him.

He hurried past them just as the light blurred into a million, tiny crashing stars.

He ran a hand over his wet cheeks, and rounded the corner toward the spiral staircase.

21.

Tahir

I watched Arulu's mental anguish, the pain he was now left with, as if it were my own. I could actually see glimpses of it with my physical eyes, running red in rivulets over his head and around his face and neck. Like some lightning force, it zagged about his clothed body, sinking through the fabric. I was tuned to him because it was still so soon after healing him. I saw it. I felt it. Altogether different, and possibly worse on some levels than his physical pain which I absorbed, it comprised itself of nightmarish mourning, bitter loss, and a mind crying out for an identity it had been deprived of for twenty years.

As he ran from the room, I tasted his tears as if they were my own.

126

Still worn out, I got up and went to my bed. I needed more rest and the day was not yet over.

I could not sleep. I lay gazing out the window again. So much night. The dark enfolding. I'd never been afraid of the dark even as a child, but right now things were grim and I could only stare and think, *Too much. Too much.*

I needed more of a plan. Dealing with Arulu in his desperation, and with the side effects of what such incredible pain had done to his mind after so many years, was going to be unpredictable at best.

What would he do if he found out that Arku's ghost might be entirely manifested by the splinter-bomb entity? Yes, I'd humored him, told him I'd give him every bit of my effort to help him find his brother in spirit. That protective streak came out in me with a rare few of my patients. Usually, I was over and done with them quickly, and they were out of my mind. But some lingered: a tendril of emotion, a scent, a heart-tug. I never really analyzed why that sometimes happened. It just seemed to be "one of those things."

Arulu was different, I told myself, because he would need on-going treatment. Not only had he sought me out with questions and a furthering of the initial healing, he was key to a new experience I was having as a result. Had I, for the first time as a healer, been infected? Were there really ghosts that could manifest themselves from Sinarha's mythical Ghost Abyss? Such huge questions loomed. A cooperation between us was necessary for each of us to survive now.

I lay still under the window's stars. In the quiet I allowed my mind to rest, focused on the black night. Examined myself for flaws, pain, disease.

The medication still pulsed in my tissues and veins. I searched beyond it, focusing my attention to what I called "the left of waking," not asleep, hyper-aware.

The glade shimmered. Not green as I remembered, but grayer, the leaves and river and rocks edged in blue, with impressionist blurs. It was like getting feedback from an unreliable power source. But I could hear the chatter of the water, smell the cool air, taste the rain of a breeze that whispered through darker clouds.

A warm hand touched my shoulder. I turned so fast I almost fell back. My movement knocked his hand away. Nik and his black-wild bangs. Farmer biceps. Cool copper eyes no less intense in the dim light. The pupils were elongated, like a cat's, but then went normal again.

My heart bucked in my chest but I hid my shock, suppressed all but awareness. This was what I'd come to the left of waking to see. To assess. To analyze.

Nik smiled and his teeth, so white and straight, looked sharper than I recalled, more tapered. I blinked and they were normal again. "Aren't you glad to see me?" he asked, holding out his arms.

"Yes." I did not move.

"What? Shy after all this time?"

"Who are you?" I asked.

"Your friend. Nik. Don't you recognize me?"

"Not entirely."

"Of course you do. You don't want to hurt my feelings, now, do you? I've come such a long way."

"A long way? This is not that far. From where you live." I looked around me. Silver River flowed past his farm, through the fields that were always gold and seemed to laugh and wave in the sun and winds. Up the bank on the other side and left, if you walked about half a mile, you'd come to a dirt lane. His farm was another half-mile up, solar silver panels over red brick, gleaming. He had goats, which I loved.

He looked thoughtful for a moment, his cheeks filling with air. Almost haughty. Teasing. "You know, Tahir. This isn't the real glade where we used to meet."

I stared at him. Of course I knew. "Who are you?"

"I'm not lying to you. I'm Nik."

"No. I don't think you are. You almost are. You look almost like him."

"Not my fault. I can't explain why. There is something strange going on. But this just is. And we two are here."

"Sorry if I'm not inclined to believe you. It's not personal."

He took a deep breath. Laughed. "It's funny, really. All this."

"What's funny?"

"I'm different but the same. The glade and the beach down there, both different but the same."

"It's not real," I said harshly.

"It is real to me."

I looked at him standing there, white t-shirt, faded denim jeans that were almost white. He'd always been intrinsic to nature, earthy and wild, and I could smell that about him right now, the old Nik still very much evident. My mind was a good trickster, or "it" was. Whatever it might be.

I decided to be honest. "My friend Nik, my real friend," I emphasized, "lives very far away from here. On another arm of the galaxy."

The eyes blinked slowly and all levity in him deflated. Sharper than normal teeth lightly touched his lower lip. Very quietly, he said, "Not anymore."

"What?"

"You can check for yourself. The wave-nets. I don't live there anymore, on that farm, near this glade. Around the time you left there was an accident. Out at the farm. A fire. I died."

I kept calm. This had to be the entity! The splinter-bomb effect. It was going to go after anything you cared about to make its best attack. "You're lying."

"You can easily fact check. Go on the wave. Get up. Wake up. Go do it. I'm here now. Not alive, not like you. But here. In a different way. And I have to tell you, it is very very strange here."

"No! I won't believe it. You can't get to me like this. I won't allow it." But already I was fighting my mind, the glade fading, disintegrating to a thousand spots of snow.

The water whispering, the air dotting my face with mist, and Nik going soft and rumpled, wistfully smiling as I opened my eyes and sat straight up.

I nearly ran to the computer on the table, a hand-held screen. It lit up at my touch. My account showed me the sent wave to Zash would be received tomorrow. Still in route through space, bouncing off planet, moon, asteroid, system to system, to make its way home. I could read news a day old from that far off. But this news would've been about a week ago, after the hummingbird ship picked me up.

My hand was shaking as I accessed information from my home planet. Half-whispering Nik's full name, there it was in a fraction of a second. The page pertaining to him. The holo of him. The time and date of his death. The cause: burns over 90 percent of his body. An accident at the farm. A fire gone out of control. He'd saved all his goats and the rest of the animals, but not himself.

Tears rolled down my cheeks. That would have been the way he'd do it, if something happened, he'd make sure the animals were all safe first. He never even had to think twice. He told me once he loved animals because they had no agendas, and they didn't need gods to tell them what to do. They were just natural, perfect as they were. Yes, he would have saved them at the expense of his own safety.

I couldn't read anymore, and shut down the screen. I put my hand on my forearm, leaned my head on the table as a part of my heart died.

*

The door opened. I had not heard the chime.

I lifted my head from the table, still shaking.

All the gold light from the corridor poured through as if desperately needing a home.

Arulu stood there, looking all ruffled and put out as he spoke. "You said to come back in two hours." His usually shining hair was unruly now, as if he slept and woke and never bothered to put it back in order. The pretty hair-comb was gone.

He stepped over the threshold, frowning at me. I couldn't think for a moment. Where I was. Why. Then I quickly wiped at my face.

He saw the gesture. "The medication has left your system. Are you—" He came closer. "You don't look so well."

In my mind I could still see Nik in the bluish representation of the glade, his wild bangs and not-quite-feral grin, hear his low voice echoing in my brain. *I've come a long way.*

"Should--?" Arulu seemed at a loss. "Do you need to lie down? Is the pain coming back?"

"I-I don't think so." I was still shaking. What was happening? Ghosts. I had humored Arulu, but I didn't really believe in ghosts. This was a trick. Had to be!

"No, I don't have pain." I leaned up until my shoulder blades hit the back of the chair. It was true. The nerve endings of my skin felt normal. Not hot. Not cold. No pins or needles.

My heart still slammed in my chest. I was short of breath.

"That's good, then, right?" Arulu asked, moving closer. The door hissed shut and the room went back to its whites and violets, with browner shadows hiding in the corners. "I put the doctor on-call, but it looks like you don't need her."

"No. I don't need her. Thank you for doing that." I still couldn't think right. "But I need some time right now. I don't think I'm ready for our meeting."

Arulu stood before me. For the first time since meeting him, I saw a hint of concern in him. But he had an agenda, too.

I looked up at his gaze, the guarded brown eyes still so grim. "I just found out a friend of mine died."

Surprising me, he did not hesitate to respond. "I—don't know what to say. I—know how it feels."

Strange he did not say the usual things people say, "I'm

sorry," "You have my sympathy." "I shall pray for you." Grief. It was something he knew so intimately he could actually connect with others on that level. When he didn't move away from me, I realized he understood, and he was unmovable in that.

He said, "Ever since you got here, it's one bad thing after another. You should not have come here. We are a haunted and cursed realm." So sad, those words. My eyes filled. His face blurred under my gaze but I saw the eyes go shiny, as his limbs seemed to lose all strength and he slid into the chair beside me.

"Arulu, none of this is because I came here."

"You have stepped under the shadow of a hell we live in here on these moons. I live in it. Now you."

"I wasn't dragged here."

He leaned his head against his hand and looked at me. "Your friend. What happened?"

"An accident, that's all."

Arulu nodded. "So many accidents. We have technology to make our lives longer and healthier, but nothing to avoid those. The universe is a dangerous place. Monstrous."

I had never thought of it that way, but could understand why he did.

"How old are you, Tahir?" he asked. Surprising me again.

"Thirty."

"Me, too. How old were you when you went to live at the Temple?"

"Young. Six." I remembered feeling so small and wet in the rain.

"Both of us had our lives put on hold at about the same age, you at six, me at ten. Never able to be on our own."

"I chose—"

He interrupted. "At six? I don't think so. You were forced into a life that locked you away."

132

He would see it that way. I did not. "My gift is an amazing one. I am one of the lucky."

My tears receded for the moment and my vision returned. Thoughts of Nik remained, although in the back of my mind.

I saw Arulu's face even more clearly, thick lashes making shadows on his cheeks, the skin fine-pored with a rich, natural tan, lips of tender pink, and felt a jolt in my diaphragm. His strong chin lowered and in that moment he was vulnerable, open, and I think I saw him with more than just my eyes for the first time. Really saw who Arulu had been, and still was, beyond his suffering, and the bitterness of a stolen lifetime. This prince had been drenched in darkness for too long.

"This gift ruled your life, took it over, controlled it. Don't you wonder what choices have been taken from you?" he asked.

"No. I don't."

"And your friend? Was he or she controlled, too? Like you? Living at that Temple?"

"I said I wasn't controlled!" I didn't mean my voice to come out harsh and immediately bowed my head.

Arulu never flinched. His fine, long hands lay against the table palm-down, steady. Had I created that steadfastness? Had my healing made him stronger in only a single day? Was this the same glowering prince I'd met just yesterday?

"Tahir," he said gently. "Tell me about your friend."

I could not resist the tone. I wasn't sure what was happening, but my response to him was immediate. I didn't think. I just spoke. About Nik and his goats. The way he tilted his head and his lopsided smiles. The yellow-green summer by the glade when we'd swum naked in the glittering Silver River. I'd never told anyone this much.

Arulu's face looked more relaxed than I'd ever seen it. He listened and said nothing for a long time. Finally, when I paused long enough that silence gathered all around us making the room seem too small, Arulu said, "How did you find out he'd died?"

I blinked. He deserved the truth. "I was meditating. He came to me like a dream. Only different. I thought it was the entity, the one we both saw in your healing. But he told me he wasn't, and that he had come a long way. To see me." My voice broke.

Arulu's eyes widened. "We both have ghosts then. You believe it now?" He didn't say it to be mean. He remained gentle, astute. Forehead tightening in thought. "But why? Is it part of the splinter-bomb? Are we now both insane?"

Instinct took over right then. I had come to do a job. To help. To heal. "Nik told me he had died. Told me to look it up. He was right. I could not have known that. How is that insane? No, we're dealing with something else."

"I've been thinking that for twenty years. No one would ever have believed me, though, so I kept it a secret." He looked perplexed and relieved at the same time.

I didn't think. I simply reached out and covered his hand on table. "Well now someone does."

I saw his throat move as he nodded tightly.

"What do we do next?" he asked.

This time it was my own face that heated. I knew what needed to be done, and how I operated. The empath's kiss. Always, when healing, it was an impassive act, something I did that awoke the gift and made it operate properly. I conducted it all in a business-professional manner.

But this felt all-too personal now.

The side of Arulu's mouth twitched.

"The empath's kiss again," I said. "To wake whatever it is in both of us. And talk to it. If it's the entity, it needs to be dissipated."

"I know." But his eyes narrowed.

I forced a smile. "It won't be any different than the first healing." I lied. Somehow, already this was different. His closeness, our talk, our griefs. I'd just found out my former

134

lover had died. The vulnerability of all of that made me shaky. And Arulu himself was so obviously not prepared. If he were to find out his brother was some mystical ruse by a weapon no one in the known galaxy understood, what would that do to him?

"Now?" he asked. "You said you needed some time. I can leave and come back tomorrow. There's a dinner with my parents anyway. They wanted me there."

"If you need to, go."

His brow rose. "If you ask me to, I will."

I was feeling better having had our talk. Things were coming together for us, a sort of trust and energy it might take time to rebuild if we held off a day. My emotions were fresh and intense, making me restless. I wanted to do something to figure all this out. Now.

"No. I'm not asking you to leave. Not anymore. I'm too curious to delay this any longer, if you're up for it."

He leaned toward me. "I want to know. I have to know."

"So do I."

The kiss was going to be more intimate than any healing kiss I'd ever done. For several reasons, I already knew that.

I watched him fiddle with an oval necklace he wore. It was a silver and gold communicator on a long chain and had an interesting design on the outside, like filigree, to make it look like jewelry. He looked up after a moment. "I cancelled dinner. They'll have to wait to see me until tomorrow."

That's how important Arku was to him. He didn't want to wait, either.

I thought about making tea to calm our nerves, dragging this out, giving us both a much-needed reprieve, or more time to change our minds, time to still back out. But delays would never help.

I stood, all too weak, but determined. Arulu mirrored me, standing quickly. "Should I go lie down on the bed?"

"It's easier that way. The position of the healing. You need to be relaxed. In as secure as position as you can be. I need to see you are open and ready. I need to take the lead."

He shrugged, but his head turned away as he sat on the edge of my bed. "Okay." He sounded casual but his words were followed by a gush of air. Like the beginnings of apprehension. Anxiety.

Arulu lay back, stretching his long legs out. My heart thrummed in my throat. The black pillows. The gentle purple light. The soft flowing dusk-blue satins of his long coat and trousers. All like a watercolor about to fade. Too much beauty. I needed to touch it to bring it back to life.

My veins began to hum. Because of his beauty, I could almost believe him unreal. In this moment his very presence undid all my professional thoughts, my routines. I shouldn't be seeing him this way, thinking these thoughts. But I had no time to chastise myself like a little boy. But how could I not see how lovely he was lying there in the gloom of the dome and the far-off despair of the city?

I stood by the side of the bed near his shoulder.

He looked straight up toward the ceiling, shifting his body a bit, no doubt gathering his composure. The communication necklace fell to one side, the chain across his neck glistening. He said, "So how will this work?"

"There is some kind of mental aberration in both of us. Something that you may have recovered from but that I am still dealing with. To better understand, we will connect again, as I said before, through the empath's kiss."

He grimaced a little, glanced toward me. "I know, but I mean will I feel anything?"

"Not pain, I assure you that."

"It's a strange way to heal someone, a kiss." He paused. "Don't you think?"

I shrugged. "You get used to it." But Arulu was different. He brought out a protective instinct, and a tenderness in me. As well as a strange flush. Was it just his

136

beauty that affected me?

No more of these thoughts!

He said, breaking my train of thought, "And it's not an aberration. It's real. You already know that. Your friend appeared to you and told you something you did not know but later verified. It's real."

My eyes misted. "I do understand that is how it appears."

Did his gaze actually soften?

He took a breath. "Okay."

Sitting on the edge of the bed by his hip, I placed one hand on either side of his head, near his shoulders. I thought I could already smell the sweetness of the glade.

I lowered my head. His lips were parted a fraction. His eyes half-closed as I moved nearer. The heat of his body radiated into my arms and chest. Our faces were so close my heart began to jump. It wouldn't do to let that show, or to be embarrassed. I just let it happen.

First our noses brushed. I let my lips descend, the touch bringing our chins together. He remained passive, letting my mouth brush softly.

I felt him tremble. The clothing on our upper bodies met in a soft shush.

In a few trembling seconds, I was in. In an abstract way, his mind and mine met with a meshing of color and light. Blue from Arulu for echoing loss. Along with cinnabar and garnet vestiges of pain. I was ivory, of course. He saw me that way because of my hair. My so-sudden grief for Nik wavered in a crisp greenness. One could call our minds stormy. I marveled at how alike we were.

I concentrated on reading him for purposes of healing, but found myself confronting my own stubbornness to just want to bask, float in Arulu's presence, which resonated with me like no other in my life.

I didn't want to move any further than that.

By some natural instinct, this had moved into more of a

lover's kiss than an empath's kiss. It shocked me.

How different Arulu was from my first assessment. In healing mode, I found him to be angry, sad and lost, but with a rare strength that had allowed him to survive for so long relatively intact. He had a longing in him so fierce it brought tingles of adrenalin from my belly to my chest. I wanted to cry out. My fingers gripped the coverlet at his shoulders. I deepened the kiss. Thought I felt him arch up.

This had never happened to me before. My honest intent had not been to arouse him. That went against my personal healer's code, one that trod a fine line because of the very fact that my talent involved a kiss.

I saw him in my mind quite suddenly, standing before me, tousled and wide-eyed, hair partially covering his face. A blue-black aura of need behind him as if saying, *Give me the world, that's all I ask.*

All of my body responded, drawing up with an impulse to try to do just that. I knew exactly what that world looked like. Its features, its topographies, its terrible vulnerabilities. It had symmetry to Arulu. Because it was his twin.

Like Nik, Arku might appear anywhere in the landscapes of Arulu's mind. But probably he would be somewhere familiar, known, inked upon his thoughts with a permanence that would never fade.

I looked at him standing before me, the dark prince of the September Stars. In his thoughts he wore fire-red suits with trailing silk scarves, as if he were shadow encased in flame. He lifted his left arm and trails of scarlet fell from him.

"Arulu."

He gazed at me through locks of long brown hair. "Tahir." Low. Working its way around me, that voice was almost a caress. He came forward. Not like the first time when he'd been so resentful. Untrusting. Shy.

Communication could be awkward in this space. I have never done it before. But he didn't seem to mind. Or notice.

138

"Do you want to touch me?" His face flushed a little. "I mean, to help locate him. Do you need to?"

I smiled. "Already am."

He came forward, almost sheepish. "But I mean here." He swept his arm out again, trails of crimson blowing in a strange, low wind. Unspoken: *Put your hands on me.*

Was he asking because he thought it was the right procedure? Or did he want it?

I kept my hands at my side. "I need to ask you something."

He nodded.

"Where in your memory is your favorite place? A place you and your brother loved to go once long ago, a place you felt free from everything and could just be kids?"

"We loved the woods outside the palace. Even had a tree house. But our favorite place to play? The throne room." His eyes turned stricken.

"On Lyric Prime?"

Lips pressed tight, he finally stuttered, "Y-yes."

Now I moved forward. All my empath strengths and instincts came alive. I knew this was where he had been attacked. Where his brother died. I put my hand, palm curved, against his upper arm. I said softly, "That's where we will find him, if he exists."

"It's utterly destroyed."

"Not in your mind."

"And your friend? Do we look for him as well?"

I shut my eyes tight for a moment. He had been here only a short time ago, a distorted version somewhat, but real enough to tell me he'd died, and prove it.

But I still did not trust any of this. It was associated with a splinter-bomb effect, and therefore unpredictable at best.

I opened my eyes. "He is in my mind. But it's Arku we're looking for now. All right?"

He nodded. "I can't feel him anymore. He left when

you took the pain." I heard the accusation implied in his words.

Still, gripping his arm, I tugged at his red coat. "Come on. Focus. We're going to the memory of your throne room."

"I don't know how."

"Focus on what you loved about it, a favorite section or hiding place, how it smelled, the way your voice echoed within that room--" Before I finished speaking, the amorphous, colorful nothing we had been in faded into: hard floor, golden sun-lit rays from high, six foot windows stabbing the air, giant columns of white marble, stone walls of intricately carved sculpture depicting towers, trees, fantastic winged ships, creatures of myth, the heads of gods.

We stood with my hand still clasping Arulu's arm, side by side, staring around us. Echoes of children's voices haunted this place. Whispers. Tiny running feet. The wind of laughter.

Suddenly a little dark-haired boy ran up to us. He had sweet big eyes and a pointed chin. An elfin creature with no worries, no strain. He laughed once. Then skipped around us in a circle, his feet tapping the floor in a little dance. He came to rest in front of us again, arms crossed over his small chest. Smiling, he began to morph. His arms and legs lengthened. His body grew bigger and his head changed from innocent child to an almost mimicry of Arulu with pointier features. Then the skin began to peel away in large flaps. The eyes bulged. Blood dripped down his arms and legs behind tattered, holey clothing. His mouth opened blackly. "Hello, brother."

Arulu's body sagged in relief. He took a breath, then reached out and hugged his brother to him. "Arku."

"Thought you'd lost me, huh?" The mouth spoke clearly even though the lips were half-gone, and the tongue looked severely damaged.

Arku stepped back from the embrace, looking from Arulu to me. "Thought you were going to kill that bastard."

Arulu said quietly, "He's helping me."

"But I'm not in you anymore. So he hurt you. And me. Or are you turning your back on me?"

"No!" Arulu glanced at me.

I still didn't know for sure that Arku wasn't in Arulu's mind as a mere memory embellished by fantasy. Our minds were merged but this place was definitely from Arulu's memory, not mine. It was all Arulu's scene now, and I could not know if it was real or not.

"I took away his pain," I said to Arku. "That should be good news to you."

"The pain brought me to him," Arku countered.

"If that's the case," I said calmly, "taking away the infection of the splinter-bomb would not affect you."

Arku said, put out, "Arulu, are you listening to his hooey-gobblety? It's ridiculous. This healer. Here. In our private place!"

Arulu clasped his shoulder, pulling him close. "He took away my pain. After twenty years. How is that ridiculous?"

"You should know." The ghost-twin shuffled his feet and they clicked on the hard floor. "His actions separated us."

Arulu moved closer to him, as if to embrace him again. I stood just watching.

"I don't want us to be apart, but the pain—"

"I always hated your pain. But look at me!" Arku cried.

Arulu gasped and I realized he was weeping. "I didn't want this for us!"

"I'm dead. You're not. Nobody wanted this," Arku hissed.

I stepped forward. "Arku, what are you? Do you even know?"

He looked at me askance, distrusting. Arulu was trying to hold back his emotions. Arku's hand curved about his neck, absently stroking the long hair, as he said, "Shh, Ari." He paused, his tongue lolling darkly. "Of course I know. Didn't he tell you? I'm a fucking ghost."

"How is that possible?"

"You tell me, oh master healer monk whatever you are."

"You came out of him when I took his pain. That was you and I saw you coming at him. That was you I felt come through me?"

"Yeah. You fixed him, all right. And then you kept me from staying within him. I had nowhere else to go but into you. So I guess you fixed me, too, and we aren't together anymore."

"Honestly," I said. "I'm not your enemy. If what you are saying is true, I'll do all I can to make it right. But the splinter-bomb—" I stopped, afraid to say too much. "If you are causing his pain, then—"

Arku interrupted. "I am not the device itself. You have it all wrong. But the splinter-bomb itself is a doorway of sorts. In order to do as much destruction as it can, it channels death."

Arulu's head came swiftly up. "You never told me that."

"You never asked," said Arku. "I might add, also, it channels the dead."

My mouth opened and stayed open. Amazement. Shock. Awe. I didn't know which feeling was strongest right now.

"Then you are linked to it?" Arulu asked.

Now Arku's head bowed. "I don't know." He hesitated. "Possibly."

"So when it completely dissipates from Tahir, you'll dissipate." Arulu said it as a statement, not a question, his voice forlorn.

Arku gave a shrug with his bony shoulders, the skin that was left on them red and oozing.

"Arku," I said, looked at his ravaged body. "You don't have pain, do you?"

"No."

Strange. As I looked at them, I could see that it was as if Arku received the burns, the horrible death, but Arulu, still alive, received his pain. All the pain that Arulu described and I felt when I healed him was equal to how Arku's ghost-body looked.

But now the remnant remained, the ghost, the specter, the revenant.

Arulu looked at me, dark eyes glimmering with tears. "Can you help us?"

"I don't know." I still couldn't reason a few things. Nik had been burned to death in his accident. But his ghost did not visit me with flaking skin. Nor did I feel the burn of his mortal injuries except at the very beginning, when I'd taken Arulu's pain. My gift had made the pain disintegrate. It had never been Arulu's pain I'd felt, but Nik's through my own connection with him.

Tears spilled down Arulu's face. "I can't lose him. I know he's dead but I just can't let him go."

"Hey, brother, I don't want to go, either." Arku put his tattered arm around Arulu's shoulders.

A thought occurred to me. I wasn't sure I could do it, but I had my gift, its power, its hope. I had no clue how to transfer something like an infection back into a patient, but I said, "Maybe I could hold onto him here for you. Keep him safe. Here. In my mind."

"But I don't like you,"Arku said, then snickered.

"Shut up," Arulu said. "If it were the only way, would you say 'no'?"

Arku looked me up and down. "He's kinda cute, in an odd way."

Arulu winced. Cheeks darkening.

"Okay," Arku said quickly. "When are we going to prove to him that I'm real? Let's get to it. Make it be so I get to stay."

How to do that? Both establish his reality, and keep him from dissipating when the entire effects of the splinter-bomb left my system? I felt my reasoning powers slipping.

But for grief-stricken Arulu, my natural empathy combined with my gift made it impossible for me not to try. Help others. My motto in earnest.

I approached the two brothers, hands out, open. "Then you both have to make me understand what is going on here so I can do everything possible to help you."

We stood in that throne room until the rays of the sun turned copper, then orange, then cinnamon. The sculptures on the walls tossed shadows of strange shapes onto the floor. From the first question I asked, "When was the first time you were aware of each other in this state?" to the last, "What do you two think death actually is?" we discussed, we analyzed, we agonized.

Arku no longer wanted to kill me. But I was still afraid. Afraid I'd fail them, that there was really nothing I nor my talent could do to heal the biggest and most insidious disease of all: death.

22.

Arulu

There was a fever in his mind. Arulu's heart whipped up a pace as if it housed the strongest winds.

Arku was there, real, and talking to them in a memory of a dead throne room in a palace that had exploded into a million smithereens. Lyric Prime no longer existed, it, too, bouncing around the cosmos in tiny, frozen fragments that would go on forever into eventual heat-death.

And yet they stood on that planet in that room. The floor felt hard. The walls looked solid. The sunlight bounded warmly at them. He could even smell the amber incense their

144

father the king used to burn every morning. Sweet and deep and ashy.

He could remember the excitement of this room. The power. As a little boy, he'd come here often, alone or with his brother and sisters. People told him he'd rule here one day, though he was too young to believe it, or to know what the word "rule" actually meant.

Then the nightmare came, the attack. Followed by more nightmares of death and more death. His brother dying in his arms, in pieces. His pain sending him screaming into red spaces he never really emerged from even with good medication.

Arku had come to him on the second month of his hospital stay, a patchwork boy in pieces haphazardly put back together. He kept Arulu company, comforted him in the worst times, grew up with him in hell. Arulu grew used to his appearance, after the first year no longer screaming at his twin brother's ruined face and body. Now, for his life, he could not bear to lose him again.

Tahir listened, to all of it, their entire life story, the tale of two brothers, two mirrors ripped apart, and though it had been less than two days since the healing, Arulu began to trust him.

Tahir made statements like, "I can't make promises I'm unable to keep, but I promise you I will do everything in my power, access all of my gift, to keep you both safe, each in your separate form."

So lucky, he was, that this healer had ever come to him all the way from the backwater stars at the galactic edge. Lucky his father had ever found this strangely talented and beautiful man.

Beautiful, yes. Arulu could admit that to himself now that he trusted Tahir more. Now that Tahir had met Arku and didn't run away yelling for escorts or doctors to lock Arulu up once more at night when his screams interfered with their own grieving silences.

When they'd all finished their questions, their stories, a strange thing happened. Tahir beckoned Arku by his side.

Arulu watched, quiet now, done with all of his questions and worries, relaxed, for now, against his fears.

Tahir's gentle voice came. He liked it. The tone like a low chime, this man from the distant stars.

"Arku, may I see if I can give you the healer's touch?"

Arku, always the rudest of the twins, laughed at him, sneering but now in a more playful way. He'd never been shy, even as a boy. "You mean the empath's kiss?"

Tahir said, "Yes." And waited.

Arulu watched.

Arku sauntered up to him, grinning toothily, torn lips flapping. It was a testament to Tahir that he did not even flinch. "Plant one right here, then," Arku challenged.

And Arulu watched as Tahir did just that, taking him without warning by the shoulders, pulling him chest to chest, and with no hesitation pressed his lips to what was left of Arku's mouth.

It took only seconds. He released him gently.

Arku gasped in air. "Fuck," was all he said. As they'd grown older, the ghost had picked up cursing somewhere. Arulu didn't mind it, even found it endearing.

Tahir said, "I've done my best. Brought you to me with the touch. But my gift dissipates what it senses as disease. I don't know if it worked. I thought I might've felt our minds latch. If I don't let go, and you don't let go, maybe this will work. I wish I could do better for both of you, but I don't know how to link you to Arulu."

"Ari can visit me through you," Arku said.

Tahir's smile was tender. "Yes, I hope he can."

Arulu was overcome again, his tears heating his eyes. He tried to blink them away, ran a hand over his face, his red sleeve dampening. It was so real here. He couldn't believe this was only mind-stuff.

The throne room and Arku began to fade then.

146

Arulu began to panic. "What's going on?"

"Don't worry," came Tahir's voice from the increasing shadows. "It's just my energy waning."

Arulu felt the warmth at his chest from another body. The upper body of Tahir leaning over him. Beneath him the bed cushioned him, a perfect give to the mattress and covers. Lips on lips. The sensation both alien and wonderful to him. He'd been alone so long.

His body thrummed with sensation. Electric and hot, but like night and day when compared to the lightning of his pain. This was being bathed in warm liquid, surging, the embrace of solace and promise and hope.

Tahir.

His far hand reached up and over his stomach, touching Tahir on the hip. And then he did something completely off, completely crazy. He lifted his head slightly and kissed Tahir back, moving his lips, using them to feel the other's mouth more fully.

He started to wonder what Tahir might be thinking, or if Tahir was even capable of thinking after using his gift. Part of him felt embarrassed, which only made the fever of his body increase. Part of him didn't care.

After a few seconds, he felt Tahir push himself up. Arulu gripped his hip harder, fingers digging into his soft trousers, trying to communicate. *Don't leave.* He did not want to be alone right now.

Tahir lifted his head and said, softly, "Sorry, this never happens."

Arulu could see the sheen in his pale eyes, and how moist Tahir's lips had become. How flushed and swollen.

"It's—it's—" Arulu tried to speak. Couldn't.

"I didn't mean for this—"

Arulu lifted his head and cut off his words, kissing him again. He wanted that touch to stay. No matter what.

Of course he had no clue what he was doing. He'd never made love to anyone before. And rarely even to himself, his drive for that killed as well by the splinter-bomb, along with everything else in his life.

The surges of his body sparked at every nerve. An intense pleasure he could not have conceived of before today. His hand clung to the fabric at Tahir's hip. He pressed up, hard with his mouth until he felt teeth.

He shuddered. Sudden tears fell across his temples and into his hair.

Tahir lifted again. "Easy," he said. The hand by the left side of his head that supported Tahir's weight came up and brushed at the side of his face. He let his fingers trail his tears. Whispered, "Ah, I didn't mean to do that to you."

Arulu was thinking, *But I did it!* Didn't want to feel angry, then, and didn't want to cry, just wanted more.

It was like seeing stars for the first time. Or touching rain-scented grass. Or learning that the universe went on into infinity.

He couldn't explain it. He just wanted it. He held tightly to Tahir's hip, tugging, seeing questions in Tahir's face. Tahir pulled back a little more.

Arulu could not abide that. He whispered, "Don't!" *Don't leave me. Don't go.*

It was Tahir's bed. It was Arulu who should be leaving despite the way the dark window glittered behind Tahir's body, and the way the purple light filtered through his soft, white hair making him want to touch it, touch him. He should leave. Now.

Tahir said gently, "I have a code. I can't—"

Arulu said, voice sounding strangled, "I should just— you can't leave me yet." Just yesterday he had hated this man. Now his body seemed like it was raw and open, the veins singing. He'd never wanted anything like this.

Tahir's chest expanded with a deep breath.

"I feel like I'm dying," Arulu whispered, embarrassed the words came aloud.

"You're my patient."

148

Arulu reached up then, placing his palms on Tahir's shoulders. Pulling gently. "I don't care."

Tahir pressed his lips together tightly, his eyebrows narrowing in such beautiful concern.

The heat burned along every inch of Arulu's skin, but pleasantly now, like the quick warm licks of a hundred candles. His muscles were tense but in a kind of thrilling anticipation. Something hollow turned over in his stomach as he said, "Unless you are repulsed."

"That's not the problem," Tahir replied quietly. His head fell back and he murmured something that sounded to Arulu like, "Gods help me." He looked back down at him. "I thought you hated me."

Arulu pulled him closer, hands gripping him now. "Me, too." But Tahir had risked everything to help. And they were both grieving now. It was so easy for him to see how alike they were. Lost childhoods, one to violence, one to an incredible gift. Both their lives planned for something special by others, neither given much choice. And now both haunted by ghosts because of an alien weapon no one understood.

Tahir's lips formed a small smile. It took Arulu's breath away. Through his life of anger and resentment, he'd never asked for anything like this. Now, in total disbelief, he heard himself say, "Please."

Tahir lowered his head. Touched him lip to lip, just a brush. A gesture Arulu felt as reverence, and slow acceptance. His body reacted with a pleasured thrill that waved through him, head, heart, groin. This time he grabbed, pulling Tahir down, hoping the healer might bring his whole body onto the bed so he could press against him.

It was pure instinct. All he could think to do. He'd never done anything like this before.

Tahir wore a pretty white shirt designed in the current fashion for the moons, no doubt purchased by the king from the best stores on Firgone. It made his skin look all the more coppery. It had one flap that fastened below the breastbone leaving the throat bare. Along with the gray trousers the outfit gave him a stark, handsome look. The aquamarine jacket Arulu had seen him in earlier had been draped over a plush, low chair by the bed.

His hands slipped over the fabric that now seemed in the way of what he really wanted to touch, pretty as it was. His thoughts wanted to go further in their imaginings. Tahir naked before that dark window, an angular sculpture of bronze. That sculpture enveloping him. He shied away from the image.

He did not feel Tahir in his thoughts as he had awhile ago with that different kind of kiss, but he still worried the man could see everything. He felt his body flush again, shyness first, then in a sort of multiplying pleasure.

He wanted to see him, like that vision, but he wanted to feel him more. There was a freshness, too, a scent of green newness, and something deeper, woodsy, that brought him secret, special memories of childhood. Comfort. Home.

Tahir was like something he'd been starving for but never knew it. Arulu was discovering within these very moments that everything about this man was exactly what he'd craved forever, without knowing he craved it. The textures, scents, the dim salt of so-soft lips.

He had the thought: *Let what is happening keep happening.*

When he finally felt Tahir's knees breech the bed and that long body lie down to match his own, he was both relieved and even more fervent. What would he do next? What would either of them do next?

But he was lost in the kiss for now, and that was fine because it was opening him up so gently, so tenderly. His heart. His body. His lips parting slightly to try to take more of that kiss, deepen it. And no idea what he was doing.

Tahir met him in every move, opening his mouth, too, and Arulu thought maybe he was doing something right, then, as he felt the inner recesses of his lips nipped, caressed,

150

and his tongue curiously sought to taste.

Tahir jerked when he did that. When he licked.

Arulu stopped, found air, a voice. "Sorry."

"No, it's nice. I didn't expect you—" He paused, looking into his eyes. "You've done this before?"

Arulu didn't know how to answer. Thought maybe he'd be wrong no matter what he said. A lie was a lie. But the truth might be evil. He felt the other man on his lips, still, the slight tremble of what could only be called lust.

"No, then," Tahir answered for him, looking thoughtful.

Arulu's heart sank. He'd done something wrong then. He was thirty years old and even this eluded him. And somewhere else inside him, where love and friendship did not reside, a stinging shame expanded.

But then Tahir said softly, "Truly, no one has ever made love to you?"

Arulu frowned, trying to hide his real emotions. "I don't like to be touched." His head fell and he lay back, taking his hands away from Tahir, although Tahir remained pressed against his side, and on his right arm.

"That is—understandable."

Arulu tensed, thinking Tahir might quit right then and there. But Tahir reached out and put his hand on Arulu's chest, resting it there.

"Did I do something wrong?" He hated asking. Wanted that question back as soon as it was out.

Tahir shook his blond head and placed a tremulous kiss on his cheek. "You are doing everything right. You surprised me."

I'm desperate, Arulu thought. He felt bumbling. Idiotic. "I don't mean to surprise or—unless that's good?" Another question he immediately wanted to take back.

But he quickly forgot about that when Tahir kissed him gently again, and he felt the tongue lightly licked. That was when he knew it was okay. What he'd done. How he'd done it. He was not a complete buffoon.

He turned his head. Raised his left hand over Tahir until he touched the center of his back.

The lips moved and he mirrored them. And there he was again, body and mind, as if sliding into infinity. It got even better when Tahir's hand moved up, caressed his cheek and the side of his head, fingers tangling in his hair. Just that tiny tug, and his hair being smoothed like that. He decided right then and there he might be dying, or maybe this was coming back to life after so long alone only half-participating in existence.

He did not know how much time passed as they kissed. It definitely wasn't healing, this. Yet it was. Like feathers ruffling, taking wing. Like air coming into a long deflated soul. He was a breath away from something more his body anticipated but his mind refused to latch onto.

He knew the whats and whys of his body's reactions. Of course he knew what sex was. But he had never experienced anything like this. The rushes and coursings, the way his body seemed caught in half a dozen different rivers at once. They didn't talk about this in e-texts.

He didn't know exactly when Tahir had moved more heavily over him. Only that he liked it a lot and that now both his arms surrounded him, like a hug but even deeper. Tahir's knee was resting on top of his thighs, close to Arulu's knees, not uncomfortable or too weighted, and he wanted to feel that more, too. His legs spread without him thinking too much about it, to allow that knee and the rest of Tahir's leg to be trapped between his own. Another hug.

The heat in his groin seemed close to pain but never quite getting there, radiating instead an urgent pleasure, a ripple of energy that tremored as if it had waited too long to be acknowledged.

His vision became starry. He closed his eyes, saw the necklace of moons where he lived, and the furnaces of suns that made up the galaxy, spinning. Tahir's tongue tasted him.

152

He tasted back. How hungry he had been without even knowing it.

Tahir pulled away and Arulu felt instant loss. But then Tahir's hand touched his throat, one finger tracing down. His other hand still rested in Arulu's tangled hair. The finger tugged at his collar. Tahir moved up, kissed Arulu once more, and then both his hands were undoing the buttons and ties on his satin shirt.

Arulu leaned up on his elbows. His coat fell away from his shoulders. If he were going to get it all the way off, he'd have to sit up.

Tahir moved back, letting him up, helping with the coat. The edges of Arulu's shirt already spread apart, shushing over his skin, exposing his entire chest. It was heaving, he realized. Hard to get air while kissing. Or maybe the kissing by itself made him breathless.

He tried not to grin. Half-failed. Was met with a beautiful smile in return.

Tahir's hand touched him in the center of his chest, crazy warm, and his exposed nipples hardened. He fell back again, arms still in his sleeves, trapped. Yesterday, he might have panicked. Today was a different day.

Tahir's hand moved over him, caressing right to left, the tips of his fingers catching on his nipples in a way that hardened him even more between his legs.

He wanted. He needed. More touch. This skin on skin thing was too wonderful. It had to continue. His hands lifted Tahir's shirt at the waist and went up under it, stroking along his lower back.

Tahir let out a quick laugh, said, "Sometimes clothes get in the way."

"Yeah," he agreed.

He sat up again, straddling Arulu's right thigh, and quickly pulled off his white shirt. Tahir's chest shone in the gray light, pale gold as a sun dawning, or the antique edging on the pages of thousand year old books.

Arulu reached up and ran his fingers over the rippling of the ribs on each side of the sternum, the skin so warm and alive there, smooth, then up to curving muscles and pale brown nipples, which went taut and erect at his touch. He ran his hands further up, raising his head a little, and touched breastbone, clavicle, the sides of the neck. He drew his hands along the line of jaw, framing the beautiful face, leaned up further while gently pulling.

Tahir moved down so he could reach. This time Arulu initiated the kiss. Hands finding more skin, shoulder blades, knots of spine. Their upper arms clashed, rubbed as Tahir pushed his hands under Arulu's still caught shirt. Arulu felt them now against his naked back, the shirt all rucked up under the back of his neck. Finally, as if tired of fighting it, Tahir took hold of it and pulled it up, bringing Arulu's hands away from his body. The shirt came over his head. His arms went up as they left the sleeves. Tahir tossed it hard over the bed and it made a hushed sound as it hit the floor.

Arulu's head fell back again, sinking against a plush pillow. Tahir kissed him on the throat, the chest. His hand wandered over Arulu's stomach, not tickling but pressing, petting. Wings seemed to pump inside his abdomen. Over and over the sensations clawed inside him as if he held inside himself some trapped beast who comprised all his yearning and loneliness and lost hopes. It wanted out. Had held its breath for too long. Died and came back to life too many times to count. It was going for total freedom from all the things that held it trapped, now. All the prison bars melting.

Fingers tickled, tugging at his waistband, undoing the clasp, the soft zip. Pushing aside the flaps.

Arulu gritted his teeth as a groan escaped him. He had not ever heard his own vocal chords make that sound. This was not pain or frustration or rage. This was unyielding pleasure in its purest form.

He didn't want to panic now, but he felt if Tahir touched him there, right there, he'd fall apart into so many pieces no one could put him back together again. Not ever. Parts of him would fly up and soar out the window all rocketing in separate directions never to be found again.

"Tahir," he gasped.

The hand froze. Tahir leaned over him, nipped at his jaw, found his lips for awhile. Pulled back again, and said, "You're beautiful."

Dizzy. Clasping warm, slightly moist flesh at shoulders and back, Arulu pulled Tahir to him. Hated that he suddenly wanted to cry again. He felt the other's heart beating rapidly against his own and knew he was not the only one in such a state.

Softly, Tahir whispered in his ear. "It's okay. A touch to ease things. We can do it again. Take our time. But the first time—let's get that done."

"Yes." The word came out as a long sigh.

Tahir lifted his weight up, and Arulu followed, arching his hips. Hands pulled his trousers down until they were below his knees. Palms swept up the tops of Arulu's thighs and everywhere Tahir touched felt like flame, but not the torture, scarring kind. The flames that took his skin now were dream-flames, encompassing, circling, warming. Summers in a dappled wood. Grand sunsets viewed from windswept porches. Hearths of cherry fires to keep away the darkest nights. All the best of childhood memory.

Tahir's hand moved up, gently on him now, stroking slow. He felt so hard. Straining to hold back. But the fingers ran along his groin, cupping him, and the skin to skin sensation was too much. But so great. Arku would have said, "Fucking wonderful."

He tried to keep quiet as his mind spun up. A sensation as if all his bones turned liquid. Cries snarling in his throat. His legs parted further not because he willed it, but because he couldn't help it.

He reached out blindly.

Tahir moved up, but did not stop those wonderful

caresses. Arulu grabbed onto him as Tahir pressed against his side, the hand ever-moving "down there" and deftly tightening as the strokes quickened.

Arulu couldn't hold back. His head came up, eyes unseeing, nothing but white, and touched his forehead to Tahir's naked chest. He pressed his face into the heated skin, his arms pulling the healer closer.

An indescribable feeling so huge within him tightened, then let go. He felt himself orgasm sharper than he'd ever remembered such a sensation could be, even the very few times he'd felt it quickly with his own hand, and his cries echoed upon the gray-black shadows.

The ecstasy shook him to his core. His heart raced and his mind sang.

And you shall worship at the dawning heat of my skin.

The thought came to him from a poem he'd read once, years ago, and thrown across the room as garbage.

Garbage. Wholeness. Garbage. Trust. Garbage. Serenity.

All those things did not exist for him, and so he dismissed them as easily as the accumulation of trash from daily living. None of them were real. Until today.

He breathed rapidly against Tahir's chest, felt the other's arms come around his head, holding him tight against his heart, and rock him like he was a baby. Which he most certainly was not. But he still liked it. So strange. Such a feeling of being so revered. Taken care of. Healed. One of Tahir's hands pressed along his jaw, fingers under his chin and tilting it up.

Arulu allowed it, seeing those pale eyes once more as Tahir lowered his face and kissed him before his breath had had time to slow. He moved into it smoothly, mouth opening, more assured than in the beginning, that kiss like oxygen. A necessity. A new addiction. Life itself.

The kiss explored more boldly now that the barrier of held-back tension had dissolved for Arulu. Tahir appeared

156

more in control. He wasn't jealous of that, just impressed.

Tahir moved over him, and Arulu felt the slippery sensation of his still trouser-clad loins pressing against his overly sensitive crotch. The cloth against him felt good. Confining but not. He loved the oddness of the idea of being held down and kissed until the everlasting end of the Age of all Ages.

Tahir moved to kiss him all over his face now, sweet presses of lips against his cheeks and jaw and throat.

Arulu ran his hands down the smooth back, clashing with the waistband and pushing down on it so he could feel more. His fingers managed to move underneath the fabric and clutch at rounder, softer flesh.

A small fire began to grow again inside him as he touched the other man more intimately. He loved the texture, the pliancy, the firmness to the curves of him.

Tahir moved his lower body up, hands going to his pants and undoing them, pushing them down. He stopped the kisses for only a moment, saying, "Must get rid of these." In the process, he pushed Arulu's trousers all the way off as well, and both sets of soft leather boots, kicking them onto the floor.

He was so ready for more contact now. Arulu wanted to feel him, all of him, and Tahir complied, hovering over his body, then pressing his full length against him. Lowering flushed and eager lips again.

Skin on skin. The soft moistness. The sharpness of hip and rib; they were both so lean. The muscles on Tahir were thicker than Arulu's, more defined, while Arulu was maybe an inch or two taller, all of it in the length of his waist.

The hardness of Tahir became evident as he pressed against Arulu, the length of his erection trapped between their abdomens, and Tahir moved gently for friction.

Seeing what the goal was, Arulu moved too, trying to help. Pushing up, rubbing with his groin and stomach, alternately clutching and caressing the finely-textured buttocks.

Tahir pressed down, thrusting back and forth. Arulu held him, now using his own lips to kiss beyond Tahir's face. He mouthed neck and clavicle. He let his teeth nip the thick muscle between shoulder and neck, tasting salt, wanting to help the urgency, and free Tahir to his own euphoric release.

Tahir's head drew up and back as Arulu licked, kissed, sucked and bit on the taut skin just beside his throat. He slid one hand from Tahir's buttock and snaked it in between their bodies, feeling the warm sweat on both of them now, cupping his fingers and palm around Tahir's straining organ. Tahir pushed into his hand and Arulu squeezed just enough, pulling on taut flesh until he heard Tahir begin to groan with every breath. Then he held strongly pulsing flesh and the wetness between them expanded, a warm flow, slippery as they moved together, as Tahir's voice moaned into the air.

Finally, Tahir collapsed on top of him. Arulu's hand was still trapped between them but he barely felt it. He thought he fell asleep for a second or two. They lay clutched to each other, dozing in and out of alpha-states for long minutes.

Slowly, Tahir moved until they lay side by side. His hand caressed the length of Arulu's body, jaw to hip, and Arulu grew hard again, as if he might never stop wanting. This. The touch. The trickles of pleasure rampant inside him. This. Tahir.

Arulu mirrored the touches, his vision focused now. He could see Tahir better as they lay side by side, not kissing. Wide shoulders, hairless chest surprisingly firm for someone Arku had called a "monk." Flat stomach. Compact hips, and all that fine bronze skin beneath such blond hair. Even the pubic hair was golden, springy to his touch.

They made love a second time, moving together. Just pressing. Slow at first. Speeding up. Using hands again until the final spill. This time was more relaxed, took longer, which was utter bliss. Arulu wanted to bask until the stars went out.

But the light stayed, growing cooler.

Not knowing what else to do, Arulu got up. He had to pee anyway. By the time he was on his feet, a flight instinct came to him. He needed to walk, or run, or something.

But before he left he took off his necklace, the little lights of it pulsing crimson, gold and pink. He handed it to Tahir.

"I have another one he said. You can contact me with this. If anything—happens. You know. With Arku. And your friend."

He had gathered his clothes and rapidly dressed in the bathroom. Now he hurried to the door. His heart breaking.

But he didn't know what else to do.

23.

Tahir

Tonight I had held onto Arulu for a lot longer than I ever imagined I could. Before he got antsy, nervous. Before Arulu bolted from my room after giving me his beautiful necklace, the communicator.

Tonight should not have happened. And yet I now saw it had to. We shared a cloister of sorrow and reprieve, the two of us alone in a universe of monsters, clutching, damp skin slipping against damp skin, muscle to muscle, strength and desperation, clutching. It had been too long for me. For half-wild Arulu, never.

It should not have happened. But it was right that it did.

I had felt the others, too. The ghosts. Nik and Arku. They'd been there, but distant. Not really present, but aware.

I lay back in my bed half-awake and worrying. About Arulu and how quickly he'd left. And about how much time our ghosts had left to stay with us. The splinter-bomb effect still remained in the back of my mind, but was fading. Because it was the thing that channeled them, most likely they would fade with it. I had latched my mind to Arku's, but no guarantees. I'd never done anything like that before.

It was easy here, where the light was always dusk, to lose track of time. Of the days.

After Arulu left, I slept some more. Not caring much about eating. Or checking in with the king. I woke to shower once, and went straight back to bed, sleeping naked, luxuriating in the fine sheets and fuzzy coverlets. Apparently, the last two days had taken a lot out of me.

I slept with Arulu's necklace around my neck. I dreamt of frozen pieces of planets glinting on black skies. Of moonswept eyes. Of virgin-pink lips pressed against mine.

Several times I woke clutching the necklace, looking at the moving lights, the blank tiny screen. Hoping for a message. Finding nothing.

Neither Arku nor Nik bothered me, but they were not gone.

And once I woke thinking I saw the two of them standing over my bed staring at me. But the image faded as my eyes re-focused from sleep to waking.

I realized I was cold and went to turn up the heat.

Another shower. Then I sat at my table and looked at my wave-screen to see if Zash had written. Nothing. Just blue stars against my favorite setting of purple back-light.

Something chimed against my heart. I looked down. Saw the tiny blinking screen on the necklace charm. It read, *Touch for Voice.* I touched the clear crystal face.

Arulu's voice said, "My father wants us both to attend the main meal of the day. It is at 2."

"Okay, I'll be there."

There was an awkward silence. "The escorts will show you the way."

"All right."

160

The screen went blank. My heart fell a little. I had hoped Arulu would escort me. He had sounded too formal. I longed to see him, but decided to wait.

*

I dressed for the dinner appropriately, and deliberately chose a white shirt, remembering how Arulu had liked it. The style of it. The flap. Leaving my throat and a small 'v' of skin below it bare. The fastener was a gold crescent moon. I chose red trousers and a matching apple-red velvet coat that fit me like a glove, tapering at the waist. I'd never had clothing like this in my life.

I super-glossed my hair and it hung like bright, short ribbons about my ears and the back of my neck.

After I looked at myself in the mirror, finished and ready to go, I felt stupid. I wanted to attract Arulu. But I was the palace healer and, more importantly, Arulu's healer. I was being idiotic.

I had been here only three days, now.

My body could still feel the warmth of Arulu's skin pressed to mine. The way he had clung to me. The power of his arousal off the charts because no one had ever touched him like that. But most of all I could not forget the sound of his cry of release as he pressed his face against my chest.

I couldn't stop the remembering. With every thought of him, my skin heated, cooled, heated, cooled. I had healed fevers that seemed cold by comparison.

The escorts took me through the golden hallways of the royal floor where, in the distance, I could hear voices buzzing through the wavering air, and the clink of cutlery, stemware. As we neared the royal dining hall, I smelled the sizzle of meats, and other aromas that were sweeter: wine, fresh baked bread and cakes.

We rounded one more curve and the banquet hall appeared, a huge room filled with long tables, round moon-

161

lights on streamers across the high ceiling, and a dais with another table for the king and the queen and their son.

At least two dozen people were already there, not counting waiters and servants who stood to one side all in black, or who busied themselves with bringing in plates of food for the buffet tables along one wall. On the gray, moon-rock wall were ancient-looking spears. There was candlelight on every table in round bowls that changed color with every second. The light looked like that of tiny, trapped suns forced to create endlessly recurring dawns. Wine decanters at every other place setting held a purple liquid.

The room was filled with the sounds of the shiftings of silks and velvets, of lace on leather, of quilted padding rubbing against metal bracelets, of chrome and feather, a half-dozen fashions from ten moons.

My eyes scanned the party and fell immediately on Arulu, who stood to one side of the dais in a purple and green coat over a black shirt and trousers. His long brown hair was still loose, unbraided, unlike everyone else in the room with their braids and their glittering hair ornaments.

Arulu's eyes met mine, still a little too sad for my liking, and looked me up and down, then glanced away. His body tensed a little. Nervous? Or something else?

I started toward him when I was side-lined by the king and some of his entourage.

"Tahir, welcome. We are so happy to have you. And for everything you have done for my son, Prince Arulu, I am in your eternal debt. In a way, this banquet is for you, though you deserve so much more."

I bowed my head. "You've given me so much already."

"You are to sit with us at the royal table. At the right hand of Arulu. Please, I insist."

I could not help but wonder what he would think, or how he would behave toward me if he knew that I had gone beyond healing with Arulu. This was the prince. His son. I was a stranger. I really had no rights here. And none where his son was concerned. Would he see me as morally bankrupt, or worse, interfering, manipulative?

I knew Arulu would not have told his parents. Yet. He was not close with them. But I did not like the thought that maybe I was the disruptor here. And this kingdom had already had more than its fair share of disruption.

So I was to sit next to Arulu through the dinner. How fitting to contribute to my unease. Not to mention Arulu's, who had not budged from where he stood, as far from the guests as possible.

Kean and I exchanged more dialog, none of which I remembered a minute later. I kept my peripheral vision on Arulu. Thought I was losing it. My mind and body ached for him.

Just then a hush fell over the great room. The queen had entered in all of her white skirts and scarves, with her black hair in the most elaborate tangle of braids I'd ever seen. She seemed to glow. I had not yet met her and found her to be amazing to look at.

Immediately, Arulu went to her. They exchanged a light embrace and he kissed her on the cheek. She held his hand and spoke to him, but everything about her demeanor looked stiff. He nodded. I wondered what she said.

For the moment, she ignored the king, clearly favoring her son.

Finally, the pair turned toward me and Kean.

The queen introduced herself as Winter and took my hand. Her fingers were cool, her palm slightly damp. "Thank you for healing my son," she said.

"It has been my honor."

She smiled but the sentiment did not seem to reach her eyes. But I could see in them other things, a distance that kept her enthroned upon her own brand of pain, a long-ago grief that never waned. Her worlds had been shattered. She had repaired but it would never be the same, for there would always be cracks, dents, scars. I was sure parts of her mind were pure, white dust slowly dissipating with time.

Arulu stood at her side, the tall shadow in the room that everyone admired and still worried over. It was all so sudden, so soon, his return to real life, his reprieve from pain.

Arulu never looked straight at me. He wore another necklace identical to mine, flickering green and gold. It reminded me he'd given me his, to keep in contact. It was a connection between us. A secret link.

I took a deep breath and realized I hadn't done that since entering the hall.

"All right, then," the king said. "We shall begin."

He led us to the dais and servants began to bring the food before we even sat.

The guests moved around to find seats as soon as they saw the king ascend to the higher table.

The purple wine was poured. Bowls of soup were brought, the steam blurring my vision. Plates laden with salads, succulent meats, gravies, vegetables were all brought.

The room before us was vibrant with color, from the fashion of clothing to the styles and jewelries of the hair. The moon-lights above gave everything a soft glow. The guests talked like buzzing bees. I drank some of the wine and fell in love with it, my tongue and throat craving more. I ate a bit of everything, but still felt little appetite.

I didn't dare look at Arulu, though I saw from the corner of my eye his graceful fingers handle silver spoon, fork and knife. I saw he, also, drank deeply of the purple wine. He did not speak.

The king and queen exchanged a few words I didn't overhear.

There was a fire in my belly. The wine mellowed me at first, then seemed to make the sensation stronger.

Dessert came. Piles of cakes, pies, and creams in little gold dishes. I could barely look at it all. Wonderful, of course, but my stomach recoiled.

Before we could all partake of the sweets, the king

stood. He made a toast to me.

"To Tahir, who came very far to heal my son who has suffered so much. He will be held in the highest esteem of this court always."

The guests all stood. As did the queen and Arulu. The king held his goblet high. I stood last, mouthing the words, "Thank you." Everyone drank to me, and many gave loud cheers.

I was happy but not proud. My gift had been born into me. And it was Arulu who had withstood so much. Not me. And then there were the ghosts. And our other secret, and as they all cheered I felt my cheeks flush, and tremors of liquid lava in my veins.

We all sat back down. I stared at the many desserts, unable to think of eating any of them even as servants placed delectable-looking bites upon my plate. I longed for tea, and just as I had that thought it was brought in steaming white and blue teacups. I could stomach that, and sipped some, only to immediately burn the tip of my tongue.

A hand placed what looked like a white, powdery cookie on the edge of my plate. "Try this. Just one bite."

Purple and green velvet sleeve, tan wrists, long fingers. I looked at Arulu as he drew his hand away. One side of his mouth twitched as if he were holding back a smile.

My breath caught.

I could only nod as I picked up the cookie and forced myself to take a small bite. A buttery sweetness instantly invaded my whole mouth.

"Good?" I heard him say close to my ear.

"Yes. Good." I swallowed and automatically took another small bite as if Arulu's recommendation for the best of the best of desserts had somehow saved me. Or soothed me.

Then Arulu took a little cream from a cloisonné pitcher and swirled some into my tea for me. "Now you can drink it." He spoke low. Only for me.

I picked up the cup and washed down the rest of the cookie with the now cooler beverage. "Thank you."

"You never have to say 'thank you' to me. Ever. You saved me."

But I wanted only to thank him. Over and over again. For letting me touch him, hold him. For letting me in.

For this man had let no one into his soul for twenty long years with the exception of a ghost.

I was finished with eating. But I sat and waited, not knowing what else to do. The greeting and the meal had taken almost two hours. I was half-drunk on the purple wine, but fully drunk on Arulu who sat so close I could feel the heat pouring off him.

The king stood again and made some more toasts to some of his most special people, those in his entourage, and those in the business ends of things who worked with the queen. He also toasted the queen herself, who rose gracefully and said, "On that note, I must get back to work. I have responsibilities."

She left to applause.

Kean said to me, "Thank you for joining us. Of course you are officially invited to any banquet or gathering."

"Thank you," I replied.

He started to move away from the table, turned and said, "Arulu, come."

Arulu obeyed without a word. I was left alone to descend the few steps to the floor where guests were congregating, still discussing their lives, their stories, their events.

I moved slowly toward the door, alone, and passed by a curtained exit reserved for royalty only. My escorts waited to take me back to my own room where I had no idea what I would do. It seemed I was not called upon to do anything right now, my job with Arulu enough for the time being.

Something touched my arm, and I turned. A hand snaked out from the black velvet-curtained exit and grabbed me by the forearm, pulling me into a shadowy alcove.

Arulu stood there, hand still clutching my arm, then slowly, almost shyly, put his other arm behind my neck and pulled my face toward his, eyes half-closed, mouth tense as if unsure. He kissed me fast and hard. He smelled like fresh pine in winter, and delicate fires on a cool wind. I pushed into the kiss, welcoming him, and he immediately relaxed. Then he pulled back, flushed, his eyes sparkling. "I have no time today or tonight. I'm sorry."

I was caught so off-guard by the ambush and the amazing kiss, I couldn't speak.

He saw my shock. More assured now, he leaned in and kissed me again, moving his mouth over mine boldly. Had I taught him to do that so well in just one night?

When he pulled back again, he said, "You hardly ate."

I opened my mouth to respond that I wasn't really hungry, and said instead, "You look beautiful."

Still no smile from him, but his lips pressed together as if in pleasure.

"Any sign of Arku, or your friend Nik?" he asked.

"Only a glimpse. But I can feel they are still here." I tapped my head.

He looked around desperate. "I can't stay." He swallowed hard, said, "You look beautiful, too."

I wanted to say more, but he quickly said, "I have to leave." His hands fell away from my arm and neck.

He turned and vanished behind a door, leaving only trails of purple, like an afterimage on my eyes, and the scent of his heat.

*

I needed to walk off the wine. And the after-effects of Arulu.

My escorts took me on a tour. Taridia and Sullen, my kind and gracious guardians.

When we left the palace and moved onto the black dusty pathways of the moon, we didn't have to go far before we came upon the first hydroponics building. A combination arboretum and aviary. I was struck by the colors first, no more dun moonscape and ashy dusk. So many shades of green! A hundred, maybe more. And the fuchsias, saffrons, lemons, of all shades as well. Flowers blooming with golden centers. Dragonflies with wings of blue.

Birds chattered everywhere. The foliage was so thick in places I could not see the ceiling or its sun-lights.

A huge waterfall poured its heart out. My body jolted. There, I saw Arku and Nik, sitting on a rock under the mist. Arku in his skin drifts and Nik in his t-shirt and jeans. They waved at me.

This was the first time I realized they could appear and disappear at will, but to my eyes only.

Taridia and Sullen had moved up a ways into some trees. I had told them I wanted to walk alone for awhile.

A narrow pathway of dirt and stone led up to the misted rock. The ghosts looked real to me. So real that tiny beads of water from the air rested in their hair and on their cheeks.

I sat down next to them.

They both said, almost in unison, "Hello, Tahir."

"I'm awake, right?" I asked.

They shrugged. Arku said, "It doesn't matter. Does it?"

Maybe not to them. But it mattered to me. Maybe it was too much purple wine.

"There are many layers of reality," Nik said.

My heart lifted when I heard his voice. He was dead and yet here he was speaking to me. Who could be more fortunate than I to have this experience?

"I have never seen you while I am in an awake state before."

Arku said, "I appeared to Arulu all the time." His grin was not meant to be macabre, but I had to drop my gaze.

Nik, too, was himself as before, not quite right. Slitted pupils. White teeth that looked too sharp, those differences fading in and out.

Nik said to Arku, "We have to tell him."

Arku said, "Fuck."

The water crashed around us, an encompassing tide. The air was moist and cool. Prisms and dancing light. Green moss on slick black rocks.

"You look nice," Nik said to me. "Your new world suits you. Fancy party or something?"

"Something like that."

"Look," he said. "We have things to do."

Arku followed up with, "Other worlds and places to be."

Then they both said something that strangled language so badly I could not understand them.

"What?" They weren't making any sense.

"He didn't understand us," Nik said.

"See, it's simple." Arku leaned toward me, bone fingers tapping my thigh.

"I don't understand you guys. Communication is better in dream, maybe?"

"No," they both replied.

"The very pure truth now," Arku said.

"How it's happening," Nik added.

Then together, they said, "We're fading."

My heart caught in my throat.

"I hung out for Arulu because I was trapped by the splinter-bomb, too, and because he needed me," Arku explained.

"I came to you when you took the splinter-bomb essence from Arulu into yourself. It opened a door and there you were. How happy I was to see you!" Nik grinned.

"But now the effects are dissipating," Arku said. "And Arulu has a new life. I'm sorry, but the link between us hasn't worked to change a thing. We both see, and we've discussed it at length, that we are fading. Arulu is moving on. This is the way it was always going to be once we were all freed from the splinter-bomb's effect."

"Arulu will not understand!" I insisted.

"But he has you, now," Nik said.

My greatest fear was this. For Arulu, mainly. "No," I said. "He's not ready. It will break his heart."

Arku said, "You know, I'm the one who told him to kill you first off. I don't apologize for it, because I sensed this would happen. But now I see this is really better, as hard as that is to say, and you're going to be there for him. He has you to help him now."

"No, it's not the same as his illness. Besides, I promised him I would not take his emotions with my gift. This will set him back. And I don't know what help there is for that."

"No choice," Arku said. "I love my brother and will miss him more than anything, but it's happening."

Nik nodded. "We are not strong enough to stop the fading."

They both spoke again, and nonsensical, meaningless words came out of their mouths.

"What?"

"We don't have words," Arku said. "And the ones we come up with you can't understand?"

"The cycles are new," Nik tried to explain.

This couldn't be happening, this surreal conversation, the two of them so strange but so real. I stood and faced them, feeling the gusts of the air the waterfall made in its fury against my back.

I stared at them. They seemed so casual, sitting on a rock under a man-made waterfall. And yet as I had that thought, tears appeared on Nik's face. Arku was trembling.

"You can't leave until you say goodbye," I finally said, not knowing if Arulu could stand it, but knowing he would have no choice.

Nik said, "Tonight?"

"No, he's busy. I'm not seeing him tonight."

"We will try to last another day," Arku said softly.

I shut my eyes. My fingers closed to fists. "How do I tell him?"

They didn't answer.

When I opened my eyes I was alone under the shivering mist. Sullen stood at the edge of the pond calling my name.

*

My room in perpetual twilight, co-lit by the dark purple lightning of the dome: shadowed floor, pink-blue-gray walls, the bed incased in folds of blue and silver-furred satins. All the weirdness of the light made it feel so empty.

I had no one to talk to. And still no wave from Zash.

So little time had passed since I had arrived on this strange moon. Yet so much had happened.

I took tea to my bed, and my flatscreen. For a long time I stared at the black sun on the wall, the way it spiked into the shadows as if wavering between two and three dimensionality.

So many worlds. So many unknowns. Humans had conquered a galaxy but still knew so little of what lay beyond the physical, what comprised pure mind. I had been taught rules at the Temple but all that seemed moot here and now. Arulu. The splinter-bomb. Ghosts. The hot-cold brushstrokes of a new-forming love.

My mind was a mess.

First Arulu wanted to kill me. Then kiss me. I needed something more solid to cling to.

But only the empty room stretched before me.

*

I don't remember when I fell asleep. Hours had gone

by, perhaps. I had wanted to dream of Arku and Nik but did not. Everything was a blank. But I still felt something had startled me awake.

I sat up and immediately the distant dark city came into view through the velvet-framed window above my bed. I felt all shivery inside, as if I wasn't completely awake, not completely put back together after being so dead asleep.

Then I heard the beep. Somewhere just below my head.

I wasn't wearing my shirt but I still wore the necklace, a beautiful pendant of silver and gold framing a crystal screen. The coolness of it rocked against my skin. I lifted it up to see the lights chasing each other around the rim in pink merging to gold.

The words on the tiny screen said, *I've changed my mind. The escorts will bring you. They are discreet.*

Changed his mind about what? Then I remembered. He'd said he had no time. Today. Tonight. Now it was the middle of the night, and he must have found himself restless and awake.

Even after the cloistered kiss this afternoon, I still wasn't sure he was sure. He'd run from my room so quickly the night before. And he'd made excuses to run off today, even if they were legitimate ones.

I got up and put on the white shirt, the trousers, the red jacket. My fingers shook as if I was in a hurry. But part of me was so afraid. For Arku. For Nik. For Arulu.

And for myself.

*

They did not say a word. Sullen and Taridia, still on shift. *They must work long hours,* I thought.

The door to Arulu's room opened at my touch. He was not there at the entrance to greet me. I looked around the dimly lit interior. Saw the rumpled bed the same as it had been when I'd first healed him. The soft restraints still dangled at its sides. I saw movement.

Arulu sat up, hair untamed at his shoulders and back, arms and chest bare.

One look from him, darkly saucy, and that was it. My body became deluged with darting pleasure. I moved across the floor to him, to the edge of the bed, leaned down and took him in my arms.

24.

Arulu

Arulu looked up as the door automatically chimed in a low zinging tone before it opened.

Tahir stood framed in gold light, the rays of it shining through his pale hair and making it shine. All dark shadow otherwise, he was a silhouette with an aura of incandescence.

At the sight, a clawing need possessed him.

With a rustle of shifting fabrics and a sure step, Tahir came to him as the door slid closed behind him. Arulu reached for him but Tahir was already leaning against the bed's edge, already holding him.

Arulu moved into the embrace as Tahir lowered himself to sit on the bed. Arulu whispered, "I can't stand it when you're not touching me. You've taken away one agony, only to replace it without another."

"I'm here," was all Tahir said.

So many feelings came at him at once, yearnings he'd never known his whole life. What was this? Different images came to him as Tahir stroked his back gently, held him, began to kiss the skin of his forehead, the sweeps of his eyebrows.

He remembered once when he was very small and on a Lyric Prime ship gliding through the huge system of his people. They moved past a cluster of lights that, when they came closer, turned into ships. Hundreds of them brilliant and fiery in ancient starlight.

"What is that?" he'd asked of his father.

"Derelicts stripped of all that is of value. Waiting to be scuttled."

In the void-pastures of space, he was gazing at dead starships.

As a kid, seeing them all useless but still beautiful, had filled him with a strange sad yearning. The dead starships that would never fly again. The dead starships in their forever-floating graves.

It was a feeling like that now. Yearning after something. Loving something too great to master. He had a strange fear that Tahir might leave. Leave him to the black fields of his mind. A love bereft. He could only think of clutching him tight. Holding him in love, and in his sleep.

He'd left far too quickly last night, afraid, unsure. He'd run from Tahir's bed and into the cold again because that was what he knew. The known, even if it was hell, was often better than the unknown.

Now he leaned into Tahir's too-padded chest; there was way too much clothing there right now. He wanted to touch him. Burned to touch the naked skin. The other man's head tilted down so they could brush lips. Ah that wonderful scent of him, of nature fresh and new. And a taste like clarity on a rainy day.

Tahir brought sanity back into his realm.

Tahir brought memory, breath, love.

He pulled the man too him and into his bed. Fully clothed, a body and a man now filled his arms, his soul.

But Tahir was tense. He could feel it beneath his palms as he ran them down the velvet coat-back. Could feel the hesitation even as their lips warmly merged.

Arulu's body raged. But Tahir pulled back too soon and fell to the side, stretching his legs out, and said, "I have to tell you something."

174

Arulu followed the body with his own, pushing naked against him, the covers falling away from his bare hips. "Later." He kissed him again. He had never felt such impending need.

"Ahch." Tahir made an indecipherable sound but allowed the kiss, even returned it with zest, and rested his hand on the bared skin of Arulu's hip as Arulu tried to roll on top of him.

Arulu wanted more. And immediately.

Tahir said, "Arulu, wait—"

Arulu said, "Call me Ari. Please. You're so perfect right now. Let's talk later."

"You're perfect right now, too." Tahir kissed him on the side of the mouth, teasing. "*Ari*. I like that."

Arulu whispered into his mouth. "I hate my name."

Tahir tried again. "I need to talk to you."

Arulu did not want to talk right now, though. He pushed the other man down so he could move on top of him, looked down at his ice-henge eyes, ran his hands through candleflame hair. "No." He moved his hands down the still-clothed chest and began to undo the shirt's fastenings. "Just this. Right now."

Tahir sighed but allowed the slow undressing. Allowed Arulu to pull the shirt from his trousers, slip it and the coat off his arms and pull them out from under his weight.

Arulu loved the texture of the other man's chest. Firm and bronze in the dim light, the ripple of ribs under soft skin, the tightness of the quivering stomach below.

He kissed him all over, chest, nipples, sides, and made slow kissing-licks around the belly button.

He felt the hardness beneath the trousers as his forearm brushed the crotch, and couldn't wait. He undid the fastenings and tugged, working until Tahir was finally as naked as he was. The room seemed misty and warm with desire.

He touched Tahir's hipbone and trailed his hand lower

to spread his hands over the thigh, and heard Tahir groan.

Tahir really was quite lovely. A vision Arulu had never dreamed to see made real. Straining. Wanting. Aroused and gorgeous in his bed.

His hand slid up to brush across the beauty of the dark and straining erection. The tip matched the pink of the healer's lips.

Tahir covered his eyes with his forearm and gave another groan.

Softly petting, Arulu felt himself grin, realizing he did not remember the last time he'd smiled more than half-way, even at Arku's jokes.

He kept his hand firmly on his prize and leaned over Tahir again, kissing up sternum and breastbone to throat, chin and mouth, only to be rewarded by a returned embrace as Tahir wrapped his arms around him.

Arulu loved it that Tahir wanted him. He'd been worried that maybe it was he, so deprived, who needed this more, that desire might be one-sided and the healer had taken pity. He hated pity. It was one of the reasons he'd panicked and run from the room that night. He had not been able to think, let alone reason. So he'd left.

But then he saw Tahir at the banquet, like a burning ruby jewel as he entered the feasting hall. He wondered if everyone could see that glow. Decided they surely did. He had felt he himself was glowing, and his eyes hurt every time he looked at the healer.

It was only at dinner when he had seen that Tahir had little appetite, and very little to say, that he thought maybe, just maybe Tahir was having the same sensations, the same needs. It had to be either that, or regret. But he hadn't looked regretful. He'd looked merely lost, as if waiting for something. Standing in a room full of people alone. It was that observation that spurred Arulu to sneak him behind the curtain for a quick, hard kiss. And it had been the best decision of his life, because it was then he knew for sure that

Tahir reciprocated his feelings. The way the man had responded. The breathless tremble of his lips.

It had hurt Arulu's heart to have to tell him he was too busy for the day. And well into the night. Too busy to get together. Be together. And do again those wonderful things they'd done the night before.

All day he had thought only of Tahir. He had heard maybe one-third of what his father had to tell him. Paid little attention in the meetings with staff which he now shared in because of his new-found health. No one had mentioned his inattention. Too polite, he'd guessed. And probably understanding that he'd only just recovered from a twenty year ordeal. People went on holiday for much, much less!

He'd gone to bed late and could not sleep, tossing in a fever, his body awash with desire. That was when he broke completely and called Tahir on the necklace communicator, hoping he was awake.

It had taken awhile for Tahir to respond.

But he was here now. And Arulu wanted him so badly his thoughts seemed to run all red and tangled. All he wanted in this moment was Tahir, to touch, taste, smell, listen. He wanted to see him naked and out of control. In this room. In this bed. His bed which he'd shared with no one but a ghost his entire life.

The cover was wrinkled beneath them, gray and red stripes faded in the gloom. Dark pillows lined the wall on one side, and Tahir's head lay cushioned by the very one Arulu used to hug to his own chest as he slept. He could not have imagined this any better.

Their kisses melted into each other. Their cheeks pressed. Their hair mingled. Eyelashes fluttered against hot skin. All he could think was: *I want. I want.*

And: *You are exquisite. You are stunning.*

His hand trailed against Tahir's groin, not urgent yet, just touching. The stiff length. The fire there.

Tahir's hand ran through his hair and cupped the back

of his head. That embracing palm, those fingers at his nape, sent thrill and need coursing through him. Over and over he felt these surges for this man, thinking they might never end. Hoping for that very outcome.

He wanted to hold, press, rub. A sort of growl escaped him. He worked his way down Tahir's body again, inhaling the dusky fragrance of his arousal, and this time refused to let shyness overcome him.

He licked at the thighs and then further up, let his tongue stroke the base of the organ. Then slowly moved it around, tasting the heat of it, the sweat, the tart richness as his mouth encircled the straining tip and his tongue moved forward and back over the satiny smooth skin, delving into the small crevice. Moving over and around, daring to press his lips down and give a smooth suck. The flesh hardened even more.

Tahir sat up, both hands in Arulu's hair now, and said, eyes blinking rapidly, "Oh you are sweet."

Arulu loved the praise. But was unsure. "I haven't ever—"

Tahir smiled and pulled him up so he could take him into his arms. "You're fantastic. Wonderful. And I'll let you do that more but—" His eyebrows narrowed and Arulu peered at him.

"But what?"

Tahir kissed him gently on the cheek, then the chin and pushed him down. "I think you should have the experience of what that feels like first. I mean—" He took his face in his hands, framing it. "—because you haven't—I mean no one's ever done that for you."

"Because of my inexperience?"

Tahir's smile did not waver. "Because I want you to feel it first." He moved over him, pushing Arulu flatter onto the bed, and Arulu watched as that magnificent body, all copper and grace, straddled him.

Was Tahir going to--? He couldn't finish the thought. If

178

he did, he would explode. Already his erection bobbed in anticipation. And he knew he was going to feel that mouth very soon, and the tongue on him, and he couldn't manage to take that thought further for fear everything would just go black. And, well, that wouldn't do at all because he'd miss the entire experience.

Tahir kissed him thoroughly and Arulu touched his waist, gently stroking, and moved his hands over the soft, taut backside. He was already groaning before Tahir began to move down his body, licking and kissing as he went. It was like being on the very edge of a cliff, his weight held back from falling only by the wind, and his balance was so precarious that he knew he would fall at any moment, but the wind kept softly pushing against him, circling, caressing. Like floating.

When Tahir's head moved lower and his chin brushed Arulu's aching penis, he instinctively spread his legs, knees slightly bent. Tahir knelt between them. And the whole moon spun. Their world. Their dark, planetlet of ghost and dust.

"Try to relax," Tahir's voice was almost a whisper. "It will last longer. The pleasure."

Arulu lifted his head, saw only blond light from Tahir's chin-length hair bow mid-way down his body, and fell back again, gripping the covers at his sides.

Something damp and wet touched below the base of his erection, teasing the sac there, tonguing. He thought he might come from just that, and bit his lower lip to distract from the overwhelming sensation. He wasn't going to come until he was damn ready.

He had the thought that if his hands gripped the sheets any tighter, they would most certainly tear.

The tongue swirled slowly upward until it lapped the length of him. Lips closed over the head.

The wind at the cliff was weaker, barely holding him up. He was going to fall. Any moment now.

One of Tahir's hands was on Arulu's thigh and one was

179

pressed flat against the skin above his penis. Tahir's mouth slid over him just right until all he could feel was liquid warmth. As the lips moved down, then up, a gentle suction began and he rode wave after wave of intense pleasure, trying to remember to relax, to breathe, but the pleasure increased sending him high on the air, as the wind suddenly grew stronger, buffeting him. Windborne now, he soared higher, the cliff far below. Ecstasy spun him until he knew nothing but light and air and a glimpse of unending white paradise.

He cried out, half in warning, half not caring, and came as Tahir's mouth tightened, drinking all the liquid that pulsed from him, keeping him aloft for as long as possible while the orgasm rippled through him.

Overcome, he could do nothing for many moments but lie there as if in stasis. Eyes closed, all he saw were endless wellsprings of prism-light against the backs of his eyelids. He realized he was breathing hard as if he'd been running.

He felt his body embraced, held. Felt Tahir kiss the sides of his face and his forehead. Then they were kissing again and he never wanted it to end.

Tahir whispered against his lips, "Pretty good?"

"More than," Arulu answered lazily, rolling tighter against him and fitting himself along the lines of that incredible body. His erection never fully receded, leaving a dull ache of wanting within him, desire shyly awaiting the spread of a new flame. It wouldn't take much to get that wind to kick up again, either. He was young.

After awhile, he sat up, pushing Tahir down with his hand flat against his chest.

Tahir smiled and went easily to the sacrifice, laid out and laid bare, skin glistening with a soft sheen. Arulu watched the room's shaded light skim the planes of golden flesh. He leaned down, hair falling over his lover's chest, and tasted. The center. The curving muscle. A nipple that budded as his tongue flicked over it again and again. Taste of rain. Taste of boyish charm too long sequestered.

180

Arulu moved down, feeling the way with his tongue and mouth, wanting to get back to what he had started earlier, where his mouth had been ready, salivating, eager to learn how to give pleasure to this man. He kissed toward the straining column at his center. He wanted to take his time but he could wait no longer. He needed to know. Scent. Taste. Texture.

He put his mouth right up to the tip and moved his lips in a gentle caress, then opened to take him inside, moving down and down, deep as he could go without force, without choking.

He opened his eyes as he began to suckle.

Tahir had thrown his arm over his face again.

Arulu pulled up and gave lavish attention to the head, licking and sucking, then steadied himself to take the length again. He felt awkward at first, but went slowly, learning. Gradually, he found a rhythm that was pleasurable to sustain, and it seemed even more pleasurable to Tahir, who squirmed and groaned and exhaled with loud hisses. Arulu could only hope he was losing his mind, all in a good way.

So good. So good. He decided he loved what he was doing, the power it gave him, surprised at the thrill of it. And his own arousal flared up tight once more, batting against his stomach.

His tongue pressed tight against the ridges of the head, rimming it. When he went down again and again, he could feel the veins pulse, the organ throb. He loved the response. Reveled in the all-new sensations. Hoped he could give Tahir the same pleasure he'd just been given.

Inspired, he tested out a few moves. He shook his head back and forth, letting the rounded tip brush the insides of his cheeks. He pulled all the way off a few times, nipping and licking at the indentation at the very tip, tonguing the tiny hole, which was open and damp and leaking tart fluid. He gladly took it in, drank it. Wanting more.

Tahir tossed his head on the pillows. He cried out.

Soon, thought Arulu. He would taste the elixir of bold, pure desire. Here. In his bed. All affection and sexual need focused on him, the one who could give him what Tahir needed, bring him to completion.

He sucked harder, letting his saliva form a slick coating on the firm flesh.

Tahir's reaction was to bend his knees, grip the covers, and buck. Arulu wanted it, took it even as Tahir tried to push him back, warn him. He didn't care. He was going to drink every drop. He wasn't going to be suddenly shy about that, or anything else now. This was the experience he had desired more than anything when he'd called Tahir to his rooms tonight. Teasing. Tasting. Sharing this pleasure that was too great for words.

Like rain, like sleet, like a storm on high, Tahir came, spurting so hard it coated the back of Arulu's throat. He swallowed and swallowed, and thought he would die not from too much of Tahir, but because he so badly wanted to laugh, and he couldn't yet with his mouth still full.

He licked and sucked until he decided the skin was clean, and Tahir was tugging at him hard, saying, "Stop. Oh gods, stop, I can't take any more."

So, he thought, *my lover is sensitive after he comes.*

The idea of that made him even happier. He lifted his mouth, still lightly licking shaft, head, his own lips.

Tahir pulled him up until Arulu was lying on top of him, chest to chest, his re-enflamed erection pressing between them. He felt Tahir soften. Tahir caressed his cheek, smiling that sweet smile of his that Arulu was growing to love more and more, and said, "Kiss me."

25.

Tahir

Ari. He had told me to call him that.

Ari. The sweetness of him. His dark tousled hair against my shoulders. The urgency of his kisses. I had never ever expected this.

I held him for awhile, until I got some of my strength back, and then flipped him onto his back. This time it was slower for him, and I had him moaning and writhing in abandon, his long legs flung apart, my hands caressing all over his body as I sucked him for the second time tonight. I could see in his eyes a drugged look, different from when I'd met him, this newer gaze bereft of torture, pain, anxiety. When his pleasure burst hard it was so intense, and lasted so long, I couldn't swallow fast enough and pearly fluid spilled over.

I got up for a towel and brought us back a glass of water to share.

He drank absently, rarely taking his eyes from mine. When I set the glass aside, his hands were already on my face again, pulling me into another kiss.

We simply could not get enough of each other.

We needed some rest, but desire still rippled our skin. The air of the room seemed to sparkle. I thought I saw the outlines of two people, two young men standing by the window that overlooked flat square buildings and desperate badlands. Arulu's view was not of Xia, but of the hydroponics buildings. The sky was purple, the dome the only thing between us and the minus 170C degrees of the dark side of Firgone and space.

The two specters faded the moment I looked directly at them. But I could feel their lingering presences in my mind. Their longing. They had not yet left. They wouldn't. Arku certainly wouldn't without talking to Arulu again.

The prince lay curled at my side now, half asleep but still reaching for me, never wanting to stop the kissing. I'd brought the covers up to our waists. I turned to face him, stroking one shoulder. He burrowed tighter against me. He wasn't running away tonight. Of course, it was his room.

I knew I had to tell him about Arku and Nik fading. But this moment, so peaceful, so right would be spoiled.

Tears warmed the corners of my eyes.

As if reading my thoughts, Arulu said sleepily, "Would it be possible to talk to Arku through you? Tonight?"

"Yes."

He glanced up at me, smiling. Saw the look on my face and frowned, body stiffening. "What's wrong?"

I lowered my gaze. "He's here."

"Well, good then, right?"

I could only nod.

"We do it with the kiss, right?"

"Yes. A different kind of kiss than this." I brushed his lips gently, chastely, with my own.

He leaned in and affectionately touched his forehead to mine. My chest heaved in a held back sob.

"Okay," he said. "I'm ready."

I wanted to warn him. But chickened out. I decided Arku was the one who could best impart the bad news. Arku would know what to say, how to say it.

I had not much time to prepare. Energy depleted by sex. But I was also continually energized by all my newly forming feelings for Arulu. That untamed desire when I was with him. It filled that spot in my brain where my gift resided. That did not surprise me. One of my favorite sayings I'd learned at the Temple was: *The King of Healers is Love.*

I took a few seconds to focus and it was a lot easier than I thought to gather myself, to concentrate on and access my gift. I leaned forward and breathed in Arulu's heady fragrance, then initiated the empath's kiss.

184

He lifted his head to accept it.

There was a rush of darkness. Like falling through a long tunnel, through a wind of ice and fangs.

I still felt Arulu in my arms, lips on mine, the breath from his nostrils moving against my cheek. The bedcovers bunched about our hips and legs.

But in my mind I had lost control. Like hurtling through space blind, directionless. I almost pulled back to stop the kiss when suddenly we were surrounded by blinking lights, a starfield maybe, or a whirlwind of dancing embers.

Two figures materialized before us. Beautiful Nik with his black hair tossing in the gale against the night, jeans and t-shirt-clad, and damaged Arku, trailing scarves of flesh. Though everything was weightless black, they stood before us as if on solid ground. When I myself tried to move, my feet felt an invisible floor and my dizziness stopped.

I looked around. Arku and Nik stood framed by strangely shaped shadows, a dimmer darkness upon the deeper depths. I tried to make out what they were. Chunks of ice, maybe? Asteroids. I focused harder. No, not meteors, either, or space debris. These were ships. Hundreds of them.

Arku took a step toward Arulu, who stood beside me dressed in a fine suit of red and amber. For some reason I appeared in my own mind dressed in my black Temple robe.

"Brother," Arku said to Arulu. "Do you remember this scene, this place?" He held his arms out and turned toward the ships.

Arulu came toward him, arms out, smiling. "Only hours ago, I was just thinking of this field of dead starships."

"I know," Arku said, taking his brother into a swift embrace. "I'm still with you always in spirit, even when you can't see me."

"I can see you now," Arulu said. "I'm so glad you're here. And that I can still talk to you after the healing brought you into Tahir. But why are we here?"

Arku smirked. "Don't you think a graveyard is fitting

for ghosts?"

Arulu shook his head. "It's all just fine on the moon, in the palace, in my rooms."

Arku said, "Do you remember a conversation we once had when we were little about this place?"

"I don't quite recall," he said slowly.

Nik and I stayed very still, watching the brothers, listening to their every word. Letting Arku pave the way gently toward breaking his twin's heart.

"We said one day when we were bigger we were going to fly back to this place and put all the souls back into the ships. Make them fly again. We thought it would be so grand, all these antique derelicts forming their own archaic fleet. All the worlds would weep to see such art."

"I don't remember that," Arulu said quietly. One arm still circled his brother's waist.

"You loved them. All those blackened ships. Don't you remember? You had artbooks full of designs for remodeling them, and for making new ships. You were more like our father than I ever was."

"Well," Arulu said, voice calm. "Not anymore. That was a long time ago."

"But now you have the freedom to go back to that dream if you want to, Ari."

"It's a dead dream. Father wants other things for me now."

"After only a couple of days?" Arku asked.

Arulu shrugged.

"But I want you to be happy," Arku said.

The starships floated, lazily turning in the cosmic nothingness, their gray and blackened-silver hulls glinting now and then in the light of distant constellations. I could make out various shapes. One looked like an actual clipper ship from old-Earth seas. Another resembled a teacup tipped to one side. One looked like it had antlers. Another looked like a tree. All serious works of art, but all retired, broken, the sights gone from their computer eyes.

I wondered what Arulu would have made, if he'd designed such creatures as these.

At my thought, he looked directly at me, and I saw it all at once, past-present-future, like a zip download, all the yet-to-be-designed starships in his eyes.

This man was my lover, but it had been such a short time since I'd arrived, and I realized I still barely knew him.

Arulu looked back at Arku, brows narrowed in suspicion now. "Why are you saying all this to me right now?"

"Because my beloved brother, my twin, heart of my hearts, I'm ready to go on now. And Nik here, too. The splinter-bomb no longer has me trapped. And I am helpless before all possibilities."

"No!" Arulu grabbed onto him now with both hands at Arku's waist. Holding him in place. "You aren't leaving. You can't!" He glanced over his shoulder at me. "Tahir, you promised."

I bit down hard on my lips, my eyes stinging.

"Tahir!" Arulu shouted when I didn't say anything. "Tell him. Arku," he turned back to his brother. "He promised this wouldn't happen."

"I don't think so. He promised he would try to keep me here. That was all. But even though I rocked that kiss he gave me big time to try to link us, --and he does kiss well, eh, brother?—he doesn't rule me. He doesn't own me. And by the way, neither do you."

"But you can't—" Arulu's voice choked up.

Nik shifted his feet on the invisible ground, looking uncomfortable. I went to him and put my hand on his shoulder. Together we watched the breaking of Arulu's heart.

Arku's bone hand touched the top of his twin's head, scratching lightly. "Ari, you needed me all this time. But now this is what I need."

Arulu pushed him away violently and Arku tripped

backward, almost falling. Then Arulu bowed his head and plunged toward him. At the last moment, when I thought he would knock his brother over and tackle him to the floor, he grabbed him, burying his face at his neck, and with trembling arms held him tight as if he'd never let go. I heard him make a low sound that traveled through the airless space of our minds and entered us with a sadness like the very distance between the stars themselves.

Arku stroked his back and said "shh" now and again.

Nik bowed his head. "Even though we haven't seen each other in years, I'll miss you, too," he whispered to me, tears on his face. "I miss my boy self teasing you strange Temple kids from across the road. And I miss you, Tahir. That summer we turned twenty was the most wonderful summer of my life."

Something wet splashed my own face. I looked up and the constellations were spinning again.

Arulu was saying in a strangled voice, "Just not yet. Not yet."

"A day or two at most, Ari. That's all I can say. The pull is too strong. We have to leave."

I heard Arulu say, "I can't lose you. I'm not ready."

The bone hand combed through his long brown hair. "You're ready. You just don't know it yet."

The dead starship graveyard, and all the tiny flickering lights beyond, began to fade. A glittering stillness overtook me. Then I found myself back in the warm bed, Arulu trembling in my arms. The kiss ended.

I looked down at him. In that moment he looked so young, his eyes tightly closed, the lashes glued with tears to his cheeks.

After a moment, he pulled away. He slid the back of his hand across his eyes, then looked at me with an unsteady gaze. "You knew."

What could I say? This was never going to be easy.

"Why didn't you tell me?" he asked bluntly.

"I tried."

"When?"

"Tonight, when I first came in."

His eyes darted around the room; he seemed to be trying to remember. "You should have insisted. You should have told me!"

He leapt from the bed all gleaming and long-limbed, and threw a long silver robe over his head, the satin rim brushing the backs of his ankles. Barefoot, he headed for the door. It chimed open and he rounded the corner and was into the hall and gone before I could utter even one word.

The door closed. I slid from the bed and searched for all my clothes from the mix of our belongings tossed in the heat of desire on the floor.

*

It was still the middle of the night. The hall looked the same as ever, though, golden light pouring from the mouths of flickering dragon sconces. A new batch of escorts I'd never seen or met stood conferring by Arulu's door as I came out.

They looked up.

I said, "Which direction did he go?"

One of them in a gorgeous blue suit pointed down the hall. I turned, saying over my shoulder, "He's okay, just a little upset. I'll find him. Please don't follow me."

Of course I had no idea where I'd find Arulu. I just wanted privacy for my search. And for us if I did manage to find him.

I walked swiftly down the passageways, listening for footsteps, rustling fabrics, anything. On this level, the royal floor of Arulu's room, I ran into more escorts around every corner. The ones who had seen him were quite helpful when they saw that I was the much-lauded healer in the king's favor, and motioned me in the direction Arulu had gone.

I came to the spiral stairway, a great open structure, a

marvelous feat of artistic design. Xia loomed in the distance like a drowning city treading stars. Right now it was asleep and cold. Arulu stood, arms on the banister, looking out over the moonscape. His robe was a cape flowing behind him. A silver cloud. His hair picked up glints of light from the hall and from the trail of moons always on the rise outside the dome.

Though my step was light, he'd heard me. His body stiffened but he did not turn. "Leave me," he said quietly, facing the dark.

I stood about ten feet from him. "I wanted to tell you. I tried."

"How long have you known?"

"Today. Just today"

His head bowed. Both hands were on the curving banister, palms down, his body leaning forward. The moonling prince, the would-be king, looking out over the land.

"You promised me," he finally said, low, dejected.

"I didn't. I couldn't. I said I'd try to link to him. I failed and I'm sorry."

"I don't care if you're sorry."

"I don't know anyone who can keep another from death forever, or who can even heal death." I didn't mean to be defensive. But love makes us all weak like that sometimes.

I heard a sob escape his throat.

"Ari—"

"I don't want you to call me that anymore."

"All right." The sting in my eyes was back. He'd only just told me I could. I loved that nickname for him.

"You know," voice strained, "ever since you came here you did what you promised. You took away my pain. But it's brought me pain in return as well. What good is that? What good is any of it?"

I tried to remember my teachings, the classroom, Zash. All my experience. But this was outside my professional

190

education. It had become all-too personal. Right now there was nothing for me to fall back on but my own heart. My feelings. And I was as vulnerable about them all as he was. I was an alien here on Firgone, everything strange, new-born.

I could only think selfishly in this moment. What good was any of it? he'd asked. Well, it had brought us together. For me that was all that mattered.

But any trite response like that to his question would make things worse. I also knew better than to say things like, "It will pass," or "Give it time." And something like grief, especially for a twin, well, that never went away. It might ease up after a time. It might be distracted for awhile, but grief never leaves.

I walked up to Arulu but didn't touch him. Instead, I stood beside him on the stairwell, hands on the banister, and looked out over the hills and valleys of shadow.

"What good is any of it," I said, echoing his words back to him. "A question asked by the greatest and the most forlorn of the galaxy. There is never one sure answer."

Very softly, Arulu said in a broken voice, "He's all I've known for twenty years. He kept me company even in my pain."

"I didn't know that before I healed you."

"I care for no one but him. No one!"

Those words stabbed at me.

His knees bent and his weight fell more heavily onto his hands. "Do you hear me? No one."

"Yes." I swallowed salt and pain.

He began to gasp. Held his breath before the words blurted out. "Why did you have to come here?"

As he spoke, his body collapsed. I reached out just in time to catch him, holding him up by his arms, my own around his chest and back.

"Let me go," he sobbed.

But he didn't fight me. Instead his hands slowly came around me. "Let me go," he said softer. "Tahir. Tahir." His body shook. "Don't. Touch. Don't. Leave."

He sobbed into my neck and shoulder. I lowered my face to the top of his head and pressed my tears into his hair.

*

Night went on, unbroken. We stood there for a long time. He clung to me like a child. It was then I knew he'd said those words about not caring, about wanting me to leave, out of anger and pain. As much as they hurt, I knew they weren't true because he held onto me so hard, and kept clutching.

His breathing finally slowed. The shoulder of my coat was wet. When I tried to move, he lifted his head and moved with me, strands of tangled hair about his face. Docile now. Calmer.

He allowed me to lead him back to his room. I led him to his bed, made him sit, and pulled the robe over his head and folded it, placing it at the foot. Then I made him lie down and covered him. He turned onto his side, reaching for me.

I took off my coat and climbed in with him, still in my shirt and trousers. For a long time, side by side, I held him. He finally fell asleep as I stroked the side of his head.

I lay awake for a long time watching his chest rise and fall. Watching him breathe.

They both stood at the foot of the bed looking down at us. Nik. Arku. Half in shadow, half in light from an unseen source, as if they stood on another planet far distant from this moon and were gazing through a magic window and into our realm.

"Ari, my love," Arku whispered. Forlorn.

His lidless eyes sought mine. "Please love him well," he said to me.

Nik said nothing but he looked sorry, adrift.

"We leave tomorrow," Arku said to me. "We would like a final goodbye. Can you do that?"

I nodded.

"Thank you, Tahir."
Slowly, they vanished, like clouds melting under the sun.

*

Arulu woke several times before morning. His blank stares meeting mine. No expression. He would look around once or twice, then simply close his eyes, burrow into me, and go back to sleep.

He was mad at me, of course. But like some strange child, he wouldn't let go of me.

It was a sad but good sign. I slept little. Afraid to look away from him. Afraid he, too, might simply vanish from life like those ghosts. I made sure he did not get cold. I made sure the covers stayed in place over his naked body, and that he had enough pillows to support his back and head. I made his tortured, fitful sleep as comfortable as possible. Sometimes he butted his head against me and moaned. But only when he was very still would he open his eyes. Maybe to see if I was still with him.

*

I looked down at the beautiful charm, the dancing lights that encircled it. The doll-size screen remained blank. I had thought briefly about sending Arulu a message. "Arku wants to say goodbye." I quickly dismissed the thought. I could not send such a terrible and personal message like that through some stupid, digital icon.

But after we both woke in the morning, Arulu left at the beckoning of his father, saying nothing. He had dressed and exited the room so quickly I had not been able to even try to say the words. "Arku wants a final meeting to say goodbye."

I'd wandered the palace for some hours, learning my way around, but mostly bored. It seemed like every five seconds I checked the necklace to see if Arulu had called. Just in case I'd missed the chime. Just in case the entire universe had altered from one second to the next and everything was all right again and we were talking.

It hurt me to even think those words, "Arku wants to say goodbye." How could I utter them aloud to Arku's very own twin?

So I waited.

No wave from Zash, though I checked several times. Just silence. From everyone.

Finally, in the late afternoon, I got a message from Kean. The king requested me to dine with him, his family and a few guests at dinner. I wanted to decline. But etiquette demanded I go.

It was in a smaller banquet hall this time.

Arulu was already there when I arrived, sitting at a large dining table alone, aloof. He was dressed like an ornament in golds and blues, his hair a shining flag down his back. Mouth tight. Features carved in stone. He looked like a beautiful doll, high cheekbones, perfectly curved dark brows, waiting for someone to give him a command. He breathed. He moved. But all without a life of his own.

Had I done that to him? Had I healed a man only to see him wither in his soul?

Without a word, I went to him and sat beside him.

He made no acknowledgment that he knew I was there. But of course he did. He could hear me. His peripheral vision could not miss the ornate purples and greens of my coat, which I'd already decided was the best piece of clothing I'd ever owned along with the red velvet jacket.

I made a splash on the air with the colorings of that coat. He had to notice.

I picked up a curved, crystal chalice of water and drank half of it before setting it back down with a clink.

He just sat there, doing nothing.

I decided to challenge that a little. I reached for his

wine glass, which was full but untouched. Mine was still empty, the servants not yet noticing I'd arrived.

I said, "You going to drink that? Because I think I need it."

He did not reply, but as my hand touched the stem of the glass, he reached across his empty plate and pushed at my wrist, shoving my hand aside. He picked up his own glass and put it to his lips. He drank the tiniest sip, tipped it level but still held onto it.

"Okay, then." I put my elbows on the table and leaned into it. Looking around. Finally noticing my need, a servant came over and poured me some wine of my own as I held my glass up.

I drank, letting the salt-sweet taste coat the roof of my mouth and my throat. Waiting for the effects of it to mellow my mood.

Even just sitting next to him, my skin felt the fever again, running up and down my back, my arms, my legs. Coiling inside my stomach. Sweet surges into my groin.

Arulu could hate me, I decided, and I'd still always want him.

I don't know what that made me, as a healer and friend, but I could not deny the stirrings within me now. And I never would.

I took another sip of the wine. We were still alone. People congregated, laughing, by the door. I turned and said to him what I'd been trying to say all day, "Arku wants another meeting."

Arulu lifted his chin. He still held the wine glass. The purple liquid wavered. "Yes," he finally uttered, like a hiss.

"Tonight, then," I said.

A curt nod.

"Just one more time," I said, pushing the barriers between us. "Then you can send me away as you wished in the beginning. I'll go willingly, no matter what the king desires."

His body stiffened. He said nothing.

"Okay, then." I took a huge gulp of the wine this time. Then another.

Arulu remained frozen, holding his just an inch off the tabletop.

I couldn't take any more. I scooted my chair back and stood. "Please tell the king I am feeling under the weather tonight and I'll take a rain check on the dinner."

Arulu started to look up at me.

I couldn't meet those eyes. The resentment. The sadness. Even though I held him all the long night, even though he never pushed me away during those long, sleep-tortured hours, I feared that he really did hate me now.

"Chime me," I said, "when you want to do this. You know where I'll be."

I turned away and walked toward the door. I didn't look back, but I heard the wine glass tip over with a soft clunk, and saw the servant rush over with a cloth to wipe the spill away.

I wasn't happy with leaving, but I truly did feel sick. Sick because I didn't know how to do this right. I had done everything I knew to help, but it seemed my presence from now on was only going to make everything worse for the prince of the September Stars.

26.

Arulu

Arulu could still smell him on his skin. Tahir. The healer. Tahir. The lover. Who had healed him from outrageous pain he'd lived with for so long. Who had awakened his body for the first time in ways he had never dreamed.

196

He wanted to keep that fragrance on him, inside him even though he was in a new kind of agony because of Tahir, even though he was so angry right now.

And then there was the grief. He couldn't even begin to put voice to the pain of that.

He'd clung to Tahir the rest of last night, beside himself in turmoil and not wanting to be alone, but he was so unsure about everything right now.

He'd worked for his father today again, seeing nothing, hearing nothing, sitting in on meetings, nodding when expected to nod, and that was it. No one required much from him. But they didn't know he was dealing with his dead twin. They didn't know he'd been haunted his whole life.

He should have been happy. No pain. A new lover. But every time he thought of Arku he wanted to burst. Sorrow and despair were not words enough for what he felt.

The dinner that evening was a nightmare. Tahir had come and gone so quickly that Arulu had had no time to think, to speak, to figure out what to do. He'd been so upset he spilled his wine.

When they all sat to eat, Kean sat beside him. The queen had decided to sit with friends at the other end of the banquet table.

Kean said, discreetly, "Tahir is absent?"

Arulu shifted his gaze to his plate, studying the food there, all of it unappetizing. "He said to give you his apology and that he was feeling under the weather."

"He has done much for this family. For you. I hope you have properly thanked him."

Arulu was silent.

"Well?" Kean asked. "Have you?"

"Have I what?" Arulu asked, only half hearing his father's words.

"Thanked him."

He thought deeply about that and realized that possibly he had not. He had never actually said the words "thank you." But after everything, were they absolutely necessary?

"I—I might see him later. A follow-up of sorts. I'll make sure to say the words."

Kean took a breath. "I am so grateful that he has helped you in something so horribly beyond our control. I know you are, too."

Arulu could only nod.

"And remember, Tahir is new, here. Alien to our ways. I'm sure he must be feeling awkward, even lonely. You would do well to take care with him, make him feel at home. It would not do for such a man, one who has done us a great favor and honor, to be made to feel at all unwelcome or alien here. Not from any of us. We owe him a debt we can never really repay."

Arulu's cheeks felt suddenly hot. He wondered if his father saw. He wondered how much his father already knew about him and Tahir, spending long hours together at night, all night. Who knew what the escorts, although mostly trustworthy, reported to the king?

"Yes, sir," was all Arulu was able to say.

He ate very little that night. The king pretended not to notice, and left him alone after that, conversing casually, in happy abandon, with his dinner guests who surrounded him and his son.

Arulu suffered quietly, until the dessert was served and he found an unobtrusive moment to declare himself finished, and politely took his leave.

*

The sleeve of his blazer was sticky where some of the purple wine had spilled upon it. Stains on silver satin. Like tears that wouldn't dry.

His instinct was to run from his own devastation, as if the pent up negative energy could be expunged by motion.

But he kept hearing Tahir's voice in his mind: *You can send me away as you wished in the beginning.*

He took the steps of the spiral staircase two at a time, going down flight after flight, his clothing and hair rippling in the breeze he made. Round and round. He felt like he was flying. Spinning. The dusk of the moon was the breaking sea all around the ship of the palace.

He could almost smell the salt of that sea, the black ash waters storming all around him at ground level where he stood heaving, trying to catch his breath.

He looked back the way he'd come. The spiral, like a giant seashell, rose up and up. He took a deep breath and determined to make it back to the royal level, two steps at a time, at a jogging pace. He began to move, undaunted by fatigue, and stopped only for a minute half-way on a landing to take deep breaths, one after the other, and correct the stitch in his side. After that, no more stops. He went further then, past the royal floor, and on up to the guest level.

The voice followed him. *I'll go willingly, no matter what the king desires.*

Round one corner, then another, eyes on the dragon-head sconces, wincing at the bright brass light that poured from their mouths. The sconces made great shadows upon the walls, like monsters all around. Round another corner. Past an intersection and straight through, then to the end of the hall and right.

Just one more time, Tahir had said.

He ended up at Tahir's door. Two escorts stood about fifteen feet away. They saw who he was immediately, and pretended to ignore his presence to give him privacy. He wanted to laugh. As part of the royal family, privacy was a joke. Of course he knew he was always watched.

He didn't want to do this. He didn't want to be here.

He pressed the chime button. Much to his frustration, the door did not open immediately. He glanced down at his necklace as he chimed a second time. If Tahir were not inside, he could always use the necklace to find him.

But this time the door opened. Tahir, all in black and white again, having removed his lovely coat, moved away from the door, turning toward the kitchen area as Arulu entered. He was making tea.

Arulu felt awkward as he came inside, and even sadder now after trying to wear himself out on the staircase. He watched the back of Tahir, who kept his hands busy with cups and hot water. Two cups, Arulu noticed. So Tahir was going to play the good host.

Tahir said nothing, which Arulu knew he deserved after behaving so rudely at the dinner. Grief was a reason but not necessarily an excuse. Not after everything Tahir had done for him. Kean had been right. Arulu had never properly thanked him.

His hands formed fists under his long, tapered sleeves. Under the silver still stained with purple wine. He opened his mouth to speak. Nothing came out.

It was all too much. Too much! He closed his mouth. Steeled himself. Fingernails dug into the beds of his palms. His head grew slightly dizzy. He focused on the teacups and Tahir's hands. Watched the way the shirt played across his back as he prepared the hot drinks. That back he had touched, skin on skin. The smoothness over knots of spine. The firmness of the waist and lower.

His eyebrows knitted. There was a thickness in his throat that made every breath he took quiver inside his lungs. He wanted very badly to run again.

Tahir poured hot water into the cups.

Arulu wanted to say, *I'm not hungry. I'm not thirsty. I just want to get through this.*

How long was Tahir going to make him stand here, so calmly preparing the tea as if nothing else mattered? The awkwardness he felt made his legs weak. He either needed to pace, or he needed a chair.

Just as Arulu was ready to turn and run away—for

what? To only delay the inevitable?—Tahir turned, two cups in his hand. He held one out in offering to Arulu.

He automatically held out his hand to take it. Maybe the warmth would comfort him for a moment, along with the honeyed scent of the boiled leaves. But just as he started to wrap his fingers about the handle, it slipped and fell.

He watched it, as if it all happened in slow-motion, tip and spin and float down, down. It shattered, topaz liquid and glass splattering all over the floor.

Arulu gave a startled, "Ah—" and swayed.

Tahir caught him one-handed, quickly setting his own cup unscathed on the counter so he could use two hands to steer him away from the mess.

"Come. Sit," he said softly, leading Arulu not to the table and the chairs, but to the bed.

Arulu couldn't fight him. He had no more strength where this man was concerned.

"Okay, okay." Tahir kept speaking softly to him. "Let's get your coat off." He pulled at the flaps, and Arulu allowed it, moving his arms back a little so that it slid off and to his waist. Tahir took the coat and folded it neatly, placing it on a chair. He turned back to Arulu and put his hand under his chin, tilting it. "Open your eyes. Look at me."

Arulu obeyed.

"All right. You're okay." Voice pleasant and smooth. Comforting.

"No," he managed to reply. "I'm not."

Tahir nodded slowly. "But you didn't fall."

"I feel like I'm falling still," Arulu retorted.

"And I will catch you. Every time. Until I go."

Arulu panicked for a moment, a new pain washing over him at those last three words. "No. You promised." *Don't go.* "You aren't going to touch my emotions."

"Not what I meant," Tahir said quietly. "I have not forgotten that promise."

Arulu needed to focus, concentrate. He was totally

losing himself and he didn't want that. Not for this last encounter. His last goodbye to Arku.

He looked at the puddle on the floor by the counter. The eggshell curves of the broken china jutted up in sharp little peaks. The sight of a simple mess grounded him. "I should get a towel for that."

"Don't worry about that right now," Tahir said, bringing him back into the moment.

He blinked at the pale eyes of the healer, fretting about what was to come. He didn't want to go there, into Tahir's mind. Not yet. The longer he could hold off seeing Arku, the longer Arku would remain here even if he could no longer see him except through Tahir's gift.

At the thought, he wondered how often Tahir saw them, Arku and Nik. Were they here this very minute? Watching this pathetic fiasco?

Slowly, Tahir sat beside him on the bed, the weight against the mattress causing Arulu to sink toward him.

Tahir said, "You don't have to do this. You do have a choice."

Arulu said nothing, head bowed, chin nearly touching his chest.

"But if you don't, I think you'll regret it for the rest of your life."

"Don't tell me what I will and won't regret."

"I am not telling. I am suggesting."

He knew Tahir was right. The terrible moment must be endured so he could go on with the rest of his life. He took a deep breath. Best to get it over with.

"Go on, then. Let's do this," Arulu said. He heard himself as if from a long distance away.

Tahir turned to look at the foot of the bed as if seeing something there that Arulu could not. A creepy tickle ran down the prince's spine. The hairs on the backs of his hands stood up. Tahir turned back to Arulu, bending at the knee and pulling his leg up onto the mattress so he could face him full

202

on.

Arulu said, "I don't want to lie down for this."

Tahir simply nodded. Reached out with one hand and cupped his cheek and chin.

Don't touch me, he wanted to say. But the touch was only steadying. Necessary. Still, his breathing grew ragged. And Tahir seemed so damnably calm. Hesitant but firm. Gentle but persistent.

The fragrance of Tahir, like a freshness that came from real live planets, not the fake settings of moons, washed over him. Almost immediately, his skin tingled in a different way from the feeling which overcame him when he had seen Tahir looking toward the foot of the bed. He couldn't help it. He couldn't stop it. Even in his abject grief, he wanted Tahir like he'd never wanted anything else in his life.

Maybe it surprised the healer, maybe it didn't, when he lifted his face up to meet the kiss. Lip to lip, the warmth, the sweetness. It was as if none of this bad stuff was happening, and Tahir had never left his side all day. As if they fit perfectly and understood each other through and through.

Of course that was his own wishful thinking. They'd known each other only just four days.

The warmth of the healer's mouth, a sort of serenity and lightness combined, flowed over him. It was not like the last time when he had spun into space and the starship graveyard.

Immediately, Arulu's feet set upon the stone floor amid the sun and shadow of the great palace throne room on Lyric Prime. His body felt real, solid. The air came into his lungs fresh and cool.

He spun to get full vision of the great room, the elaborate carvings on the walls, looking for the others.

Arku stood by the giant thrones that were carved from a black meteorite. And there was Nik by the arched window. Tahir stood in shadow beside the window, about five feet from Nik. He wore his black Temple robe.

Without preamble, Arku said, "Hello, brother."

Arulu's head swam a little, but he approached his brother quickly, reaching out. Arku, in his ruined body, reached for him as well and they walked into each other's embrace.

"The room's intact here," Arulu said into his ear.

"The palace still stands, yes," Arku agreed. "For as long as we remember it."

"When I dream this place, it's a horror. A—" he paused. "A slaughter house."

"But it lives on, untouched by evil, in the old folds and crevices of time itself. Even Tahir doesn't understand how or why he can bring us here. But he does it somehow through us, a connection of sorts. Don't you feel it?"

"Yes." Arulu pulled back so he could see his twin's face, wrecked as it was. "If this room in the past lives on in old time-folds, then so can you. You don't have to leave me."

"So insistent that I stay. After everything."

Arulu frowned, confused at the words. "But I—I love you."

"I know. It's kept us close for all these horrible years. Companions through hell and beyond. But now things have changed. Neither of us is trapped; anymore."

"But we can stay together, surely—"

"Did you not hear me?" Arku sounded annoyed but his voice remained soft. Arulu pressed his lips tight. Tahir was on the peripheral edge; he could still feel him pressed against him on the side of the bed even as he saw him standing in the shadow by the window. He wanted to push away from them all except Arku, whom he wanted to pull close, bind to his heart forever.

"There is a call beyond," Arku said. "And I can't resist it. Look at me. Can't you see how trapped I am?" He held up his arms, mostly bone, the meat swinging at the elbows.

Fighting what he heard, Arulu said, "If the room is intact, so you can be. A memory of you from before, but now grown. I'm identical to you. Use me as a model. We'll make you whole. Tahir is a healer. We'll work it out!"

Arku laughed without humor. "Listen, Ari. Please, listen! I have other places to be now. I am not an extension of you."

"That's not what I mean." Arulu was desperate, though. Arku could stay, he believed that, if they could just find a way that worked for them both.

"I know what you mean. I can practically read your mind, twin. You'd keep me here if you could. Even if it meant binding me up. Trapping me."

"You're misunderstanding."

"No. I know you and have depended on each other in our strange states. Of course you don't want that to end. But it must." His smile barely showed. There was little flesh to smile with. "And I'll miss you more than life itself, Ari, my love."

"Then don't leave me," Arulu pleaded.

"Shush." He reached out to touch Arulu's shoulder.

"Just don't. Decide to stay. For me."

"And what about me, you idiot?" Arku said sweetly. "You're making a scene, and you're making this harder on me. Ever think about that? I don't want to leave you. You're my brother. I love you." Tears rolled from the lidless eyes and onto boney cheeks. "Ever think how I'm feeling? You're not the only one who has suffered, brother."

Arulu was stunned. "But we're of the same mind."

"Sure. But you forget one crucial thing."

Arulu shook his head.

"I'm dead," Arku said. "You're still alive. You need to go on and I need to go on."

"But I can't bear it. Not without you."

The sharp hand stroked down Arulu's shoulder to his arm, his wrist. He took his hand and held it tightly. "You must. For us. For me. Because if I know you continue to suffer, I will never be happy wherever I am. Is that what you want?"

Slowly, Arulu shook his head no.

"And," Arku continued, "you have Tahir now."

Quick breath of denial. "No."

"You do. I've seen you with him."

Arulu closed his eyes, didn't want to hear.

"Brother," Arku said firmly, resolutely. "He's so good for you."

Voice a whisper, "I barely know him."

Arku huffed. "You know enough. And you can't deny he cares."

Arulu felt the sobs come up, out of his control.

Arku merely shook his head. "Don't. Please don't do that."

But how could he make a promise to his brother he wasn't sure he could keep? Move on. Be happy. Just words that meant nothing in the face of the emotions he now grappled with. But the thought of Arku in pain, forever trapped. That was inconceivable.

He swallowed back his tears and looked his brother straight in the eyes. "I'll try." It felt like a lie. He wanted to defy everyone now, even his own brother, and not try. Just curl up and not feel ever again.

Arku squeezed his hand. "Make me believe you."

He said it again. "I will try."

"And you'll let Tahir help you when you need him?"

Arulu nodded tightly.

He heard Nik and Tahir speaking softly behind him, too soft for him to make out the words. But he understood the tone. They, too, were saying goodbye.

"It's time, then," Arku said.

Arulu wanted to hold onto him. His fingers clasped bone. But Arku pulled back, then let go. And Arulu felt like he was falling as the throne room seemed to sway and became less solid.

"Arku!" He called out. His brother was there still, but wavering. He saw him fully now, smiling, and as his image shimmered Arku became a whole man for the first time in twenty years. Face smooth and tan, unmarred, hair long and dark, arms and legs full. A black suit formed over his features and he stood tall, finely dressed, glowing, an image that would be burned into the memory of Arulu forever.

Nik came to stand beside Arku. Tahir approached, stopping when he reached Arulu's side. Together they watched as the ghosts grew brighter until they vanished in a golden flash of light.

Arulu and Tahir stood in the vast room as the light around them began to dwindle. A wind blew through the chamber, neither hot nor cold, and it was not constructed of air. It was more of a thought form. An eerie laugh echoed. It circled the moon prince and the healer in a swift cyclone that died as soon as it appeared.

Arulu knew what it was. The pain and the grief and the horror of that monster weapon, a rent of blackness that in their language was called a splinter-bomb. The thing that channeled death.

The offensive, destructive energy moved along the walls of the room like a lazy, snaking shadow. A howl filled the room, ending in an echo. The window was dark now. It slithered toward it, moving through it and into the depths of the dead galaxy of its origin, rebuffed.

Arulu gasped, and opened his eyes to find himself still sitting on the edge of Tahir's bed as Tahir's lips moved away from his. He breathed hard, as if he'd been running a long, long distance. He could not control the shivering of his body. It felt as if all his muscles were collapsing.

Tahir said, "Lie back. Just rest." And put his hand against Arulu's back to steer him into the pillows.

Arulu sank gratefully into the soft nest, pulling his legs up, and curled onto his side facing the low wall that supported the bedroom window. He stared up and out that window toward the darkness swathed with intermittent purple flashes. Dampness trickled over the bridge of his nose as he tasted the bitterness in his throat. He had been crying.

Was still crying deep inside.

He felt the weight of Tahir leave the bedside. After a few moments, the sounds of Tahir cleaning up the mess of his broken cup and the spilled tea surrounded him. He heard the clinking of broken glass being gathered and faint swishing sounds of towels mopping. Water running. Soft footsteps.

He closed his eyes to those ordinary, strangely peaceful sounds and drifted into a sad but tired sleep.

Awhile later, he woke, not knowing how much time had passed. He opened his eyes, turned over, and saw Tahir sitting in the big chair by the bed, legs drawn up, head tilted toward his chest, one hand resting on the chair arm, one hand clasped into a fist against his chest. He'd obviously been watching over Arulu before falling to sleep himself.

The necklace Arulu had given him hung to the side of his white shirt, just below his ribcage, the lights all gold and pink faintly chasing each other around the rim. He noticed Tahir had never taken it off since he had given it to him.

Arulu fidgeted about his neck, pulling his own necklace straight and untangling it from his hair. Using deft, practiced touches, he created a message in pale blue letters that said, simply, *"Thank you."*

Then he got up and gathered his folded coat from beside the sleeping Tahir, and silently left.

*

The next morning Arulu arrived at breakfast in the royal banquet room. He noticed a place had been set for Tahir but the healer had not arrived.

When breakfast began, with cutlery ringing and the scents of fresh bread, meats and eggs being served, the seat remained empty. Arulu turned to Kean. "Where's Tahir?" He raised a glass of juice to his lips and drank a small sip.

The king turned to his son and said, "He's gone."

"What?" Nearly choking.

Kean's eyebrow rose. "Not off-moon. He just went into Xia to visit for an undisclosed time. He has some prospective clients there that I helped him set into motion."

"He's not living here?"

Kean stared at him for a moment longer than was comfortable. He replied, "His rooms are still his. Everything I gave him remains. It won't be touched until he decides to return."

Arulu set down his glass and turned away, staring at the far wall of the hall, seeing nothing. The pain of Arku leaving was still deep inside him. But the pain of Tahir leaving was almost more than he could bear. He felt his father's gaze linger, heard him give a soft sigh.

It was at that moment he became certain that Kean knew. About him and Tahir. And once more it seemed the father was disappointed in the son.

27.

Tahir

Xia was an old-fashioned city, with gas-lamps deliberately designed to decorate the high-end sections of the downtown area in its ever-impending dusk. I got myself a fancy, furnished room, thanks to Kean's gracious salary, and haunted the city like the curious alien I was, marveling at the baroque architecture, amazed at how the buildings looked like strange animals poised to attack, or in some extreme cases, bristled with spines as if defending themselves from predators. Some doors and windows were round, or triangular. Awnings stretched over the walkways like the ribcages of giants. I grew used to the black dust that settled upon the streets, and the shadows the city grew on its own sidewalks and walls that made my own nightmares look tame.

After that final night with Arulu, knowing we both needed space, I'd hastily packed some of the fine clothes that had been given to me, and a few other necessities. I had a quick meeting with the king that went well. He supported my decision to seek some work outside the palace for a time.

I had been here two weeks and had done some simple healings for a few people who were pleased to have me. In my spare time, I explored. Stores. Restaurants. Strange dark parks.

On a corner close to the building I lived in was a fancy lounge, a place that seemed clean, happy and well-lit. They served that purple wine I had grown a taste for and I frequented the place all too often, enjoying the ambiance, and the clientele.

The lounge walls sported murals of what looked to be cultural myths, stories I didn't know or understand but that were nonetheless familiar, since every culture had them. In one picture was a ruler with a scepter of stars and a dragon on his head, the tail inserted in the ruler's mouth. In another was a figure holding a plate of what looked like cookies, except they were moons of all colors. One had a bite taken out of it. A small creature huddled underneath the tray, the laughing mouth exposing great fangs.

I did recognize one of the paintings, however. The Void-God Sinarha who had risen from the Ghost Abyss. Ruler of Aeons. Ruler of Death. In this depiction, he looked a lot like Arulu, with long brown hair, unbraided, and lots of scarves decorating him in silver, scarlet and gold. I decided that had been a deliberate tribute to the royal family by the artist. Despite Arulu's inability to function as a ruler, he had remained all along the Crown Prince of his people.

I wondered if that was where Arku and Nik had gone. To the Ghost Abyss. Was it even real? The ghosts of the dead could come back. I knew that now. But after that, where did they go?

It made my heart ache to look at that wall-painting, but I went back every night, ordering purple wine, sitting in a happy place. And my eyes were always drawn to it.

The stark, cool wine held no answer. But I loved the taste.

Every night I had a routine. A nice dinner. The lounge. Maybe a conversation with a stranger that would leave me with new knowledge. And the purple wine.

When I grew tired, I'd head for my room. I'd check my waves. I had heard from Zash finally. We were writing fairly regularly, though the delays were two days or more to receive waves. I told him some of what had transpired, but nothing personal. Still, his insights had helped me a lot, and all tragedy aside, he was fascinated by what I had learned about splinter-bombs.

After that, in my routine, I would sometimes shower if I felt like it, or simply strip and climb into my bed. Before I turned out the light, I would pick up the necklace that I had placed on the nightstand. I no longer wore it. I would check it for messages. There never were any.

Then I would let the darkness fall, pull up the covers and try to sleep. Sleep did not always come easily. Sometimes it took me an hour or more of full, concentrated meditation.

My heart was raw. It seemed I couldn't heal myself.

But my routine remained undisturbed. Which meant I was making it easy for anyone to find me, should anyone decide to come looking.

*

It took 16 days, 12 hours and twenty-two minutes, give or take a minute, for him to arrive at the lounge, his head down to avoid stares, scarves all aflutter.

My heart clenched hard. My throat caught so I couldn't, for a few seconds, breathe.

I saw his eyes scan the place before his gaze ended at

me.

His face gave no expression, but he was as beautiful as ever, the long flashing hair, the dark, deep-set eyes, high-boned cheeks, perfectly winged-brows. The graceful lines of his body were offset well by his tight fitting suit of amber and red, the scarves fastened to him like belts and extra sleeves, and ties trailing off the back of his neck.

Just to see him like that, my eyes heated.

He came toward me, ignoring the whispers that came over the place at his arrival, shoulders back, unpained, and moving with the ease of someone in the prime of youth and health. Someone who had not moved like this since he had been ten years old. Someone who was a prince.

That had been my doing. And if I had it to do over again, I wouldn't have done it any other way.

He sat down next to me but did not look at me. Instead, he glanced at my goblet of wine, then motioned the bartender over.

He ordered the same I was drinking, which almost made me smile, until he added, "For him. For me, I think I'll have a cometjoybackslutbanger." Or at least that's what it sounded like. I'd never heard of anything like it, and when it came it had a rainbow of layers, a side assortment of speared fruit, and a loopy, plastic straw.

He absently stirred at the layers of liquid with the straw, which remained undaunted in their ability to perform the perfect rainbow, and said still staring at his drink, "I'm still pissed off at you."

They were the first words I'd heard from him in over two weeks. He used an archaic term for "pissed off" which meant sort of "as enraged as a full bladder after a night of drinking" and I was grateful for such a thorough download of the dialect these people spoke in Galactic Standard.

I could only blink, unsure how to reply. He'd searched for me and he'd found me. It could only mean one thing.

Now he turned his head slightly, but still his eyes did

not meet mine, and instead seemed to study the bartop. "I realized," he said quietly, "there was something I needed to do and never did. Well, I sort of did, but not in person."

I finally blurted, "I don't know what you're talking about."

"I never thanked you. In spoken words, I mean. Not on a stupid screen."

"Thanked me." I let out a puff of breath. Impatient. "For what? It was your father who hired me."

Finally, his head lifted and he looked directly into my eyes. "He didn't hire you for everything."

To my shock, my face instantly heated. Arulu raised an eyebrow at my blush but did not smile. He glanced back down at his fancy drink.

As calmly as I could, I lifted my drink and took a sip. Then I said, "You don't have to thank me. It's not all about you, you know."

He stopped stirring at his drink, quite frozen by my words. I couldn't tell if people were staring at us, or not. Did I care?

"What then," he said. "You're thanking me?" But he turned his head and gave a little smile to take the sting out of his words.

Maybe, I thought. But I didn't say that aloud. And yet after sixteen days I could still feel his warm skin against mine, the taste of his lips, the scent of his arousal. All of it embedded into me, my flesh stored with his essence.

I had never loved like this. Love, if that's what it was apart from mere mind to mind mixing, and the chemical response to that which might only be temporary obsession.

But whatever it was, it wasn't just my body that wanted him. I felt this longing to my core. This thing inside me that had missed him so much.

"I live about half a block up," I said quietly.

"I know," he responded.

I gave a short laugh at the thought he'd been spying on

me. "Well, then let's get out of here."

"Okay." He got up at the same time I did, motioning for the bartender and putting a money card in his hand. He had never touched his drink except to stir it. He left the card with the bartender and did not look back.

Our walk was silent, up the dim and dusty street side by side, while the purplish dome flashed overhead reflecting in pools of lavender on his hair. There were a few people out, but far away from us, some moving slowly by in open, floating cars. The gas-lamps, all constructed for pure ornamentation, flickered in a line of pale, gold stars. This was the kind of night that back home would have been a prelude to a storm. This kind of night could either wash the ash from your heart, or churn it into black mud. Here it was ordinary. The endless black mouth of it. The night where gods who preferred the sun did not walk.

Well, we were not gods, but just men. And our hearts had bits of ash, maybe, and bits of brokenness, but were not yet so dark. Or, in Arulu's extreme case, no longer quite favoring that absence of color.

I'd helped him get at least that far.

Ten moons behind a thick barrier of defense and paranoia. Ten little worlds from which some of the greatest art in the design of starships had ever emerged. A culture having spawned on a large planet that was now adrift in pieces. But the soul of its people lived on.

Arulu embodied that in name. And in a penchant for design, as Arku had briefly alluded to, saying his brother had made decent drawings of ships even as a child. And had dreamed of making dead starships live again.

But he was just a man. Scarred and flawed. Just a single body among billions who had managed to survive.

Still, I thought he was the perfect representative of his people now. Even if he was still in the process of finding that out for himself.

Yes, this perpetual night of Firgone was not for gods.

214

But it was for men. Like us.

I turned into the doorway of my building. It recognized me and opened its doors to me, letting us through. We went up a sliding stair to the fourth floor. The doors to my place, again recognizing me, opened. I waved Arulu through.

He barely looked at my room's interior, instead going straight to my wide, floor-to-ceiling window, saying, "You have a balcony." He went immediately through the windowed door, which slid open at a touch, and explored the jutting edges of the outdoor ledge's perimeter. Its waist-high walls with little decorative knobs. Its four planters, each with an individual grow-light, spilling over with cascading green leaves. Creeping-crawlers. Ivy.

How well he distracted himself from the inevitable. As if he didn't want to talk. Or couldn't. The mess that was between us too flinty to touch. Or too tender, maybe.

As he looked out over the moonscape, my gorgeous view, for I'd grown to love these valleys of shadow and clenched hills and secret darks, my chest quaked with love for him.

In the distance his palace reached for the horizon, a castle of dark fantasy, sleeping beauties, a crouching and endlessly unfolding fairy tale. Straight out of the dusks of a billion tomorrows.

I could see the future here. It wasn't all dark.

"So," I said boldly. "You came to see me, or the view from my balcony?"

"My father sent me." He stood very still, unflinching.

If it was true that he didn't come of his own accord, it hurt. "Why?"

"He thinks I rejected you and he let me know he was disappointed." He leaned against the wall reminding me of his demeanor on the spiral staircase the night he'd run from my room after Arku told him he was fading.

I reached out to touch his hand which was clenched against the wall's edge. I didn't know what I was going to say,

but I began with the nickname he'd forbidden me to use.
"Ari—"

Before I could even think of uttering another syllable he whirled on me, flipping his hand over mine, grabbing it up and using it to push me back across the balcony, forcing me with his whole body, his weight now against me as I stepped backward to keep my balance. In less than two seconds he had me up against the cobbled wall, its uneven rocks digging into my back and buttocks.

His free hand came up to my shoulder, pushing harder, holding me there as he pressed against me, chest against my chest, stomach against my stomach.

In what was an amazing and powerful gesture for Ari, and one I had never seen him commit to before, he tilted his head forward and caught my lips with his own in a furious and searing kiss.

His mouth opened, moist and hot. I tasted the remants of bitter grief, but also sweetness, need, affection.

Slowly my arms went around him. All the built up tension of the last couple of weeks drained from me and I let him hold me there, let him say what he wanted to say without the complication of words.

My fingers slid up the satin of his jacket, tangling in the scarves and his hair.

It was a long time before he finally pulled back, his rich brown eyes tensed in a kind of agony mixed with a question.

I understood his question clearly. He didn't need to speak. And I? Well, I simply nodded. "Yes," I said. "Yes."

The End

 Wendy Rathbone has had dozens of stories published in anthologies such as: Hot Blood, Writers of the Future (second place,) Bending the Landscape, Mutation Nation, A Darke Phantastique, and more. Over 500 of her poems have been published in various anthologies and magazines. She won first place in the Anamnesis Press poetry chapbook contest with her book "Scrying the River Styx." Her poems have been nominated for the Science Fiction Poetry Association's Rhysling award at least a dozen times. You can visit her blog at: http://wendyrathbone.blogspot.com/

Her recent books include:
Lace, book 1 in the vampire fairy series, m/m romance.
Scoundrel, science fiction m/m romance novel.
"Beneath the Blue Dusk and the Sea," short story collection.
"Turn Left at November," a brand new collection of poems.
"Letters To An Android," science fiction novel.
"Pale Zenith," science fiction novel.
"Moltenrose," 2 stand-alone novellas in the Pale Zenith universe.
"The Foundling," male/male romance novel, book 1 of the Foundling trilogy.
"None Can Hold the Dark," book 2 of the Foundling trilogy.
"The Lostling," book 3 of the Foundling trilogy.
"The Secret Sharer," science fiction romance novella.
"Unearthly," omnibus collection of 7 out-of-print poetry booklets.
"The Vampire Diaries: The Myth," available from Kindle Worlds.
"The Vampire Dairies: Deep In the Virginia Woods," available from Kindle Worlds.
"My House Is Full Of Whispers," erotica short story collection.

Upcoming:
The Moonling Prince, a science fiction m/m romance.
"Bitters," a collection of vampire short stories.

Look for more novels and short story collections coming up in 2016.
She lives in Yucca Valley, CA with her partner of 35 years, Della Van Hise.

Dear Reader:

Thank you for reading "The Moonling Prince." If you enjoyed it, you may also enjoy the sequel, "The Moonling Prince: Shadow on the Moon" which takes place right after this book.

As always, you can find me on my blog here: http://wendyrathbone.blogspot.com/

My Facebook page: https://www.facebook.com/wendy.rathbone.3

My author page on Amazon.com contains a list of all my books as well.
http://www.amazon.com/Wendy-Rathbone/e/B00B0O9BMS/ref=sr_tc_2_0?qid=1435096235&sr=1-2-ent

In greatest appreciation,

Wendy Rathbone

LETTERS TO AN ANDROID
Wendy Rathbone

Cobalt is a created human, vat grown and born adult, with no human rights and indentured to serve others for the duration of his life. Liyan is a young man with wanderlust in his eyes, embarking on a career that takes him to the furthest regions of space. The two become unlikely friends and create a memorable long-distance correspondence. Through Liyan, Cobalt gets to explore the universe, living vicariously through his friend's wave transmissions. A strong bond develops between them that not even the stars can put asunder.

Now you know an android who writes poetry.

This is all your fault. Did you not read my last wave telling you extracurricular activities for my kind are discouraged? Of course this is harmless and strangely enjoyable and does not necessarily require me to leave the hotel. Pel would not care if I wrote lines of equations or nonsensical juxtaposed words. As long as the act does not bring my mental state into question.

However, in history, poetry is often written by the rebels.

So we can keep this to ourselves.

Let me know about your lieutenant's test.

And to give you peace of mind, I never believed you observed me as anything other than human.

Some people are and always will be hateful bigots. Most people are simply uncomfortable in speaking to "property." And anyway, friendship, like poetry, is also discouraged.

Your friend,
Cobalt

FROM THE AUTHOR:
www.eyescrypublications.com

ON AMAZON:
http://www.amazon.com/Letters-Android-Wendy-Rathbone/dp/0989693872/

SCOUNDREL
Wendy Rathbone
A male/male romance

Antares is a willing sex slave, trained in the harems of Anada since the age of 18, and owned by a wealthy master who spoils his slaves. But all that changes when Empire soldiers invade Antares' world and he is taken away from the only life he's ever known.

In a colonized galaxy where starships are as common as houseflies, and a dark Empire seeks to control thousands of civilized worlds, there are those who fall through the cracks and refuse to be conquered, including the pirate, Slate, and his crew.

Out in the darkness of the unknown, among Empire soldiers and scoundrels, will bad fates befall Antares and his fellow captive companions?

Will Slate finally find the love he's been looking for his whole life?

Can Slate and Antares ever see eye to eye?

A male/male romance to end all male/male romances!

FROM THE AUTHOR
www.eyescrypublications.com

ON AMAZON
http://www.amazon.com/Scoundrel-Wendy-Rathbone-ebook/dp/B014BU7V42/ref=sr_1_1?s=books&ie=UTF8&qid=1440660148&sr=1-1&keywords=scoundrel+wendy+rathbone

PALE ZENITH
Wendy Rathbone
A Science Fiction Novel

On a far-flung "Earth" in a parallel universe, two factions are fighting a decades-long psychic war. Young talented psychics are being temporarily kidnapped from present day Earth, seemingly at random, to serve as part of one side's psychic army. They are put under the control of spychiatrists, mysterious machines with many limbs that have a programmed ability to travel time and space and universes to kidnap and control carefully selected humans. The humans never know they are being used; when their missions are completed they are brought back to their universe through time and placed back in their beds, their memories wiped.

The shadows wound the tall corridor in muted gold, varnished brown. It seemed as though they were in the bowels of a giant serpent coiled outside time, outside space.

When they left the palace, a familiar sun flourished in a clear, blue sky. But this wasn't their sun. Not Zack's sun. It was an alien star burning within a different galaxy in an all too distant universe. Zack looked up squinting, trying to see if he could peer beyond the sky, beyond the pale of midday and into his own timespace, but there was nothing. Only sunlight. Only the thin atmosphere of an Earth not his own.

His back knotted again. Leo's presence was a gelid space inside his chest, empty. Always before he'd felt a warmth there, a sort of pressure like someone's hand pressed gently to his heart. He'd taken Leo for granted knowing, the way a shadow falls when you block the sun, that he was there around him, inside him: blood, air, salt, brain, soul. They were genetic duplicates, twins, spiritual halves. Without him, Zack knew the first icy tugs of panic.

FROM THE AUTHOR
www.eyescrypublications.com
ON AMAZON
http://www.amazon.com/Pale-Zenith-Wendy-Rathbone/dp/0976689790/

The Foundling
by Wendy Rathbone

WENDY RATHBONE

The Foundling

Diego is a powerful man with a tragic past. Out on the expansive ocean in his private yacht, he discovers a beautiful and mysterious man adrift on a raft, near death. The bond that forms between them in the aftermath of Alec's rescue is one of fierce passion, though lacking in trust. Can they make it work, or will Alec's amnesia bring forth secrets so disturbing as to tear them apart? A passionately erotic love story of desire and darkness, exquisite and explicit.

———————————

I can see his struggle between gratitude and uneasiness. He is buffeted by all things new and strange. He does not know where he is from, who he is or what happened to him. He does not know me. There has not been enough time to transition between strangers and friendship.

This isolation of his is something I can identify with, but it is also a feeling no one can help him with until or unless he gets his own life back. And his memory.

If that doesn't happen, then it will take time for him to build a new life. He is polite to me, even friendly, but even a night together during a storm with his arms wrapped tight around my waist doesn't calm the surge I see inside him, the emptiness, the loss, possibly even panic. That night may have reinforced some trust in me, but so far not enough for him to completely relax.

He seeks me out, though. That's something. He sits by me at dinner when he can have any seat of his choosing. I watch him closely when he does not realize it. At dinner the following night after we had only 'slept' together, and before we go to bed again in separate rooms, I notice everything about him, how he moves, the way the air warms when he is closer to me, the dry sheen of his lips as they part for more air when he is reacting to something, or speaking, or eating.

His hands still shake. Anyone else might not notice because he keeps them clasped into fists at his sides or, while sitting, pressed tight to his lap.

I spend another fretful night alone. I dream restlessly, wild, loud and colorful visions I cannot recall at all as soon as my eyes open. All I know is the dreams leave me unfulfilled, impatient.

www.eyescry.com/html/publications.htm

None Can Hold the Dark
Wendy Rathbone

In the eagerly-awaited sequel to Wendy Rathbone's homoerotic romance **"The Foundling,"** Diego and Alec meet new challenges in private and from the outside world. Diego is being investigated by the local police for murder. Meanwhile, Alec's amnesia and the trauma of his kidnapping by white slavers continue to plague him. And the danger to Alec is not yet over.

Distracted by their new love, both men fail to see certain threats until it is almost too late.

"Why do you keep doing this illegal business?" Now Alec's gaze turned toward him, open as the day and lit with a sad frenzy, a challenge. "You could go anywhere, do anything, be anyone."

Diego had asked himself that question on rare occasions. In truth, he got used to what he was, what he did. Even a dangerous known was perhaps preferable to the unknown. "People depend on me."

Alec shook his head, but smiled a little as he said, "That's so weak." He leaned forward, over the arm of the chair, and put his shaking hand on the back of Diego's head. The kiss was cool, lingering, moist with salt. When Alec pulled back, he said almost matter of factly, "It's like there's sharks and there's goldfish and one can't decide to become the other."

Diego was still stunned by the kiss. But the words hit him hard. In them was the unfair conjecture of a locked fate. He believed in making his own fate...or luck. Did Alec think only one kind of man lived inside him and that was all there was to it? To life? It hurt. Badly.

Diego sat back on his heels, catching himself with his hands on the smooth floor. "So, Alec, which am I?"

Alec frowned.

Diego said, "I made choices in my life. I made them No one made them for me. If I need to be strong I'm strong. If I need to be vicious I can be that too. So what? I'm stuck there? In a pattern, a role...with no free will?"

Alec watched him inquisitively now.

"Because," Diego went on, "I'm solely responsible for my actions. Me. Could you say the same of the shark?"

They both waited, the silence covering them in muggy discomfort.

"You think you understand me?" Diego finally asked.

The Lostling: Alec's Story
Book Three in **The Foundling Trilogy**
by *Wendy Rathbone*

The Lostling takes place directly after *None Can Hold the Dark*, as Alec and Diego relocate to San Francisco. There, amid salty winter wind and fog, Alec's lost memories slowly return and he must relive some of his most painful and terrifying moments to regain his forgotten self. In agonizing dreams and flashes of memory, he finally remembers what happened to him... and why.

Excerpt*: Putting a hand on his arm or leg, I can always feel the tremor of Diego even through his clothes, an innate wildness, a life-power.*

I always believed, from the first day Diego found me unconscious and dying, floating in the middle of a sapphire Caribbean ocean, there was a core of me unhidden, unforgotten, that cried out silently to the air and everything around me communicating who I am, what I am.

I can't remember it myself. Not that core, not anything up to the day I awoke in Diego's bed, sick and panicked. In that moment, I remembered nothing more than my first name, and even that memory is suspect. But this core of me demands to take things into its own hands to be seen, to make sure it remains "I am."

I believe Diego saw it, the urgent desperation in me wanting to be witnessed, and he made a promise to that essence of me, to that heart of me, that he would see me through anything that came my way. Something in me reached up and latched onto him, a clasping energy, and Diego clasped back.

It caught and held him. He was moved. He was compelled. He was mesmerized.

www.eyescrypublications.com

Turn Left at November
Wendy Rathbone

Visit realms of diamond rain, dust-folk lands and valleys of curses and shame. Reside in the burning moonships of dream, the silt of stars, the asphyxiation of the waking day. Meet the golden android who houses your soul. Journey through tatters of stardust down roads of sorrow. Find hope in planets of candles and crazy-eyed mermen. There you will meet November in these rich and evocative poems by Wendy Rathbone.

Unmaking Autumn
Out at the excavation site
where they are taking apart autumn
leaf by fabled leaf
the searchlights try to catch us
putting the eyes back into the pumpkins
the moon back in the witch-shaped sky
We steal blood kisses
behind the naked apple orchards

Winter's Shelf
hidden pathways to the moon
the north's blue breath
star-rise
amethyst dusks
winter wind bottled
and sold here

ON AMAZON
http://www.amazon.com/Turn-Left-at-November-Poems/dp/1942415087/ref=asap_bc?ie=UTF8
FROM THE AUTHOR

http://www.eyescrypublications.com/html/november.htm

UNEARTHLY
by Wendy Rathbone

A Collection of Award-Winning Poetry

Intro by the Author: This book contains all my out of print chapbooks (mini-collections of an author's work usually published by smaller presses.)

The chapbooks published within include:
Moon Canoes, published by Dark Regions Press, 1994
(Im)mortal, published by Shadowfire Press, 1996
Scrying The River Styx, published by Anamnesis Press, 1999
Autumn Phantoms, published by Flesh and Blood Press, 2000
Dreams of Decadence Presents: Wendy Rathbone, published by DNA Publications 2002
Dancing in the Haunted Woodlands, published by Yellow Bat Review, 2003
Vampyria, published by Eye Scry Publications, 2005

She Sleeps With Vampires
She sleeps with vampires
courting velvet breaths
poem-dreams
chill-stopped hearts

Wrapped in her arms
like teddy bear thoughts
purple lips trembling
at her quiet throat
they love her more than
somber rain
more than autumn
more than ash-soft hearths of night.

FROM THE AUTHOR
www.eyescrypublications.com
ON AMAZON
http://www.amazon.com/Unearthly-Wendy-Rathbone-ebook/dp/B00B0MTIZK/

Other fiction titles from Eye Scry Publications...

Prince of Umberlight
Alexis Fegan Black

"If Prince of Umberlight doesn't rattle your cage, you're more dead than the undead!" **-Night Readers**

Thorn may be an 800 year old vampire, but he does not possess the ability to create others of his kind, and so he is cursed to fall in love with mortals, only to watch them grow old and die. Torn by grief, Thorn denounces his immortality and enters into a comatose oblivion for decades. When he awakens, he is no longer in London, but finds himself in a world spun into being by his own desires - a world where Time and Death do not exist, a world where it is forever autumn, where the Parish of Shadows and the River of Stars become his home. It is in this world of Umberlight that he meets Atom - an interloper into his private sanctuary, but also an impudent imp who is destined to reveal to Thorn the three dangerous elements a vampire must possess in order to become a Creator.

The Art of Brutality.
Submission to Dark Desire.
Love.

FROM THE AUTHOR
www.eyescrypublications.com

ON AMAZON
http://www.amazon.com/Prince-Umberlight-Tales-Book-ebook/dp/B00TRD2EHS/ref=asap_bc?ie=UTF8

The Effect of Moonlight on Tombstones

(A Dark Little Collection of Poetry Gleaned From the Gnosis of Vampires and Songs of the Muse)

Moments Frozen In Time

Poetry has never been something I consciously set out to write. Instead, it is something that comes or not, entirely at the whim of whatever it is that writers call "the muse." Over the years, I have come to think of my own poetry as a form of shorthand - an attempt to capture a moment frozen in time. A wayward leaf caught in mid-fall. A glimpse of a shadow cast by nothing at all. The effect of moonlight on tombstones.

Though I write primarily novels and nonfiction, I do find myself pleasantly haunted by what my mentor once referred to as "the gnosis of shadows." As another friend once said, "Poetry is the streaming download from the broken heart of the universe."

The poems in this anthology represent approximately two decades of those streaming downloads, most of which were scribbled hastily and in bad penmanship into cloth journals. If I have been at all successful in capturing some of those moments frozen in time, perhaps a line or two will resonate with you, hopefully bringing a smile to your face or a chill to your spine.

Candles keep journals
of time's passing
in empty books of matches.

The cemetery lies empty,
pallid headstones only coloring books
for the idle hands of time.

ON AMAZON
http://www.amazon.com/Della-Van-Hise/e/B003ZOK75G/ref=dp_byline_cont_book_1

FROM THE AUTHOR
http://www.eyescrypublications.com/html/moonlight_tombstones.htm

NO FORWARDING ADDRESS
Della Van Hise

When Terrans came to sail dark seas,
And see what stars might be...
Heaven moved with no forwarding
address,
And left this void to me.
(Children's song from Lazali)

―――――――――

A literary science fiction novel told in the voice of an empath, *No Forwarding Address* explores the lures and the dangers of love, the tragedies and triumphs stirring in the human heart.

When Crystal and Raine first meet, it is 50 years after The Great War on Earth. They are hesitant to trust, afraid to love. But even if they are able to overcome these seemingly insurmountable obstacles, is even love enough?

When a man has the stars in his eyes, legend says he must serve them above all others.

―――――――――

I knew then that it wasn't love and hate who were mirror twins. The final irony was that <u>grief</u> would always turn out to be the paradoxical antithesis and simultaneous manifestation of whatever it is that humans call love.

Crystal remained silent and walked a few steps away from Raine – further down the shoreline, until she stood under the wing of one fallen Phantom. She thought of the ship she had seen from the balcony of our home, and though it had long since disappeared over the dark and treacherous abyss of the ocean, its image lingered clearly in her thoughts. On that ship was a man, she thought. A terribly lonely man who made no great difference to the flow of time or the memory of the galaxy. A man who, like Raine, was compelled to keep moving and look only ahead and never behind. A man who could not afford the luxury of waving goodbye to friends on shore.

At last, she turned toward her beloved and watched him watching the darkness. He stood only a few feet away, yet the images in my mind said he might as well have been a million light years off in the void. He was lost to her in that instant out-of-time, just as lost and impossible to find as the light from that ship which had vanished over the horizon...

www.eyescrypublications.com
http://www.amazon.com/Forwarding-Address-Della-Van-Hise-ebook/dp/B00PEOSKJ0/

COYOTE
Della Van Hise

*A Novel of Love, Honor
and Personal Sacrifice...*

When River Willows is accused of a murder she didn't commit, her life takes a turn toward the sanctuary of a world existing at right-angles to our own. Combining the mysticism of martial arts and the romantic conflict of a young woman torn between two powerful men, COYOTE takes the reader on an epic journey of dangerous secrets, military cover-ups, and the infinite heart of the peaceful warrior.

_____

"So who's Coyote?" I asked, trying to ignore the effect he was having on me. "You?"

Steale laughed easily, though it did little to hide the torment behind that mask of indifference he wore so well.

"Coyote's a scavenger, Jack of all trades. The Native Americans call him the trickster - the one who brought chaos down on the world." He shrugged as if altogether unconcerned. "Original sin."

"Is that what you are?" I asked, keeping it light despite the growing knot my stomach. "Original sin?"

He kept his profile to me, eyes straight ahead as he drove. "Sure you want to know?"

I couldn't help wondering if I had cornered the coyote, or if the clever trickster had cornered me.

_____

By the author of **KILLING TIME** – without a doubt the most controversial **STAR TREK** novel ever published!

From the author:
www.eyescrypublications.com

On Amazon
http://www.amazon.com/Coyote-Della-Van-Hise/dp/0976689782/

YEAR OF THE RAM
Della Van Hise

Year of the Ram was described by one reviewer as... "A spacefaring gay romance full of love, angst, and longing."

Only after Star Commander Morgan Diego becomes an exile as a result of a Galaxy Corps political blunder does he begin to realize how much he valued the companionship of his second in command - the mysterious Lucien, an Alfarian who is more elven than human, with peculiar powers & abilities which begin to unfold as he, too, realizes what he has lost.

Separated by circumstance from his former life, Morgan is thrust into a world where he must survive by his wits. When he meets a peculiar little old man calling himself Kim Le, Morgan finds himself in a situation where he is required to master The Art - not only a form of human & extraterrestrial martial arts, but a way of living and being that will alter his life forever.

At the temple, he is introduced to his new teacher, another Alfarian who begins to steal his heart - a heart which is already promised to Lucien. Torn and conflicted, Morgan struggles with the world he left behind and the world he now inhabits.

Beginning to believe he may never again return to his ship and to the friends and loved ones he left behind, he is all the more frustrated and heartbroken when a new Master arrives at the temple: a man to whom Morgan is immediately drawn both mentally and physically, a man who is strikingly familiar... yet utterly alien.

Year of the Ram is a fully-fleshed novel, approximately 97000 words, with a focus on the love story and romance angle. Set against a science fiction milieu, it explores the infinite possibilities of the human and alien heart. Sexual content is explicit, though is not the primary focus of the novel.

For those who like a romance that forces its characters to contemplate the ecstasies AND the agonies of love... you will enjoy *Year of the Ram* immensely.

FROM THE AUTHOR:
www.eyescrypublications.com
ON AMAZON:
http://www.amazon.com/Year-Ram-Della-Van-Hise/dp/0989693813/

Non-fiction titles from Eye Scry Publications...

TEACHINGS OF THE IMMORTALS
by Mikal Nyght

So... You Want To Live Forever?
The teachings are presented as brief vignettes in no particular order of importance. This is not a book you read from start to finish in a single night. It is a grimoire of self-creation, intended to be contemplated slowly so as to be assimilated wholly. Pick it up and turn to a page at random. Where your eyes come to rest on the page is your lesson for the day. Go no further until you have assimilated the lesson totally.

The teachings are seduction as much as instruction. This is the way of The Dark Evolution.

The Ruby Slippers
The danger of the consensual continuum is that its natural gravity exists at the lowest common denominator of human experience, and because of this it will automatically make you forget those elusive truths you've fought to learn, and before you know it you're lost in petty dramas again, sinking into the mire of old familiar scripts.

The only way to overcome this is to be continually cavorting with worlds and events beyond human experience, journeying into the unknown so that it can become known, expanding knowledge and awareness to become more than you were, bringing back from the Dreaming those secrets which will teach you how to use the ruby slippers to transport yourself over the rainbow to the vampyre wizard's secret lair.

Perception
This is the nature of reality: to be precisely what perception dictates, as solid and whole as your interpretation of it, or as changeable and eternal as you permit it to be.

It wasn't knowledge god tried to keep from Man, you see. It was perception, for perception alone has the power to destroy god and obliterate comfortable consensual realities to create unending immortality.

Take the apple, my embryonic children. Nibble its red red flesh. Open your vampyre eyes so you may finally begin to *See*.

www.immortalis-animus.com
http://www.eyescrypublications.com/

http://www.amazon.com/Teachings-Immortals-Mikal-Nyght-ebook/dp/B00C2HY5WS/

QUESTIONS ALONG THE WAY
A Quantum Shaman Book by Della Van Hise

Anyone on a journey of personal growth and enlightenment is sure to come face to face with difficult questions that will keep them awake at night and may even plunge them into the dark night of the soul. In Questions Along the Way, Quantum Shaman Della Van Hise talks frankly with seekers on the path of heart and opens wide the door to a new understanding that lies beyond the false belief systems and cultural programming all of us must confront when emerging from the dark into the light.

Who am I?
Is there a God?
Do we create our own reality?
Does life have meaning or is it only random happenings?
Are our lives predestined?
How do I know if I'm on the right path?
Why am I here?

These are just a few of the questions along the way. This book is part of the Quantum Shaman™ series, but it also stands alone as a unique and powerful road map for seekers on the road to Knowledge and personal evolution.

On Amazon
http://www.amazon.com/Questions-Along-Way-Conversations-Quantum-ebook/dp/B01A4MPLI4/ref=asap_bc?ie=UTF8

From the author:
www.quantumshaman.com

Quantum Shaman:
Diary of a Nagual Woman
Della Van Hise

"Diary of a Nagual Woman brings a quantum understanding to what has traditionally been believed to be a mystical path alone. This book picks up where Carlos Castaneda left off to take us on a roller coaster ride of our own forgotten power..." - Michael Grove, Reviewer

When I asked how Orlando had known I would come to this remote location, and how he himself had gotten there – since there were no other cars in the tiny parking lot – he only smiled a little, stretched out his long legs, and slouched down on that cold metal bench to stare up at the stars.

"You're predictable," he said as if I should have already known. "I'm here because this is where you always come when you're mad at the world."

I attempted to engage him in a conversation of just exactly how he knew I was mad at the world, since I'd had no direct contact with him in quite some time, nothing to give him any hint of what was going on in my everyday life. But even as I began spelling all of that out to him, he brushed my words aside with an easy gesture.

"Do you want to talk or do you want to waste time looking for logical explanations for every magical thing that ever happens?" he asked. "That's what's wrong with the world, you know. Instead of embracing the mysteries and trying to determine how they might open a crack in an otherwise humdrum, pre-programmed existence, people waste their entire lives explaining it all away, attaching labels to it, filing and categorizing it until it loses any meaning."

He had a point. And I'd already been inundated with enough mysteries to know that some things simply had no explanation humans could understand. *'Magic is only science not yet understood'.* Words Orlando had written more than a year before rattled through my mind up there in the middle of the night, in the middle of nowhere, looking down on a distant world that seemed far more unreal to me at that moment than the world he had been trying to teach me to *see*.

He was there – whether physically or in some spirit-form is ultimately of no importance, for in the sorcerer's world there is no difference between body and spirit, and in any world, perception is reality.

www.quantumshaman.com
www.eyescrypublications.com

Eye Scry Publications
A Visionary Publishing Company
www.eyescrypublications.com